ALLIGATOR ALLEY

ALSO BY MIKE LAWSON

THE JOE DEMARCO SERIES

The Inside Ring
The Second Perimeter
House Rules
House Secrets
House Justice
House Divided
House Blood
House Odds
House Reckoning
House Rivals
House Revenge
House Witness
House Arrest
House Privilege
House Standoff

THE KAY HAMILTON SERIES

Rosarito Beach
Viking Bay
K Street

OTHER NOVELS

Redemption

MIKE LAWSON

A JOE DeMARCO THRILLER

ALLIGATOR ALLEY

Atlantic Monthly Press

New York

FIRST EDITION

Published simultaneously in Canada
Printed in the United States of America

First Grove Atlantic hardcover edition: February 2023

This book was set in 12-pt. Garamond Premier Pro
by Alpha Design & Composition of Pittsfield, NH.

Library of Congress Cataloging-in-Publication data is available for this title.

ISBN 978-0-8021-6052-2
eISBN 978-0-8021-6053-9

Atlantic Monthly Press
an imprint of Grove Atlantic
154 West 14th Street
New York, NY 10011

Distributed by Publishers Group West

groveatlantic.com

23 24 25 26   10 9 8 7 6 5 4 3 2 1

I finished this book in March of 2022, about the time Vladimir Putin invaded Ukraine. This book is dedicated to the brave Ukrainians fighting for their survival, and I'm hoping that by the time this book is released in 2023, there will have been a resolution to that terrible conflict.

1

The Everglades—at midnight—was the last place twenty-three-year-old Andie Moore wanted to be.

There was only a pale half-moon providing any light, and she could barely see where she was walking. She was also terrified of snakes and alligators, and there was no doubt that there were alligators all around her. She knew this because she'd parked her car on the Everglades Parkway, the highway that runs east-west across southern Florida. The Everglades Parkway has another name. It's called "Alligator Alley"—and it's called this because the damn alligators thrive on both sides of the highway.

About fifty yards in front of Andie were four people walking together, heading into the swamp.

She was following them, praying they wouldn't spot her.

The four people were all thieves.

There was Lenny Berman and his wife, Estelle, and two men named McIntyre and McGruder. The Bermans were in their forties, small, dark, and sleek; they made Andie think of two legged ferrets. McIntyre and McGruder were big, beefy white guys. They were over six feet tall, over fifty, and overweight. There wasn't anything sleek about them at all, but that didn't make them any less dangerous. McIntyre and

McGruder were walking behind the Bermans and prodding the married couple to keep them moving.

Andie had followed the four of them from Miami—they all went together in McIntyre's Cadillac—and when McIntyre parked on the Everglades Parkway and they headed into the swamp, she decided to go after them. She knew she shouldn't be doing what she was doing. She knew she was risking her life. But she had no choice. Following them into the swamp was the only way to prove to her boss that she was right.

She was holding her iPhone in her right hand, about head high, videoing the people ahead of her. She knew what was going to happen—she was positive—but there was no way she could stop it from happening. She didn't have a gun; she couldn't yell, *Stop or I'll shoot.* And it was too late to call 911; by the time the cops got there it would all be over with, and McIntyre and McGruder would be gone. But what she could do was be a witness and, with a little luck, film the crime that was about to be committed. The problem was that it was so damn dark that she didn't know if the video would show anything.

She just hoped she didn't trip. The group ahead of her could see where it was going because McIntyre was holding a flashlight in his left hand, guiding their way into the swamp, and the beam of his flashlight briefly illuminated the bough of a cypress tree dripping with a fragile curtain of blue Spanish moss.

In his right hand, McIntyre was holding a gun. McGruder had a gun in his right hand, too.

———◆◆◆———

Andie could hear Estelle whimpering and Lenny saying something she couldn't make out. He was most likely begging for his and his wife's lives.

The gunshots—four cracks and four flashes of light caused by the muzzle blasts—startled her, and she had to clamp her hand over her mouth to keep from crying out.

She stopped the video, praying that the iPhone had at least captured the sound of the gunshots and the flashes of light. Now what she had to do was get away without being seen, or she'd end up as dead as Lenny and Estelle.

She was afraid that if she ran, they'd hear her, and when they turned around to leave the swamp, McIntyre's flashlight might illuminate her. She decided the best thing would be to move a few paces off the path they'd taken into the swamp and lie in the grass and wait for them to pass—and hope that an alligator didn't decide to make her its midnight snack.

She turned and took a step to her right, but when she did her foot snagged on something and she tripped and fell. *Oh, shit!* She knew the sound of her hitting the ground and her accompanying grunt had been noticeable in the otherwise silent night. She was certain the killers had heard her.

She got up and started running.

As she was running, the beam from McIntyre's flashlight hit her and, for an instant, lit the way in front of her.

She thought, *I'm going to get shot in the back.*

———— ✦ ————

McIntyre heard something behind him and whipped his head around. He thought it was probably a big gator pouncing on something. He aimed the flashlight at the spot where the sound had come from—and saw Andie.

"Oh, shit! It's that little bitch," he yelled.

"We gotta get her!" McGruder said.

McGruder took off after her, knowing he probably wouldn't catch her. McGruder had been an athlete when he was young, and if he'd still been young, he would have easily caught her, especially with his long legs and Andie Moore's short ones. But at this stage of his life, packing all the extra pounds and wearing rubber swamp boots that were hard to run in, the girl was extending her lead on him.

———◆———

Andie was running for her life—literally, for her life—thinking how foolish she'd been to follow them into the swamp. She sprinted toward the highway where her car was parked, hoping they wouldn't be able to hit a moving target. She was also hoping that someone would be driving down the highway and the driver would see her fleeing in his headlights. A witness might stop them from killing her.

If she could reach her car, there was a good chance she'd be able to escape. She was certain that she was faster than McIntyre and McGruder. They were more than twice her age, and she'd been a sprinter in high school. She was thinking that there was no way they'd catch her unless they shot her—and that's when her foot hit a fallen log she hadn't been able to see in the darkness.

She fell hard, facedown into the marsh grass, and her phone went flying from her hand when she hit the ground. She didn't even try to find the phone. She scrambled to her feet, pushed off with her right foot, then stumbled again—striking the log had done something to her right ankle. She got up but had taken only a couple of limping strides when she was shoved hard in the back and knocked to the ground.

She looked up to see McGruder staring down at her, breathing heavily. He said, "What in the fuck are you *doing* here? Are you *nuts*?"

McIntyre joined McGruder. He was also panting and out of breath. He shined his flashlight on her face, blinding her. They stood there silently for a moment, the two big men looming over her, then McGruder said, "Give me the flashlight and stay with her while I finish taking care of Lenny and Estelle."

McGruder headed back into the swamp. McIntyre jerked Andie to her feet, then stood in the dark next to her, holding her right arm. The guy was so much bigger and stronger than she was, there was no way she could break free of his grip. She cursed her luck, knowing that McGruder would have never caught her if she hadn't hit the log.

Based on what she could hear, it sounded as if McGruder was pulling Lenny's and Estelle's bodies deeper into the swamp or maybe doing something to force them under the water. While he was doing that, Andie desperately tried to think of something to say to keep them from killing her. And there was no doubt they'd kill her because she'd witnessed them killing the Bermans.

She said, "I called my boss and told him I was following you tonight. Anything happens to me, he'll know you did it."

"Yeah, sure you did," McIntyre said, obviously not believing her. "Goddamnit, why'd you have to tail us?" To Andie it sounded as if McIntyre genuinely regretted that he was going to have to kill her.

"I did call him," Andie said. "I'm not bluffing."

"Aw, shut up, kid. Just shut up."

McGruder returned a minute later and said to McIntyre, "What are we going to do with her?"

McIntyre said, "We're all going back to that rest stop we passed earlier to talk this over and see if we can work something out."

"You sure?" McGruder said.

"Yeah, I'm sure," McIntyre said.

Andie didn't believe him—the part about them being able to work something out—but his words gave her hope nonetheless.

They walked back to the highway, McIntyre still holding on to her right arm, and when they reached McIntyre's car, McIntyre said, "Where's your car?"

"Down there," Andie said, pointing with her small chin.

"Okay. I'm going to go with her," McIntyre said, handing McGruder his car keys. "We'll meet you at the rest stop."

When they reached her car, McIntyre said, "You drive. And I'm telling you right now, you do something stupid, like try to cause an accident, I'm going to shoot you right in the fuckin' head."

They had to drive west a couple of miles to find an exit ramp where they could turn around and go east, back in the direction of the rest stop. Andie didn't see a single car on the highway coming toward them or going away from them. At half past midnight, she might as well have been on the surface of the moon. When they reached the rest stop exit, Andie saw a sign saying that the rest stop closed at nine p.m., meaning that's when the restroom doors were probably locked and any concession stands shut down. Her only hope was that someone might be parked, sleeping in a car, but she knew the likelihood of that being the case was small.

McIntyre ordered her to turn off her headlights as she drove into the rest stop parking lot, which was completely dark. Apparently all the lights were turned off at night to discourage folks from using the rest stop after it was closed. McIntyre told her to park in a space that was the farthest one away from the low cinder block building that contained the restrooms. A moment after she parked, McGruder pulled McIntyre's Cadillac into the spot next to her car.

She turned to McIntyre and said, "Okay. Here's what I'm willing to do."

She'd been thinking about what she was going to say the whole time she'd been driving. And when she spoke, she tried to sound confident, as if she were actually in a position to make a bargain.

She said, "You give me part of what you and McGruder stole. Let's say half a million, because that seems like a reasonable number. You do that, and that'll make me an accomplice and I won't have any incentive to testify against you. Plus, I never wanted this damn job to begin with, and with five hundred grand I can go do something else."

McIntyre just looked at her, his face expressionless.

She said, "You know you don't want to kill me, McIntyre. You kill me and it won't be some hick county sheriff doing the investigation. It'll be the whole fuckin' bureau because my boss will make sure of that. The smartest thing you can do is to give me some of the money so I'll be an accomplice and you won't get the death penalty for murder."

McIntyre slowly nodded his big head. "You know something, kid, that might actually work. Because you're right, I don't want to kill you. But roll down your window and drop the keys on the ground. I don't want you to try to take off while I'm talking to my partner."

"Yeah, sure," Andie said.

Did he really believe she'd be willing to cut a deal with them? Could he be that stupid? Could she be that lucky?

She rolled down the driver's-side window, removed the keys from the ignition, and dropped them on the ground next to the car.

McIntyre reached up and turned off the dome light in the car so it wouldn't come on when he opened the door. He got out of the car, holding his pistol in his right hand, the pistol that had been pointed at her while she'd been driving. By now McGruder was out of McIntyre's car and standing in front of it.

McIntyre walked around the front of Andie's car, toward McGruder, but then turned and walked to her open driver's-side window.

And he shot Andie Moore twice in the heart.

2

They stood in the dark parking lot, looking at the dead girl slumped in the front seat of her car.

McIntyre said, "Jesus, what a clusterfuck. Why in the hell did she have to follow us?"

McGruder said, "Why didn't you shoot her back where we dumped Lenny and Estelle? We could have left her with them and then gotten rid of her car."

McIntyre shook his head. "The Bermans disappearing can be explained, and where things stand now, no one is going to care that they disappeared. No one is even going to look for them. But if the kid was to just disappear, they'd start a manhunt to find her and assign a whole team that would ask a million questions, and we don't want that. We want this thing to go away fast. So what we're going to do is make it look like the crazy bitch decided, for whatever fuckin' reason, to go for a ride through the Glades, stopped at this rest stop, and some loony who was camped out here shot her and robbed her. And even if her boss suspects us, he still won't be able to prove we had a damn thing to do with her death."

"Maybe you're right," McGruder said. "But it kinda pisses me off you shot her without even discussing it with me."

"Hey, I'm tellin' you—"

"Never mind, it's done," McGruder said. He looked around the parking lot. "I wonder if this place has surveillance cameras."

"If it does, they'd be on the building where the restrooms are, and we're parked so far away and it's so dark here, I doubt a camera would be able to see us clear enough to make an ID. And if there are cameras, tomorrow we'll see if we can find a way to look at the video."

"You think we can make that happen?"

"I don't know, but we'll have to try. Let's put on some gloves. We need to wipe down her car to remove any prints I might have left, then we'll take everything out of her car—her purse, any cash she has—rifle through the glove compartment, pop the trunk like somebody was looking for shit to steal."

"Yeah, okay," McGruder said. He really wished they'd shot her back in the swamp and left the body there. There were just too many things that could go wrong.

They put on latex gloves that McIntyre carried in an equipment bag in his trunk. Five minutes later, the interior and exterior of the car had been wiped clean of McIntyre's prints, and Andie's purse and laptop case were in the trunk of McIntyre's car. They pulled the girl's pockets inside out and didn't find anything in them. McIntyre also pulled off her watch, some kind of ultra-slim thing a woman would own. They'd dump everything they took, along with the revolvers they'd used to kill her and the Bermans, on their way home.

When they finished searching her and her car, McIntyre said, "Anything else you can think of?"

"No. Let's get the hell out of here," McGruder said.

"Just take a breath," McIntyre said. "We need to make sure we're not forgetting something."

They didn't speak for a moment, both of them trying to decide if there was anything else they needed to do to keep from getting arrested for the first-degree murder of a Department of Justice employee.

McIntyre said, "Where's her phone? I know she had one. She told me she'd called her boss and told him she was following us. I think she was bullshitting me about calling anyone, but there's no doubt she had a phone. I'll check the car again. You look in her purse."

McGruder opened her purse, rummaged around inside it for a phone, and when he didn't find one, he looked in the laptop case as well. "There's no phone here," he said.

"I didn't see it in the car either," McIntyre said.

"Well, shit. Where the hell is it?"

"Maybe it slid down between the seats," McIntyre said. "Let's look again."

They spent five minutes shining a flashlight between the seats and under the seats and on the floor in front of and behind the seats.

"Fuck me," McIntyre said when they still didn't find the phone.

"Call the number," McGruder said.

"How the hell can I call the number? I don't know the fucking number. Do you?"

"No," McGruder said, "but she gave you a business card when she met with us the first time. I thought you might have it with you."

"I don't have it with me. I think I left it on my desk."

McGruder said, "Maybe she dropped her phone when we were chasing her. We're going to have to go back and see."

"We'll never find it in the dark. And it's probably lying in two or three inches of water. We can go look for it tomorrow. I'll find the card she gave me, and we'll go back when it's daylight and call the number and see if we can spot it."

"What if she really did call her boss?"

"Then we might be fucked. But I don't think she did. Her boss would never have ordered her to follow us."

"Yeah, I guess," McGruder said, although he didn't sound convinced. "Now unless you can think of anything else, let's go dump her shit and the guns, then find someplace that's still open and get a drink. I've never needed a drink so bad in my life."

"No shit," McIntyre said.

McIntyre and McGruder had done some bad things in their lives, but they'd never killed before—and tonight they'd killed three people.

And although they were somewhat worried about being caught, they weren't *that* worried.

McIntyre and McGruder were FBI agents.

3

At six the next morning, they were sitting in McIntyre's car, parked on the Everglades Parkway, a mile from the rest stop where they'd killed Andie Moore. Her car was still sitting in the parking lot, and she was still slumped in the front seat.

They were exhausted, as they'd gotten only a couple of hours of sleep last night after dealing with the Bermans and the kid, and they were drinking black coffee to stay awake. If somebody were to ask why they were parked on the shoulder of the highway, they'd flash their FBI credentials and tell whoever asked to fuck off. If their boss called and asked where they were, they'd say they were working a case in Hialeah that they'd been assigned, but they figured their boss most likely wouldn't call. Their boss hated them and avoided talking to them as much as possible.

What they expected to happen was that some tourist would drive into the rest stop, see the dead girl in the car, and then call 911. The rest stop was located in Collier County, and the dispatcher would most likely send a Collier County sheriff's deputy but could end up sending the state patrol. Then whoever responded would call for more cops, a forensic team, and probably a coroner. Because they'd taken the girl's purse, the cops wouldn't be able to identify her immediately, but then someone would find the papers for the rental car in the glove compartment that McIntyre had intentionally left there. McIntyre figured that within a couple of hours of finding the body, they'd identify Moore as a DOJ investigator, and then somebody would call the FBI's Miami field office, which was actually located in Miramar. At that point, FBI agents would be sent to make sure the locals didn't fuck up the crime scene and would probably take over the case.

But there was no way that McIntyre and McGruder would be the FBI agents dispatched.

McIntyre and McGruder were both fifty-six years old, and the mandatory retirement age for an FBI agent is fifty-seven—unless there's something special about the agent.

There was nothing special about McIntyre and McGruder.

They'd spent over thirty years in the bureau. For the first few years they'd been fairly gung ho about their jobs and had made an effort to stand out, but after a while they realized they were never going to be more than foot soldiers in the war on crime. They just didn't have the ambition, the connections, or the political shrewdness it takes to rise through the ranks to upper management. So for thirty years they put in the hours and performed adequately but without enthusiasm. What they were really enthusiastic about was fishing.

McIntyre and McGruder were a couple of fishing fanatics.

They had met at Quantico, where FBI agents are trained, and had remained lifelong friends. They hadn't usually been assigned to the same field offices, and some of the places where they had been assigned weren't considered garden spots. They froze their asses off in the Dakotas, Maine, Alaska, and upper Minnesota. They sweltered in the summer heat in Arizona and Alabama. But throughout their long careers they took vacations together—fishing vacations. They'd fished for salmon in Alaska, fly-fished for trout in Montana, and, of course, gone after the big game fish in the waters surrounding Florida. Then they managed, through a combination of luck and wheedling, to pull off what they considered to be the coup of their careers: they both got assigned to the Miami field office and were teamed up as partners.

They were not held in high esteem by their coworkers or their supervisor—especially their supervisor—and they knew it. They were considered to be exactly what they were: a couple of old warhorses just plodding along until they could pull the plug and start collecting their pensions. And because their boss had been told that she was stuck with them until they retired, she gave them jobs she figured they'd have the least possibility of screwing up. They weren't assigned to high-profile cases like those involving terrorism or big-name celebrities and politicians. In the absence of any better place to put them, they'd been placed in the unit dealing with crimes like identity theft and scammers targeting senior citizens. And Medicaid and Medicare fraud.

A lot of fraud cases require considerable computer and financial savvy, which McIntyre and McGruder didn't have, so they were typically given grunt work, like stakeouts and following suspects and executing search warrants. That they'd been assigned to the Berman case was mostly because no one better had been available at the time. That and the fact that in terms of Medicare fraud, the Bermans were considered small potatoes. In a country where health care fraud amounts to several *billion* dollars annually, the fifteen million bucks the Bermans had stolen over a five-year period weren't exactly peanuts, but they hadn't broken any records.

"Okay, here we go," McGruder said.

An old codger had arrived at the rest stop in a battered pickup, unlocked the restroom doors, and opened a concession stand where other old codgers would give away free coffee and sell stale cookies to tourists stopping there. But the old guy didn't pay any attention to Moore's car sitting at the end of the parking lot.

After a while, people starting streaming into the rest stop, and eventually one of them parked next to Moore's car. It was an elderly lady with curlers in her blue hair, wearing red pedal pushers and carrying a little rat-size dog. She put the mutt on a leash, planning to take it into the bushes so it could take a dump, when she noticed the young woman sitting in the car next to hers. There was something unnatural about the way the woman was sitting, her head lolling off to one side. She walked closer to the car, peered through the open driver's-side window, then backed away so fast she tripped and fell. She scrambled to her feet and, still backing away, pulled out her cell phone.

Fifteen minutes later, a Florida state police cruiser, its light bar flashing blue and red, its siren muted, pulled into the parking lot, stopping near the dead woman's car. In the next half hour, a second state patrol car pulled in, then two cars from the Collier County Sheriff's Office. Yellow crime scene tape was strung around Moore's vehicle. Not long after that, a coroner's van arrived.

While waiting for the CSI guys to get there, deputies and troopers milled around talking to folks, and one of them went to interview the people manning the coffee concession stand. Through his binoculars, McIntyre saw the deputy point at a camera on the corner of the restroom building, and twenty minutes later, a truck with markings indicating it belonged to the Florida Department of Transportation arrived.

McGruder said to McIntyre, "They're probably the guys responsible for the cameras."

A white van belonging to the sheriff's office pulled into the parking lot, and a few minutes later, two people wearing white coveralls and hairnets and plastic booties on their feet began to examine Moore's car.

McIntyre and McGruder sat there waiting patiently. All the fishing they'd done had made them patient men.

Three hours after the body was discovered, an unmarked black sedan that had red and blue grille lights flashing pulled into the parking lot, and three men in suits stepped out.

McIntyre said, "Well, it's about fuckin' time."

The FBI had arrived. And the arrival of the FBI meant that Moore had been identified as a DOJ employee, because FBI agents wouldn't normally have been dispatched to investigate the death of an ordinary citizen. The presence of the FBI also meant that word of her death had most likely spread through the Miami field office, which McIntyre and McGruder had needed to happen to provide them with the cover they required.

"Anybody we know?" McGruder asked.

Looking through the binoculars, McIntyre said, "I think I recognize one of them, but the other guys I've never seen."

As several hundred agents worked in the FBI's Miami field office, it wasn't surprising that McIntyre didn't know all of them.

Now what McIntyre and McGruder had to do was quietly insert themselves into the investigation.

———◆◆◆———

They waited thirty more minutes, long enough for the FBI agents to assess the situation, then drove into the parking lot. By now there were vehicles in the parking lot belonging to three different law enforcement agencies and a dozen county, state, and federal officials standing around, most of them with nothing to do.

McIntyre and McGruder walked casually over to one of the guys wearing a suit—only FBI agents would be wearing suits when the temperature was eighty degrees and the humidity about the same. McIntyre and McGruder were also wearing suits. They flashed their credentials at the agent but didn't volunteer their names.

Before the agent could say anything, McIntyre said, "Our boss sent us over here to find out what was going on because we knew her." He pointed at Andie Moore's corpse, which still hadn't been removed from the car.

"You did?" the agent said.

"Yeah. She worked for the DOJ Inspector General out of D.C. and was down here looking into a case we worked on."

"What kind of case?"

"Some Medicare thing. You know the IG's office. They were counting how many pencils we'd wasted, checking to see if we dotted all the t's and crossed the i's."

"You mean dotted the i's."

"Yeah. What did I say?"

"You said—"

"Anyway, she talked to us and a bunch of other people working fraud, and our boss was just curious about what happened to her. You got any idea who did it?"

"No."

"So what do you know?" McIntyre asked.

"Someone shot her and searched her car. We didn't find a purse or a wallet in the car, or any luggage, so we guess all that stuff was stolen. Also a watch she was probably wearing, based on a tan line."

"How was she ID'd?"

"Rental car papers."

"Any evidence at all?"

"Nothing yet. The techs say whoever did it wiped down part of the car and was probably wearing gloves."

"Shell casings?"

"Nope."

"What about the cameras? I saw one on the roof of that building over there."

"I didn't look at the video myself," the agent said, "but I heard that the only thing on it is two flashes of light at about one in the morning, which might have been the shots that killed her. The camera isn't for shit, and at one in the morning, this parking lot would have been darker than the inside of a mine shaft. The video's useless."

The agent didn't notice McGruder exhale in relief.

"So what do you think happened?" McIntyre said.

"The sheriff's guys say there's a lot of meth in this county. Also just a lot of poor, dumb rednecks. The thinking is that Moore pulled into the parking lot late at night, and there were a couple of meth heads parked here or camping out here, and they decided to rob her. What nobody can figure out is why in the hell she would have been here at one a.m."

"Well, I got one idea," McIntyre said. "When we talked to her— we talked to her a couple of times about this Medicare thing she was working—she mentioned something about visiting a friend in Naples. Maybe she drove to Naples to see her friend and headed back to Miami late at night and decided to pull in here to take a leak."

"The restrooms here are locked up at nine."

"But she might not have known that. But hey, I don't really know. Like I said, we only talked to her a couple of times, and I don't have any idea if she went to Naples or who her friend was or anything else. I'm just sayin', maybe that's a possibility."

"I'll let Atkins know."

"Who's Atkins?"

The agent pointed. "Guy over there. He's in charge of this one. Do you think this Medicare thing she was working on could have been a motive for someone killing her?"

"I don't see how," McIntyre said. "I mean she was looking at a case that was six, seven months old and had already been closed, and the people involved were doctors and guys who ran nursing homes. They weren't drug dealers packing guns."

"Well, you need to tell Atkins about it."

McIntyre took out a card and handed it to the agent. "We gotta get going, got someone we gotta go interview in Hialeah. Just tell him to call me and I'll be happy to tell him everything I know. But like I said, I can't imagine her being killed has anything to do with the Medicare case she was looking into."

They walked back to McIntyre's Cadillac feeling pleased. They'd achieved their objective: they'd learned that they hadn't been videoed killing Moore and the cops were looking in the direction of meth-snorting rednecks.

McIntyre said, "Now let's go see if we can find that fuckin' phone."

It really bugged them that the phone hadn't been on Moore or in her car. They figured the only place it could be was where they'd killed the Bermans and that she'd most likely dropped it or it had fallen out of a pocket when she was running. They drove to the spot, parked on the shoulder of the highway, put on their rubber boots, and walked toward the area where they'd shot the Bermans. Before driving to the rest stop, McIntyre had gone to his office and found the card with Moore's phone number on it.

McIntyre pulled out his phone and started to punch in Moore's number when McGruder yelled, "Hold it!"

"What?" McIntyre said.

"If you call from your phone, her phone will show she got a call from you. And if we don't find the phone and someone else finds it, they'll see you called her. We don't want that. Or even if nobody finds the phone, the phone company can probably provide a list of whoever called her."

"Yeah, shit, you're right," McIntyre said. "I'll use my burner." He meant the phone he used to talk to their other partner.

"No, we don't want to do that either," McGruder said. "Then someone might be able to get the burner number and trace it to us."

"Well, shit," McIntyre said.

McGruder said, "We need to go buy another burner. We can probably get one in Weston." Weston was a medium-size town about half an hour away. "We'll use it to try to find her phone and then ditch it afterward."

"Yeah, all right," McIntyre said.

So that's what they did. They drove to Weston, found a Walmart where McGruder paid twenty bucks in cash for a prepaid flip phone, and an hour later were back at the spot where they'd dumped the Bermans' bodies and chased Andie Moore.

They walked around the area for twenty minutes, McIntyre using the new phone to call Moore's number repeatedly as they listened intently for a ringtone. The cars rolling down the highway made it somewhat hard to hear.

McGruder shrieked, "Son of a bitch!" and pulled his FBI-issued Glock.

Twenty yards from him was an alligator that looked about twelve feet long; it was staring at him with its beady, unblinking yellow eyes.

There was a fence that ran along the perimeter of the swamp that was supposed to keep the alligators in the swamp and off the highway, but the fence in this area had been flattened by a large cypress tree that had fallen, most likely during the last hurricane. The damaged fence was the reason they'd chosen this particular spot to dump the Bermans' bodies.

McGruder glanced around and saw three more alligators. The monsters were all over the place, thanks to the fallen fence, and McGruder had the impression they were being stalked.

"What should we do?" McGruder said, pointing his pistol at the nearest gator, ready to empty an entire clip into its knobby head.

"I think we should get out of here before one of those damn things tries to eat us," McIntyre said. "Why would anyone even think of looking for her phone here anyway? How would anyone know she'd been here? And if the phone is here, the damn battery is probably dead. I have to recharge mine about every eight hours."

"Yeah, but your phone is like five years old. The new ones—"

"Hey. You want to keep looking for it, be my guest. I'm going back to the car."

Back in the car, McGruder started scratching his neck. "Fucking mosquitos," he muttered. "Can you get malaria in Florida?"

"Let's go get something to eat," McIntyre said. "Then we'll head over to the Bermans' place."

"Get rid of the phone we bought," McGruder said.

"Oh, yeah," McIntyre said. "I'm so damn tired I'm not thinking straight." He stepped out of the car and threw the Walmart flip phone as far he could into the swamp.

⬥

They stopped at a restaurant in Weston and had a couple of burgers accompanied by a couple of beers. While they were eating, McGruder said, "I saw an ad for a fifty-four-foot Hatteras in Lauderdale going for seven-fifty." He meant seven hundred and fifty thousand. "We oughta go over and take a look at it this weekend."

"What year?"

"2018."

"I don't know," McIntyre said. "A boat that old can get pretty beat up. Maybe we ought to be thinking about buying a new one."

"Hell, a new one that size would cost us more than a million. And don't forget insurance and mooring fees and having to have the bottom scraped every year or so."

"Yeah, but we have ten million."

"Still, I'd just as soon not spend that much on the boat. We'll get it inspected by some guy who knows what he's doing, and even if we have to put in a few thousand to fix things, we'll be money ahead."

This was their dream:

After they retired, they were going to go in together on a sport fishing boat, minimum length forty-five feet. The boat would have a flying bridge, the best fishing gear money could buy, and all the electronics—radar, sonar, depth finders, fish finders—available to modern man to hunt fish and not get lost at sea. They'd buy condos close to each other and close to the marina where they'd dock their new boat. And with the money they now had—hell, they were millionaires—they might even be able to attract a couple of forty-something divorcées who looked good in bikinis.

Yes, they could see themselves on the bridge of their new boat, cruising the blue-green Florida waters, beers in hand, the wind whipping through their thinning hair, poles bouncing in the pole holders, and—the cherry on the sundae—a couple of good-looking ladies captivated by their wealth and willing to overlook their many flaws. And maybe they'd get a bass fishing boat, too, and enter some of the tournaments in the South. And there was a lake in Canada you had to fly into that had a fancy resort and where you could catch five-pound lake trout. And they didn't have to limit their fishing expeditions to North America. They'd seen pictures of a fish in Brazil called a golden dorado, a fish that could weigh forty pounds and would fight so hard it could break the pole. There was another fish called a giant trevally that lurked in the lagoons and off the reefs near Australia that could weigh up to two hundred pounds, and it would be fun to go after that one, too.

Yeah, retirement was going to be heaven on earth—provided killing Andie Moore didn't screw things up.

※

They finished lunch and drove to the Bermans' place in Coral Gables. The house was in the middle of the block, set back deep in a large lot. There were large tropical ferns and small palm trees and a couple of hedges that provided privacy from the neighbors, and at this time of the day, most of the neighbors would be working and none were outside in their yards.

McIntyre parked in the driveway where his car was partially shielded by a tall laurel hedge. He looked around, didn't see anyone on the street, then unlocked the front door using the Bermans' keys, and he and McGruder entered the house. On a storage rack in the attached two-car garage, they found suitcases and took two large ones, one small one, and two carry-on bags to the master bedroom. There was a large walk-in closet in the master bedroom, and they dumped a bunch of Lenny's and Estelle's clothes and a few pairs of shoes into the two large suitcases. They left the small suitcase lying open on the bed. By the time they were done, and with all the empty hangers in the closet, it looked as if the Bermans had packed about half their clothes.

Next, they went into the living room, where there was a stack of electronics sitting on a coffee table: the Bermans' cell phones, their laptops, Lenny's iPad—all devices that might contain evidence they didn't want anyone to see. Also in the pile were the Bermans' passports, their driver's licenses, and their credit cards. Last night, before they'd escorted the Bermans to their final resting place in the Everglades, they'd forced them to hand all this stuff over to them. They dumped all the electronics into one of the carry-on bags, then using scissors and pruning shears McGruder got from the garage, they cut up all the documents and credit cards into small pieces and flushed the pieces down a toilet.

"Okay, I think we're good here," McIntyre said, but he was so damn tired, as he'd barely slept the night before, that he hoped they weren't overlooking something.

They carried the two suitcases and two carry-on bags into the garage, where the Bermans' cars were sitting—the BMW convertible that Estelle drove and Lenny's Subaru Outback—and loaded everything into the Outback. McGruder had the keys to both cars, which they'd taken from Lenny and Estelle before they killed them.

McIntyre went out the front door, making sure to lock the door behind him and, looking around again to make sure no was watching, got into his car and took off. McGruder started the Subaru, used the remote clipped to the sun visor to open the garage door, backed the car out of the garage, and closed the door with the remote. He figured if anyone saw the Subaru coming out of the garage, they'd assume Lenny was driving it.

McGruder, with McIntyre now following him, drove to a Goodwill store and gave the kid in the donation area the two suitcases containing the Bermans' clothes and the one empty carry-on bag, having already made sure that there were no luggage tags that identified the suitcases as belonging to the Bermans. Next McGruder drove to a nearby school that was closed for spring break and pulled into the parking lot behind the school. He took the carry-on bag containing all the Bermans' electronics from the car, and using tire irons, he and McIntyre smashed the Bermans' devices into small pieces and then placed the empty carry-on bag and all the pieces in the three dumpsters behind the school.

Lastly, McGruder drove to an airfield used by rich people who owned planes like Learjets, a place where nobody checked the IDs of the people flying into or out of it. He parked Lenny's Subaru outside the fence surrounding the airfield, locked the car, tossed the keys into some nearby bushes, and joined McIntyre in his Cadillac.

McGruder said, "I think it's time for a drink."

"Roger that," McIntyre said. "And then I need to sleep for like fourteen hours."

As they were driving to a bar that was close to both their apartments, McIntyre's phone rang. The burner phone, not his personal phone.

He looked at the caller ID. "Aw, shit, it's her."

"She must have heard about Moore," McGruder said.

McIntyre didn't answer the phone. A moment later, McIntyre's phone gave a beep indicating he had a voice mail.

McIntyre listened to the voice mail. McGruder said, "What did she say?"

McIntyre said, "You can listen to it yourself."

He hit the SPEAKER button on his phone, and a moment later, a husky female voice filled the car: "What did you dumb shits do? Don't bother calling me back. I'm flying down there tonight."

"Aw, shit," McGruder said.

4

John Mahoney hung up the phone and thought about the conversation he'd just had with the president of the United States. The president had asked him for a favor, and Mahoney had promised to accommodate the man. Now what he had to do was figure out how to avoid doing what he'd promised, but in such a way that he wouldn't be held responsible.

He reached for the coffee cup on his desk and took a sip. The cup was half full of Maker's Mark bourbon. The fact that it was only eleven a.m. was irrelevant, at least to Mahoney it was. He'd had his first two drinks of the day—Bloody Marys—at eight a.m. with his breakfast. Waiting until eleven to have a third one was Mahoney's idea of showing some restraint.

John Mahoney was an alcoholic.

He was also the Speaker of the U.S. House of Representatives.

There was a rap on his door. Half a beat later, without waiting for him to say "Come in," Mavis, his secretary, opened the door. Mavis was Boston born and bred and still had a trace of the Bean Town accent. She was gray-haired, sharp-eyed, whip-thin, and tougher than rawhide. When she'd gone to work for Mahoney, she'd been a teenager, barely out of high school, and she'd been a stunner. She'd certainly turned

Mahoney's head. No one knew more about him than Mavis did, and despite what she knew, her loyalty had never wavered. And it was a good thing she was loyal; she knew enough to put Mahoney behind bars for the remainder of his life.

She said, "Henry Cantor is waiting to see you."

"He is?" Mahoney said. "How long's he been waiting?"

"About fifteen minutes."

"Well, shit, why didn't you tell me he was here?"

"Because you were on the phone with the president."

"Well, when it comes to Henry Cantor, the president can damn well wait. Send him in."

Mahoney thought for a second about sticking the coffee cup filled with bourbon in one of his desk drawers so Henry wouldn't smell the booze, then thought, *Fuck that*. He was who he was.

John Mahoney was a handsome, heavyset man, broad across the back and butt. He had a full head of pure white hair—it was the only thing pure about him—bright blue eyes, and a florid complexion thanks to the amount of alcohol he consumed on a daily basis. In spite of documented instances of corruption, adultery, and untruthfulness, he'd been a member of Congress for forty years. Or maybe he'd been in office for so long *because* he was corrupt and untruthful. Whatever the case, every two years, his constituents in Boston reelected him. But John Mahoney was also a Vietnam War veteran, which explained why a visit from Henry Cantor was more important to him than a call from the president.

Henry stepped into his office. He said, "Hello, Mr. Speaker. Thank you for agreeing to see me."

No matter how many times Mahoney had told Henry to call him John, Henry always addressed him as "Mr. Speaker" or "Congressman" or "sir." Henry said that had to do with respecting the office, not the man.

"I've come to ask for a favor," Henry said.

"Anything," Mahoney said. And Mahoney meant what he'd just said. He might break a promise he'd made to the president, but he wouldn't break one he made to Henry.

Henry was dressed like a typical Washington bureaucrat, which he was, in a dark blue suit, a white shirt, and a red-and-blue-striped tie. He was a small, compact man, only five foot seven. He was about Mahoney's age and he, too, was a Vietnam vet. He had short gray hair and gray eyes and an unremarkable, unmemorable face. Standing in a crowd, Henry Cantor would be the last person you'd notice and the first person you'd forget.

He was also a recipient of the Congressional Medal of Honor.

Mahoney never met Henry when he was in Vietnam. Mahoney had been a Marine grunt while Henry had been an army officer, and they'd served at different times and in different parts of the country. But Mahoney doubted there was a man who'd served in Vietnam who didn't know Henry's name.

Mahoney had joined the Marines voluntarily; he'd been seventeen at the time and eager to serve and even more eager to leave Boston and see the world. Henry Cantor was drafted. He had no interest whatsoever in a military career and was adamantly opposed to the Vietnam War, but when his lottery number came up, he answered the call. Because he was a college graduate—or maybe it was because of his deportment—he was encouraged to become an officer. Henry Cantor was one of those quiet men who rarely raised his voice but was a natural leader.

When he arrived in Vietnam, he was a first lieutenant. The life expectancy of first lieutenants in Vietnam was about fourteen minutes. That he survived for seven months as an infantry officer before he was seriously wounded was only the first miracle when it came to Henry.

The act that led to Henry receiving the Medal of Honor occurred when he was leading a dozen soldiers, all of them frightened young men in their teens and early twenties, across a rice paddy toward a small village of absolutely no strategic importance. His mission was to search the village for a cache of weapons that an informant had said was there. Henry's commanding officer—a man who'd become mentally unhinged after three tours in Vietnam—knew the mission was a waste of time, because if there were weapons hidden in the village, they'd be impossible to find. His commanding officer also knew it was possible that the informant was actually a Viet Cong sympathizer and that Henry's men could be walking into a trap. Nonetheless, he ordered Henry to search the village, and Henry followed the order.

On one side of the rice paddy was a nearly impenetrable, untamed jungle, and when Henry's squad was in the middle of the paddy, with no place to take cover, the Viet Cong opened up with AK-47 rifles and started killing his men. Henry knew that everyone under his command was going to die that day, and he knew that he was responsible because he'd led them to their deaths. So instead of dropping to the ground or running in the opposite direction, as some of his men did, Henry charged the enemy. It was an insane act of desperation and the last thing his adversaries expected him to do.

Henry ran screaming toward the jungle, firing his M16 on full automatic. He fell when hit the first time, rose, and kept on firing. When the magazine in his rifle was empty, he pulled out his .45 sidearm and then stood motionless, taking careful aim, and killed more of the enemy as the bullets whizzed past him—except for those that hit him. He was hit four times; how he was able to stand and keep firing was an unsolvable medical mystery.

He killed six enemy soldiers that day; the others ran away thinking they were dealing with an invincible white demon and not a mortal human being. Eight American soldiers lived solely due to his valor. Henry spent nine months in various hospitals, undergoing multiple surgeries, but eventually recovered from his wounds. He walked today with a noticeable limp, had only one kidney, and couldn't raise his left arm above his shoulder.

Mahoney had encountered Henry numerous times over the years. He was an honored guest at the formal opening of the Vietnam Veterans Memorial, a ceremony that Mahoney, too, had attended. Mahoney had also seen him at the memorial several times after that. Both men, it seemed, would go there when they were in a certain pensive mood, and Mahoney had seen Henry running his fingers over the names of men he'd known that were etched into the black granite wall. Mahoney would also see him standing silently in the crowd at Arlington National Cemetery at the funerals of Vietnam veterans, some who'd achieved noteworthy status later in civilian life and others who were known only to their friends and families. On none of these occasions did Henry ever wear the medal he'd been awarded.

Today, Henry Cantor worked for the U.S. Department of Justice Office of the Inspector General; he ran the DOJ's Oversight and Review Division. He joined the IG's staff a few months after he recovered from his injuries and returned to civilian life, and he'd been there for almost forty years. Mahoney had no idea why Henry had gone to work for an inspector general. He suspected that he had done so because he had a degree in accounting that was useful in an organization that did a lot of financial audits. The most likely reason, however, was that he'd just wanted a stable civil service position that would support his family.

The Inspector General Act of 1978 created twelve government inspectors general. The mission of these high-ranking bureaucrats was to hunt for government waste, fraud, and abuse.

Talk about a target-rich environment.

Today there are at least seventy-two inspectors general. Virtually every department, agency, and commission in the federal government has one. Every department run by a member of the president's cabinet has an IG. The Central Intelligence Agency, the Federal Housing Finance Agency, the Nuclear Regulatory Commission, and the Social Security Administration also have their own IGs, but so, too, do the Peace Corps, the Corporation for Public Broadcasting, the Library of Congress, and the National Endowment for the Arts. A cynic might conclude that having more than seventy inspectors general, and all the people they employ, is a prima facie case of government waste.

These inspectors general are, of course, pretty much loathed by the organizations they work for because, well, because their job is to find instances where these organizations are wasting money, committing fraud, and abusing their authority. The IGs are critics, they're finger-pointers, they're nitpickers, they're auditors—and nobody likes an auditor. It's been said that auditors are the guys who come along after the battle has been fought and bayonet the wounded.

Many inspectors general are presidential appointees—and presidents, upon occupying the Oval Office, often fire the IGs appointed by their predecessors and hire ones who they think will be kinder to them. Presidents also fire their own appointees when they aim their gnarly, accusing fingers at them for sneaky things their administrations are doing. Being an inspector general is not an easy job.

Henry Cantor was not a presidential appointee, but he'd worked for many in his long career, and although a couple of his bosses had been fired, no one had ever considered firing him. For one thing, he was a Medal of Honor recipient. No politician in his right mind would want to fire one of those. Then there was the fact that Henry was as honest as the day is long, was rarely wrong, and had not one ounce of partisanship or political ambition in his body.

What Mahoney couldn't understand was why Henry hadn't retired. He was well past the age when he could have. He suspected the reason was because Henry had no one and couldn't stand the thought of being alone day after lonely day after he retired.

Henry's wife had died a dozen years ago of breast cancer, and his only son and daughter-in-law were killed in a car accident five years ago. That same accident had also taken Henry's eighteen-year-old granddaughter—which, in a way, was the reason Henry came to see John Mahoney.

———◆◆◆———

Normally, when people came to his office, Mahoney remained seated behind his desk.

The massive mahogany desk, his throne-like chair, and the photos behind the desk—photos of Mahoney posing with presidents and generals and movies stars, as well as plaques and certificates given to him for various achievements—were designed to impress and intimidate, to convey his power, his connections, his political longevity. But with Henry, he came out from behind the desk and took a seat next to him on one of the two armchairs in front of the desk.

"What can I do for you, Henry?"

Henry cleared his throat. "A young woman who worked for me was killed yesterday in Florida."

"Ah, jeez," Mahoney said.

"She was only twenty-three years old. She was this tiny little thing, just brimming over with enthusiasm. I interview all the people I hire personally, and I asked her why she wanted to work for me. It's certainly not a glamorous job. She told me that for people to trust their government, the government has to be trustworthy and honest—and she wanted to be one of the people who *kept* it honest. And this wasn't some canned response to a job interview question. I could tell she really believed that the role of the inspectors general was vital to a functional democracy."

Henry paused for a moment as if he was having a hard time speaking. "This kid—and she was just a kid—reminded me of my granddaughter. She even looked like my granddaughter."

Henry's eyes welled up with tears. He shook his head as if trying to toss aside his loss and misery, then took out a handkerchief and blew his nose.

"Sorry," he said, embarrassed that he'd become emotional.

"Nothing to be sorry about," Mahoney said.

John Mahoney was an impatient man, and had it been anyone other than Henry Cantor, he would have told him to get to the point. With Henry, he sat silently and patiently, waiting for Henry to regain his composure.

Henry said, "The reason I'm here is that I want somebody independent to investigate Andic's death. Oh, her name was Andrea Moore, but she went by Andie."

"Isn't the FBI investigating?" Mahoney said.

"Yeah, well, sort of. A county sheriff has the lead on the investigation, but the FBI in Florida is assisting."

"Then I don't understand," Mahoney said. "Are you saying the FBI isn't sufficiently independent?"

"Not in this case." Henry paused before saying, "I think an FBI agent might have killed her. And I think that other people in the FBI or the DOJ might have been involved, and I don't know who to trust."

"Jesus," Mahoney said. "So what do you want me—"

"When Lyle Canton was killed and your man, DeMarco, was framed for the crime—"

Normally, Mahoney would have interrupted Henry to say that DeMarco didn't work for him. But he didn't want to lie to Henry. So he didn't interrupt, and Henry continued.

"—there was a woman named Emma involved. I would like her and Mr. DeMarco to look into Andie's murder."

Aw, shit, Mahoney thought. *Not fucking Emma.*

5

Henry left a few minutes later, and as soon as he did, Mahoney pulled the bottle of Maker's Mark from his desk and added more booze to his coffee cup. He always needed a stiff drink, and usually more than one, before going to see Emma.

And he was going to have to go to her house to see her. She wouldn't come to his office. Nor could he call her and tell her what he wanted, because if she saw it was him calling, she wouldn't answer. If he left a message for her to call him back, she wouldn't *return* his call. He was certain she'd help Henry because of who Henry was, but to get her to do so, he'd be forced to drive to her home and meet with her and would have to tolerate her abuse. And there was no doubt she'd abuse him. The damn woman despised him and delighted in telling him so to his face.

He picked up the phone on his desk and punched a button.

Mavis answered. "Yes," she said.

"Track down that goddamn DeMarco and tell him to meet me at Emma's house in an hour. The lazy bastard's probably playing golf. Then tell my driver and the security guys to meet me down front in half an hour."

About three years ago a Republican congressman named Lyle Canton was killed while sitting alone in his office in the U.S. Capitol one fine night. The real killer turned out to be a member of the Capitol Police, but Mahoney's man, DeMarco, was framed for the crime. The frame was so good that DeMarco would have certainly spent the rest of his life in prison had it not been for Emma.

When DeMarco was arrested for killing Canton, Emma knew he was innocent and took it upon herself to save his malingering ass. DeMarco was hardly a saint, but he wasn't a killer. Because of who she was and the connections she had in the military and the intelligence communities, Emma got the guy who was the president's chief of staff at the time—a guy who had once worked for her—to appoint her to oversee the FBI's investigation into Canton's murder. The fact that she had the clout to make that happen was almost mind-boggling. And once she got involved in the investigation, she made the FBI look like fools when she found the actual killer and the people behind him who'd framed DeMarco.

Henry Cantor, with his position in the DOJ's Inspector General's Office, which included oversight of the FBI, knew what Emma had done, and this was the reason he wanted her to investigate Andie Moore's death. Or it was possible that Henry knew more about Emma than Mahoney did—although that was doubtful. No one knew much about Emma. She was the most enigmatic, secretive person Mahoney had ever known, and even with his political power and his contacts throughout the government, he hadn't been able to find out much about her.

About all he really knew—which was about all anyone really knew—was that she'd spent a career at the Defense Intelligence Agency, the DIA. But what she had done there wasn't clear—and intentionally so—because she'd done the types of things that were sealed in files that wouldn't see the light of day for at least fifty years. She'd been a spy and a handler of spies, and she'd been involved in those sorts of clandestine operations where the president and the Joint Chiefs were kept in the dark so they'd have deniability if anything went wrong. Even though she was now retired—although it wasn't entirely clear that she really was retired—she knew a lot of high-ranking people in the government, and many of those people would do anything for her.

So she was bright, competent, connected, and able to do almost anything. The problem with her, as far as Mahoney was concerned, was that she was so goddamn self-righteous. That biblical saying, "Let him who is without sin cast the first stone"? Well, Emma would be the first one to reach for a rock. She felt that public servants should be honest and serve the public without lining their own pockets—a position Mahoney found impractical and naive. Consequently, she let Mahoney know almost every time she saw him that he was unsuitable for *any* position in government, much less a position where the holder was second in the line of succession should something happen to the president.

Mahoney finished his bourbon. Now fortified by several ounces of liquid courage, he headed down to meet his driver, who would take him to Emma's house so she could have the pleasure of tormenting him.

6

DeMarco was not playing golf as Mahoney had assumed, although it wouldn't have been surprising if he had been on such a lovely spring day. And the fact that it was a workday was irrelevant; DeMarco played golf every chance he got. But today he was in his office—a place he avoided as much as possible—and was actually, reluctantly, doing his job. He was, however, dressed for the links should the opportunity present itself. He was wearing khaki pants and a polo shirt inscribed with the words ARMY NAVY COUNTRY CLUB. He wasn't a member of the club, but he'd finagled an invitation once and bought the shirt in the pro shop.

DeMarco was a muscular man, almost six feet tall. He combed his dark hair straight back and had a cleft in his blunt chin, blue eyes, and a prominent nose. He was a handsome man but a hard-looking one. His ancestors on his father's side were Italian, and with DeMarco's face, you could picture him being cast as one of Tony Soprano's goombahs, one of the guys in a black stocking cap, helping Tony's crew unload the goods from a hijacked truck.

DeMarco avoided his office because it was a stifling, windowless, claustrophobia-inducing box that was smaller than some walk-in closets and located in the subbasement of the Capitol. The furnishings—a gray metal desk, a gray metal file cabinet, a worn, tilt-back faux-leather chair, and a wooden visitor's chair that hardly anyone had ever sat in—were so old that DeMarco suspected they'd been purchased during the Carter administration. The file cabinet, by the way, was empty except for a bottle of Hennessy cognac that DeMarco kept in the bottom drawer for special occasions. And the reason the file cabinet was empty was because of one of John Mahoney's favorite sayings: "The bastards can't subpoena air." The bastards were, of course, those members of law enforcement who might be inclined to indict Mahoney for various and sundry things he'd done.

And although John Mahoney was his boss, DeMarco was not identified as an official member of Mahoney's staff nor was he shown on any organizational chart connecting him to Mahoney in any way. Instead, DeMarco, according to the position description on file with the Office of Personnel Management, was a GS-13 lawyer who served members of Congress on an "ad hoc basis"—whatever the hell that meant. And DeMarco actually had a law degree, although he'd never practiced law, and two decades after getting his degree, he couldn't remember any of the law that he'd been taught. What DeMarco really was was Mahoney's *troubleshooter*. Or at least that was what DeMarco liked to call himself, because "troubleshooter" sounded better than "bagman" and "fixer." Which also explained why DeMarco's office was located in the sub-basement of the Capitol and not in the Speaker's luxurious suite of offices on the second floor. If DeMarco was ever caught doing some of the things he did for Mahoney, Mahoney would be able to deny that DeMarco worked for him. Yes, John Mahoney, as DeMarco well knew, wouldn't hesitate to abandon him if he was ever caught breaking the law, which DeMarco had reluctantly done on a few occasions.

His current assignment, however, was not in any way illegal. It had to do with a Democratic congressman from Rhode Island named Stanley Freeman. Freeman typically stayed out of the media's bright spotlight and, in fact, rarely spoke to the press. He was apparently one of those guys who firmly believed in the wisdom of the adage "People might think you're stupid, but they won't be certain if you keep your mouth shut." Whatever the case, Freeman maintained a low profile and kept getting reelected; he'd been a member of the House for eighteen years. But the main thing about Freeman—and why Mahoney cared about the man—was that he always followed the party line, voting with the Democrats in the House. Or to put it a different way, he always voted the way Mahoney told him to vote.

Last week, however, Freeman had voted with the Republicans on a bill having to do with protecting marsh areas. The bill passed, but it annoyed and perplexed Mahoney that Freeman had committed an act of political treason. When he asked Freeman why he'd done this, his response had been: "Mr. Speaker, I have an obligation to vote my conscience." This, of course, was pure bullshit because politicians don't have a conscience. So Mahoney told DeMarco to find out what the hell was going on with Freeman. Mahoney suspected that someone was squeezing the congressman's undersize testicles, and Mahoney wanted to know who and why.

So that's what DeMarco had been doing: looking for reasons for Freeman's sudden switch to the dark side. Maybe Freeman or one of his relatives owned marsh property that would be adversely affected by the bill. Maybe he was getting kickbacks from some group trying to build a hotel on top of a swamp. Maybe someone was blackmailing him. DeMarco had been in the process of checking Freeman's schedule to see if he'd been meeting with greedy, swamp-draining developers when Mavis called and told him to meet Mahoney at Emma's house.

He asked, "Do you know why he wants me there?"

Mavis hung up.

7

DeMarco arrived at Emma's place in McLean before Mahoney did. He saw Emma dressed in faded, dirt-smudged jeans, a sweat-stained T-shirt, and scuffed tennis shoes, kneeling under a rhododendron bush, pulling weeds.

Emma's stately brick home in McLean was probably worth about two million bucks. How a retired government employee was able to afford such real estate was a mystery because no one knew the source of Emma's wealth. But one thing that was known about her was that she was a fanatic when it came to her yard. She employed professionals to mow the grass and keep it free of crabgrass and noxious weeds and to trim the many plants, trees, and hedges, but she was not above doing some yard work herself if she saw anything marring perfection—and Emma *demanded* perfection. DeMarco had always felt sorry for her gardeners, knowing that they must be terrified of her.

Emma was tall and slender. Her hair was short, fashionably styled, and some shade that was neither blond nor gray but something in between. She was slender because she ran in marathons and played a vicious, no-holds-barred game of racquetball. She didn't think golf—DeMarco's favorite pastime, and one where overweight men rode around in golf carts and drank beer and smoked cigars while playing—should even be considered an athletic activity.

She was probably a decade younger than Mahoney and two decades older than DeMarco, but DeMarco didn't know her exact age. What he did know was that she was in better physical shape than he was, and thanks to her former occupation, in any form of hand-to-hand combat she'd probably kill him.

He parked his car in her driveway and walked over to her. She glanced up at him briefly, didn't say anything, and continued to yank weeds.

He said, "You know, they got this stuff you spray that'll kill those little suckers and keep 'em from growing back."

Now she looked at him. She had the palest blue eyes, eyes that made DeMarco think of chips of ice.

Emma was almost as disdainful of DeMarco as she was of Mahoney because DeMarco was lazy and unambitious and because he worked for Mahoney. She tolerated him, however, because DeMarco had saved her life on two separate occasions. The other thing about DeMarco—and unlike Mahoney—was that there were moral lines he wouldn't cross. The placement of those lines could be somewhat arbitrary, but when DeMarco was personally committed to a cause, he would do whatever it took to achieve the right outcome. The upshot of all this was that while Emma treated Mahoney with nothing but unbridled contempt, her attitude toward DeMarco was more like that of a cranky older sister toward a wayward younger brother.

She said, "Those weed killers have been proven to cause cancer, and people exposed to them have won multimillion-dollar lawsuits against the companies that make them. They wouldn't have won the lawsuits if they were benign."

"Yeah, but those guys probably worked on big farms, spraying the stuff over acres, practically swimming in it. I'm talking about spritzing it in a few places. Just put on a mask and you'll be safe enough."

"Why are you here, DeMarco?"

"You don't know?"

"No, why would I?"

"Because Mahoney told me to meet him here, so I thought you'd know the reason."

"Mahoney's on his way here?"

"I guess."

"Go in the house and get my shotgun. I'm going to shoot him for trespassing if he steps onto my property."

At that moment a Lincoln Town Car pulled up to the curb in front of Emma's house. Following the Lincoln was a Chevy Suburban containing Mahoney's security detail, a couple of armed Capitol policemen built like linebackers, wearing sunglasses and dark suits. Mahoney's driver opened the back door for him and he stepped out. His security guys started to get out of the Suburban, but Mahoney made a gesture, indicating that they should stay where they were. Had they overheard Emma's comment about blasting Mahoney off her lawn with a shotgun, they would have insisted on accompanying him.

Emma stood up and said, "What are you doing here?" Before Mahoney could answer, Emma continued: "No, I don't care why you're here. Go crawl back under the rock you slithered out from under."

Mahoney said, "Before you start busting my balls, I'm here—"

"I saw you on CNN last night lying your ass off about those building contracts," Emma said, "and I'm praying that reporter doesn't stop digging until you're in handcuffs."

The John F. Kennedy Federal Building was a twenty-six-floor skyscraper in downtown Boston that was over fifty years old and needed major renovations. And nobody disagreed that the renovations were required, nor did anyone complain too much about the hundred-million-dollar price tag. And the fact that John Mahoney pushed the funding needed through Congress wasn't considered at all unreasonable. The building was, after all, in his district, and the work would provide employment for many of his blue-collar constituents. The problem was the company that had been awarded the contract.

An intrepid reporter who worked for the *Boston Globe* learned that the contract had not been awarded to the lowest qualified bidder, a company whose bid had been rejected for reasons that seemed downright whimsical. So the reporter dug a bit deeper. He learned that the company who got the contract contributed heavily to Mahoney's campaigns. Three of the people who sat on the board of the company were longtime cronies of Mahoney's and had also poured money into Mahoney's coffers. The electrical subcontractor, the plumbing subcontractor, and the subcontractor who would be pouring the cement had all written sizable checks to make sure that John Mahoney kept his seat in Congress.

When these facts were pointed out, Mahoney's response was: "I didn't have anything to do with selecting the company that's going to do the work"—which was *technically* true—"and there's nothing illegal about these guys making campaign contributions"—which was also true—but the whole situation stunk to high heaven. The one thing the industrious reporter couldn't prove was that Mahoney had gotten kickbacks from all these contractors in addition to campaign contributions—which, of course, he had—and that's what Emma had been alluding to when she said that she hoped the reporter would keep digging until Mahoney ended up behind bars.

"Hey!" Mahoney said. "Will you give me a chance to talk? I'm here on behalf of Henry Cantor."

"Oh," Emma said.

"Who's Henry Cantor?" DeMarco asked.

Mahoney and Emma both ignored DeMarco. Emma, after a lengthy pause, said, "All right. Go around to the patio. I'm going to go wash my hands."

DeMarco and Mahoney walked together to the back of Emma's house, where there was a large flagstone patio with a table and chairs shaded by a blue umbrella. On the way there, DeMarco glanced into a window and saw Christine, Emma's longtime partner. Christine was a stunning, willowy blonde, twenty years younger than Emma. She had a doctorate in mathematics but earned a living playing the cello in the National Symphony. She was undoubtedly brilliant, but DeMarco had always thought she was a bit of a ditz. Whatever the case, she had the sort of easygoing personality that could tolerate Emma's not-so-easygoing one. Emma, DeMarco had always thought, would be really hard to live with.

Mahoney and DeMarco took seats on the patio, which overlooked a backyard that could have been part of the U.S. Botanic Garden. Emma came out of the house a moment later. She hadn't bothered to change her clothes; she wouldn't have changed her clothes for Mahoney. She was carrying a tray holding three glasses filled with ice and a pitcher of pink lemonade.

She set the tray on the patio table, and Mahoney said, "I don't suppose you have any beer, do you?"

"Get to the point, Mahoney. What does you being here have to do with Henry Cantor?"

Again, DeMarco said, "Who's Henry Cantor?"

Emma said, "He's one of the most decorated veterans of the Vietnam War. Also a recipient of the Congressional Medal of Honor. Furthermore, unlike your employer, he's one of the most honest and honorable men in Washington. He works for the DOJ's Inspector General."

Mahoney said, "Henry came to see me this morning. He said a young woman who worked for him was killed yesterday in Florida. She was shot. The thing is, Henry thinks that an FBI agent might have killed her."

"Jesus," DeMarco said.

Emma absorbed this news without expression. She said, "I'm sorry to hear that, but what does this have to do with me?"

"Henry was aware of the work you did when Joe was framed for killing Canton. And he probably knows what Joe did when it came to Sebastian Spear."

Sebastian Spear was the man who had been behind Canton's murder and who had been instrumental in framing DeMarco for the crime. Spear was now dead.

Mahoney said, "He wants you and Joe to find out what happened to this girl because he doesn't trust anyone in the FBI."

Emma was silent for a minute as she studied Mahoney. She was most likely trying to decide if there was any way he could be playing her. Finally, she said, "Fine. We'll go see Henry. Now you can leave."

8

Emma called Henry after Mahoney slunk away and set up a meeting with him for that evening at the Capital Grille, a popular, pricey watering hole a short walk from the Department of Justice's main building on Pennsylvania Avenue.

DeMarco arrived first and took a seat in a booth near the rear of the restaurant's mahogany-paneled bar, admiring the plush red seats and art deco chandeliers. As the sun was over the yardarm, he ordered an overpriced vodka martini. Had the sun been below the yardarm, he probably would have done the same.

Emma got there next. She'd changed out of her gardening clothes and into a white blouse and black slacks, which hung perfectly on her slender frame. DeMarco got the slightest hint of some exotic and probably absurdly expensive perfume when she sat next to him.

A server hustled over the moment Emma sat down; DeMarco had had to wait at least five minutes before the same server noticed him. With Emma this almost always happened—instant, groveling service—and most likely because people just *sensed* that she was somebody rich and important. She pointed to DeMarco's drink and said, "Give me what he's having." The one thing DeMarco and Emma had in common—maybe the only thing they had in common—was that they both enjoyed vodka martinis.

Her drink arrived at the same time a short, gray-haired man carrying a briefcase limped toward their table. Emma rose to her feet to greet the man, and because she did, DeMarco did, too. The man stuck out his hand and Emma shook it. He said, "Henry Cantor. Thank you for agreeing to help me."

DeMarco had been expecting someone who'd received the Medal of Honor to look more imposing, more heroic, like maybe Gregory Peck in *To Kill a Mockingbird*. Henry was no Gregory Peck.

"It's an honor to meet you," Emma said.

"It's an honor to meet you as well," Henry said. "I don't know much about your career, but the little I do know is impressive."

Turning to DeMarco—the least impressive person present—he again said, "Henry Cantor, Mr. DeMarco," and shook DeMarco's hand. "Thank you for coming."

Not able to think of anything else to say, DeMarco said, "Call me Joe."

A server, the same one who'd brought Emma's drink, walked past the table, ignoring the new arrival. Emma said, "Miss"—the word like the snap of a whip. The server turned back to the table and said to Henry, "I'm sorry. I didn't see you. What will you have?"

"Tonic water with lime, please," Henry said.

They waited in silence until Henry's drink arrived. Henry didn't appear to be in the mood for small talk and Emma never was. DeMarco noticed that Henry's complexion was sallow, but maybe that was due to the lighting in the bar. Whatever the case, DeMarco didn't think the man looked particularly healthy. When he picked up his drink to take a sip, his right hand trembled slightly.

Henry said, "As I told Congressman Mahoney, a young woman who worked for me was shot and killed yesterday in Florida. She was only twenty-three years old."

Emma, although not an emotional person, was sensitive to the emotions of others. She said, "I can see this young woman meant a lot to you."

Henry nodded. "She did. Her name was Andie Moore, and she reminded me of my late granddaughter, but the truth is that I hardly knew her at all. She'd just started working for me. She was bright and enthusiastic. Also naive and inexperienced. I don't know how she would have turned out had she lived longer. All I know is that I liked her enormously and I feel responsible for her death. I had no idea what she was getting into down in Florida, and in hindsight, I should have taken precautions to protect her."

Henry took a breath. "The case she was working on had to do with Medicare fraud. A couple named Lenny and Estelle Berman ran an assisted living facility in Miami, and in a span of five years they defrauded the Medicare system of approximately fifteen million dollars. Working with a doctor, they billed for medical procedures that were never performed. They billed for prescription medicines that were not needed and never ordered. They sold opiates that were ordered to addicts. They invented patients that never existed and billed for those patients. They billed for nonexistent ambulance rides and for physical therapy sessions that never happened. In other words, they did all the things that are normally and typically done when it comes to health care fraud but on a relatively small scale."

"You call fifteen million small?" DeMarco said.

"Yes, in terms of health care fraud. Health care fraud costs are measured in the billions annually. We've arrested *rings* of doctors and other health care providers that have stolen hundreds of millions. So yes, fifteen million over a five-year period is small compared to some crimes in this category."

"And this was the case that Ms. Moore was investigating?" Emma said.

"No. She wasn't involved in the case at all. She was investigating the people who did the investigation."

Henry took another sip of his drink, and DeMarco again noticed the way his hand trembled. Emma apparently did, too, and said, "Are you feeling all right, Henry?"

Henry ignored the question. He said, "Health care fraud investigations are complicated and typically involve multiple agencies, the primary one being the Department of Health and Human Services. In the case of the Bermans, HHS saw sufficient indicators of fraud, mostly billing red flags, and they turned the case over to the DOJ and the FBI to collect the evidence needed to prosecute them. Two FBI agents named McIntyre and McGruder, working out of the Miami field office, were assigned to the case. And after a six-month investigation, the Bermans were indicted and arrested, but they were never prosecuted and all the charges against them were dropped when the assistant U.S. attorney assigned saw that there was no chance of convicting them."

Before Emma or DeMarco could ask how that could have happened, Henry said, "It was as if these two agents went to a defense lawyer and said, 'Tell us all the things we can do to screw up the case,' and then that's exactly what they did. McIntyre and McGruder have both been with the bureau for thirty years—they're not inexperienced agents—but they failed to read the Bermans their Miranda rights when they arrested them. McIntyre said he thought McGruder had read them their rights, and McGruder said he thought McIntyre had done so. The Bermans asked for a lawyer, at which point the agents should have stopped an interrogation. They let the Bermans call their lawyer, but while waiting for the lawyer to arrive, they continued to grill them. McIntyre said they just 'chatted' about topics not related to the case, but the Bermans' lawyer said that was a lie and used the recorded interview to prove it. At one point during the interrogation, Estelle Berman, who has some sort of heart condition, said she felt faint and asked for the bottle of nitroglycerin she always carries in her purse, and the agents refused to get the pills for her. So we now have the agents not only failing to read them their rights and interrogating them without a lawyer present, but also doing so while intentionally causing Estelle Berman physical and mental distress. And the list of errors goes on. When they executed a search warrant to obtain documents, they exceeded the limits of the warrant. That is, they were not allowed to look at patient records because of doctor-patient confidentiality rules, but they looked at those records anyway. Furthermore, the warrant limited the search to the Bermans' office in the assisted living facility, but they also searched the Bermans' home office. McIntyre said that the Bermans' home office, being an office, was covered by the warrant, which it clearly wasn't. I won't bore you with the other errors they made, some of them having to do with fine points of the law, such as failing to turn over exculpatory material in a timely manner, but it's like I said. It was as if they went to a lawyer and got his advice on *everything* they needed to do to ruin the case for the prosecution."

DeMarco said, "So you're saying the Bermans got away with stealing fifteen million bucks?"

"Yes. The government has the ability to freeze what's known as 'tainted assets,' and stolen money is a tainted asset. But thanks to delays and procedural errors made by McIntyre and McGruder, by the time the government got around to freezing the Bermans' accounts, it was discovered that they had only about two hundred thousand in their accounts. Somehow the Bermans made the money they stole vanish and in such a way that Treasury so far hasn't been able to find it. What's interesting about this is that it took some considerable expertise to move the money the way it was moved, and it's doubtful that the Bermans had this sort of expertise, which leads me to think that someone was helping them, but I don't know who."

Henry paused. "Okay. Now we come to my and Andie's involvement in the case. When I learned what happened, I wanted to know *how* it could have happened. At the time, I didn't think that McIntyre and McGruder had done anything overtly criminal, and they were hardly the first agents in the bureau's history to ruin a case for the prosecution.

I just assumed they were a couple of sloppy, incompetent fools. What I wanted to know was where their supervisor was in this whole mess. Where were the DOJ lawyers who should have been advising them, like the lawyer who applied for the warrants? I thought that because so many gross errors and procedural violations had occurred that we had to see if it went beyond these two men and was indicative of more deep-seated institutional problems. In other words, were the errors made limited to these two agents, or symptomatic of broader problems in the bureau having to do with training or procedures or supervision issues? So I assigned Andie to do the review, thinking it would be a good case for her to cut her teeth on."

DeMarco noticed Henry's small fists were clenched, the only indicator of the anger he was feeling.

Henry said, "Andie spent a few days in D.C. going through all the paperwork, then flew to Florida to interview McIntyre and McGruder and their supervisor. I was particularly interested in understanding why their supervisor hadn't done a better job of overseeing them. After she'd been there for less than a week, she called and told me she was convinced that McIntyre and McGruder had intentionally tanked the case against the Bermans and were planning to get some of the money the Bermans had stolen. I asked her if she had any evidence to support this conclusion, and she said the way the whole case had been handled *was* the evidence. She also told me she followed them a couple of times and saw them looking at a fishing boat that was for sale and that cost far more than they would ever be able to afford. She said more than anything else, it was their attitude when she interviewed them that convinced her that they'd deliberately ruined the case. She said it was the way they smirked at her and laughed about the errors they made, not even trying to rationalize them. In other words, she had absolutely no evidence whatsoever that they'd done anything illegal. All she had was a gut feeling based on the way the two agents behaved."

Henry shook his head. "Well, I lost my temper with her," he said.

DeMarco found it hard to imagine Henry losing his temper.

Henry said, "I was particularly upset that she'd followed these people. She wasn't trained to follow anyone and shouldn't have done that. All she was supposed to do, as I said, was look for procedural and supervision and training issues to explain why McIntyre and McGruder had made the errors they made. So I ordered her back to D.C., but I learned that instead of getting on a plane and returning home, she met with McIntyre and McGruder one more time and then was killed that same night. I guess she'd decided to take one last shot at them to prove she was right."

Henry stopped speaking and rubbed his eyes. Briefing Emma and DeMarco appeared to have exhausted him.

He said, "So that's where things stand right now. Andie found no evidence that I'm aware of that McIntyre and McGruder intentionally blew the Berman case, and I don't have any evidence that they killed her. But I believe they may have. The coincidence of her calling me and telling me that she was certain they were guilty and her being killed that very night is too much to ignore. I also have no evidence that anyone in DOJ was helping them, but I strongly suspect that they were getting advice from a lawyer."

Emma said, "Could the lawyer have been the lawyer who was prosecuting the case against the Bermans?"

"No, I'm sure she wasn't involved. She was so mad about what McIntyre and McGruder had done, and the way they'd embarrassed her in court, that she was the one who brought the case to my attention and said that the IG should review it."

DeMarco said, "You said there was a doctor who worked with the Bermans. Where's he in all this?"

Henry smiled slightly. "The doctor is an eighty-three-year-old retired physician who has Alzheimer's and lives in the assisted living facility that the Bermans had been managing. They forged all the papers he supposedly signed or had him sign documents that he didn't even know he was signing. He's still alive but barely, and he can't remember a thing he did for the Bermans. He doesn't even know who the Bermans are."

"And where are the Bermans now?" Emma asked.

"Still in Miami, as far as I know. They're no longer running the assisted living facility because the company that owns it fired them. I imagine what they're doing right now is trying to figure out how to spend the money they stole without the FBI catching them."

Henry picked up his briefcase, placed it on his knees, and opened it. He took a brown accordion file folder from the briefcase and laid it on the table. He said, "That contains a very good synopsis of the whole case and provides information you may need on all the players involved."

Next, he placed a laminated card on the table. He said to Emma, "That identifies you as an investigator working for the DOJ Inspector General. I have the authority to hire outside investigators, and I'm effectively hiring you and deputizing you. We'll skip the part where I have you swear an oath." He placed a Visa card on the table. "Use that for all your expenses. Mr. DeMarco, I didn't provide credentials for you because I'm assuming you have credentials showing you work for Congress and you can identify yourself, if you wish, as a congressional investigator."

He closed the briefcase. "If there's anything you need, call me directly. And again, thank you for agreeing to help." He stood up and said, "Please catch the people who killed that girl."

With that he turned and limped away from the table, lugging his briefcase and his guilt.

9

In a way, Andie Moore's death could be blamed on the alphabet.

More than thirty years ago, on the day McGruder and McIntyre met at Quantico, they sat in an auditorium in alphabetical order—and in between them sat Patricia McHugh.

They were all the same age, twenty-four years old at the time. McIntyre and McGruder were strapping young fellows. Not Hollywood handsome, but rugged and appealing. Patty McHugh was a tall blonde with outstanding legs and a noticeable bust. She was pretty enough to be cast in a movie, not as the lead actress, but maybe in some scene as the sassy waitress or the quick-talking secretary.

They became friends almost instantly and during the weeks of training spent their free time together, mostly in bars drinking and playing pool. McHugh was a hell of a pool player. McIntyre and McGruder competed for Patty's affections, but she made it clear right from the get-go that she had no intention of becoming sexually involved with a coworker. That conviction changed over time.

Patty McHugh was brighter than both men and just as athletic. She finished near the top of the class; McIntyre and McGruder ended up at the rear of the middle of the pack. They went their separate ways after Quantico but always stayed in touch. After five years in the field, Patty, who had obtained a law degree, decided to leave the FBI and moved to the Department of Justice. Her field of expertise became prosecuting tax evaders and money launderers, which would later turn out to be very useful.

For thirty years the trio called and saw one another frequently, particularly when times got tough and any of them needed a shoulder to cry on. Whenever the two men were in D.C., they always found time to have drinks with Patty, even after she was married.

McGruder met a girl in Bangor, Maine, married her, and three years later divorced her. Or she divorced him. McIntyre met a woman in Bismarck, North Dakota, when he was stationed there and married her. Five years later they were divorced. McGruder married a second time when he was stationed in Anchorage, Alaska. He married the woman after knowing her only a month and claimed that lack of sleep caused by the midnight sun and a shortage of unattached, good-looking women contributed to his hasty decision. That marriage lasted only eight months. McIntyre married a second time, a couple of years after his first marriage ended, then was divorced again a couple of years later. Whether by luck or a fortunate genetic defect, neither McIntyre nor McGruder ever sired a child.

Patty McHugh also married. She married a lawyer who she thought had the potential to become somebody, like maybe the U.S. attorney general. Turned out he didn't. The marriage lasted fifteen stormy, disappointing years, and after it was over, she swore she'd never marry again and she hadn't. Patty McHugh had also slept with both McIntyre and McGruder. She slept with each of them only once and blamed both occasions on depression and too much alcohol. Fortunately, two one-night stands of mediocre sex didn't destroy the threesome's friendship.

Time had also been somewhat kinder to Patty than to McIntyre and McGruder. The two men ate too much, drank too much, and packed on the pounds; the only exercise they got was fishing, which is rarely an aerobic activity. Patty had a healthier lifestyle; she worked out and watched her diet. Her problem was that she liked the sun and liked being tan, and at the age of fifty-six, her somewhat desiccated skin reflected this.

———◆◆◆———

The plot that was hatched to steal everything the Bermans had stolen came about over a year before Andie Moore was killed. McIntyre and McGruder were stationed in Miami by then, and McHugh had gone there to attend a conference and decided to stay a few extra days to play some golf and lounge around the hotel pool. They got together for dinner the first night Patty was in Miami, a dinner where the amount spent on alcohol was double the amount spent on food. The talk eventually turned to the future, which didn't look particularly rosy for any of them.

McIntyre and McGruder would be forced to retire when they turned fifty-seven, and after thirty years of working, neither had much money in the bank. They had lost money when they divorced multiple times, and they always ended up buying houses when it was a sellers' market and then selling them when it was a buyers' market. Their government pensions were only going to pay them three-fifths of what they currently earned, and they could barely get by on what they currently earned. Their post-retirement dream of going in on a deluxe fishing boat together wasn't a dream. It was a pipedream. Their future fishing expeditions would most likely be limited to casting a line off the end of a pier.

McHugh's financial position wasn't as dire as theirs. She had a modest amount in her savings account and, with her pension, would be able to enjoy an adequate post-retirement lifestyle—the key words being "modest" and "adequate." She didn't want *adequate*. McHugh's dream had always been to own a home in Arizona; she didn't want to experience another winter in Washington. And the place she wanted to live was Sedona, which was arguably the most beautiful spot in the state. She wanted a house with a pool and Spanish architecture, a house in a gated community on a golf course, where she'd mingle and play golf and tennis with affluent, stylish folks her age. And when the summer temperatures in Arizona became unbearable, she'd take cruises or fly to cooler climates, and she wanted to fly first class, not fucking coach. But real estate in Sedona was expensive, and she'd probably have to settle for a humble home someplace where the cost of living was lower, like maybe Yuma, which was basically one large trailer park inhabited by gray-haired snowbirds who made ends meet by getting their medical and dental care across the border in Mexico.

So they sat there that night, the three of them in their cups, depressed by the lives they could look forward to in their sunset years. And it was as they sat there bitching about having served an ungrateful nation for thirty years that McIntyre mentioned the Berman case, and how these two slippery slimeballs had managed to steal fifteen million bucks. He said, "What I'd like to do is steal the fuckin' money they stole."

"What are you talking about?" Patty asked.

McIntyre told her about Lenny and Estelle Berman, and how they'd been bilking the Medicare system for years and how his and McGruder's job was to gather up the evidence to make an arrest, after which the money the Bermans had stolen would be returned to the U.S. Treasury—as if the U.S. Treasury needed more money to squander.

That night Patty couldn't sleep as she thought about the Bermans and what McIntyre had said. The next morning, she called them and said, "Let's get together for breakfast. I have an idea."

The idea became a plan.

McIntyre and McGruder paid the Bermans a visit. They showed them their FBI credentials, then McGruder dropped a stack of paper on Lenny's desk.

McIntyre pointed at the stack and said, "Do you know what those are?"

"No," Lenny said.

"Those are search warrants signed by a federal judge."

Lenny said, "I don't understand."

"Yeah, you do," McIntyre said. "We know that the two of you have bilked the Medicare system out of approximately fifteen million and—"

When Lenny started to deny the accusation, McIntyre raised a paw and said, "Shut up, shitbag. I'm not finished. Tomorrow, we're going to execute all those warrants. We're going to seize your files and your computers. We're going to obtain all your banking and tax information. We're going to search your house and your office and your safety-deposit box and interview everyone who works for you. We're going to give everything we find to a bunch of smart lawyers, who will be able to prove, beyond a reasonable doubt, that you've been billing for nonexistent patients and for procedures which were never performed. Then you're going to be convicted and spend the next twenty years in a federal prison being fucked by sociopaths."

Estelle, who was smarter than her husband, said, "Why are you telling us in advance that you're going to execute the warrants?"

McIntyre smiled. "Well, we were thinking that maybe all that unpleasantness could be avoided. Well, not *all* the unpleasantness, but the part where you go to prison."

"And how's that?" Estelle said.

"You're going to agree to give us half the money you stole. If you agree, an associate of ours is going to call you and tell you how to transfer the money you've parked in an offshore account to another account that won't be frozen by the government, after which we'll split the money. In return for sharing, what we're going to do is make sure you're not convicted. What I mean by that is we're still going to execute the search warrants because we have to do that, but we're going to mess things up in such a way that you won't go to jail."

Estelle stared at him. McIntyre thought she had the eyes of a great white shark: flat, dead, and devoid of mercy. They were scary. She said, "How do we know you won't take all the money?"

"You'll just have to trust us," McIntyre said.

"Trust you?" Estelle said.

McIntyre laughed. "I'm kidding," he said. "You don't have to trust us. You see, if we took all the money, then you might be inclined to rat us out. I mean, what would you have to lose? But we figured if we let you keep half, then, well . . . then we could all be friends and help each other work out all the details so nobody, including us, goes to jail. So what do you say, guys? Do you want to keep *half* the money, or do you want to go to jail and lose *all* the money?"

As the Bermans didn't really have a choice, they made the right one.

Patty then got together with the Bermans over the phone—she never met with them in person—and moved the money they'd stolen to an account that, thanks to Patty, Treasury would never, ever find. After that, with a lot of advice from Patty, McIntyre and McGruder screwed up the Berman case to a fare-thee-well by failing to read them their rights, violating the parameters of the search warrants, and doing everything else needed to make a conviction impossible.

And it all turned out just as Patty had predicted. The charges against the Bermans were eventually dropped, the money they'd stolen was never found, and McIntyre and McGruder were given written reprimands and suspended for two weeks without pay for having fucked up the case the way they had. Had they not been so close to retirement, they would have been fired. And if they had been fired, that would have been okay, too.

The next step of Patty's plan was to get rid of the Bermans.

They could have killed the Bermans as soon as Patty moved their money but decided not to do that. First, they needed the Bermans' cooperation to tank the case by testifying to all the legal errors McIntyre and McGruder had made. But more important, when the money disappeared, they wanted Treasury and the FBI to think it was the Bermans who had disappeared it. The plan was to make it look as if the Bermans still had the money so no one would even think of looking in another direction. So the idea from the beginning had been to wait until the case was closed, then dump the Bermans' bodies into the Everglades and make it appear as if they'd fled the country.

Once the Bermans were gone, they would all retire and wait a year, then Patty would teach McIntyre and McGruder how to launder the money they'd stolen, after which they'd go on to lead the lives they'd always wanted. McIntyre and McGruder would buy their deluxe fishing boat; Patty would get her home in Sedona.

And it had all gone just as Patty had planned—until Andie Moore was killed.

10

———◆———

The day after they cleaned out the Bermans' house to make it appear as if they'd fled the country, McIntyre and McGruder met Patty at an IHOP close to the hotel where she was staying. She'd flown down the night before to find out what the hell had happened to Andie Moore.

The men arrived at the restaurant first, and she saw them wolfing down waffles and link sausages, shoving food into their mouths as if they were starving. She sat down at their table and shooed the server away when he came over. She wanted to *scream* at them, but because they were in a public setting, she hissed at them like a pissed-off, sun-wrinkled rattlesnake.

"Did you two morons kill that girl?" she said.

News of Moore's death had spread through the Department of Justice like a flash flood. FBI agents were sometimes killed, but not very often. But nobody could remember the last time a DOJ employee, much less one working for the inspector general, had been killed. And no one at DOJ had any idea as to why she'd been killed—except for Patty McHugh.

She knew the Moore girl had been investigating the Berman case debacle because McIntyre had called her and told her so. And the coincidence of the girl dying for some reason *not* connected to the

Berman case was too much for her to accept. The only thing she could conclude was that McIntyre and McGruder had killed her, but she couldn't understand *why* they would have done so. There'd been no reason whatsoever to get rid of some novice investigator working for the inspector general.

As soon as she asked the question—*Did you two morons kill that girl?*—and saw them both look away, she knew they'd done it. "Why?" she said. "Why in God's name would you do something so fucking stupid?"

"We didn't have a choice," McIntyre said. "The goddamn kid followed us the night we killed Lenny and Estelle. She saw us do it."

"She followed you?" McHugh said.

"Yeah. She talked to us earlier that day and made it clear she thought we'd conspired with the Bermans and blew the case deliberately, but it was obvious she didn't have any evidence. We told her, 'Write your little report, kid. We don't give a shit.' But we never had any intention of doing anything to her. Why would we? We did decide it was time to get rid of the Bermans—we'd put it off long enough, and we didn't want the kid talking to them—and we did everything you said. You know, used clean guns, got rid of all their electronics, cleaned out their house so it would look like they'd taken a trip. But we had no idea that fucking kid was going to tail us. I mean, those IG pencil pushers don't do surveillance work. They do audits, they crunch numbers. They're not cops."

Patty started to say something, then stopped herself, but sat there looking as if her head were about to launch from her shoulders like a surface-to-air missile.

McGruder said, "Relax, Patty. We're golden. You see, we managed to insert ourselves into the investigation and—"

"Oh, Jesus," Patty moaned. They didn't have the subtlety or the brains to do that without it coming back to bite them. "Tell me *exactly* what you did. Tell me everything."

McIntyre told her how they shot the girl and that they'd left no evidence tying them to the crime: no fingerprints, no shell casings, no DNA, no nothing. He said, "But we had to find out what the guys investigating her murder were thinking, and we really needed to know if a camera at the rest stop had recorded anything."

He told her how they dropped by the crime scene and talked briefly to one of the FBI agents, from whom they learned that the camera recorded nothing but two flashes of light. They also learned that the current thinking regarding the girl's murder was that some addict, who'd been camped out at the rest stop, killed her to steal her purse.

"Did you tell the agent that the girl was looking into the Berman case?" Patty asked.

"Well, yeah, we had to say something to explain why we were there asking questions about her."

"Oh, fuck me," Patty groaned.

"Hey," McGruder said, "the girl being down here wasn't a secret. She talked to us a couple of times and talked to our boss. Like we told you on the phone, she was here to figure out how come we'd screwed the pooch the way we did, but all she was supposed to do was look at training and procedures, that sorta shit."

"I'm telling you, we don't have a problem," McIntyre said. "I told the agent I talked to to have his boss call me if he wanted to know more, and he hasn't called and I don't think he will. Right now, the case is being handled by the Collier County sheriff, and I'm guessing the bureau won't take it over, particularly because as of now it looks unsolvable."

Had Andie Moore been an FBI agent or an agent working for any federal law enforcement organization, the FBI would have definitely taken over the case. But even though she worked for the Department of Justice, Andie wasn't technically law enforcement, and she fell into a gray area. The bureau could take over the case if it chose to, but as murder in general is under the jurisdiction of state or city cops, it could also choose not to. And what McIntyre was saying was that the FBI would most likely opt not to take over the case because the chance of solving it looked small, and if it couldn't be solved, that would screw up the bureau's solve-rate statistics. So although the FBI was assisting the sheriff, it hadn't yet taken the case away from him, and McIntyre didn't think it would.

McIntyre thought about telling Patty that the girl's cell phone was missing and how they'd failed to find it—and decided not to. She would just yell at them. And he wasn't worried about the phone. It was in a swamp, surrounded by alligators, probably ruined from lying in the water, and the battery was most likely dead. Plus, why would anyone even think the phone was in the area where they'd killed the Bermans? The only important thing was that the phone hadn't been on her and wasn't in her car, and as far as the guys investigating the murder were concerned, it had been stolen along with her purse. And there was another reason not to worry about Moore's cell phone. Even if, by some total fluke, somebody found it, they'd need a password or a fingerprint to get into it, and the goddamn geeks at Apple wouldn't help anyone get into it. No, the phone wasn't a problem and Patty didn't need to know about it.

"Do you guys have alibis for the night the girl was killed?"

"If anyone asks, we'll say we were both home alone and nobody will be able to prove otherwise," McIntyre said.

"That's not true and you know it," Patty said. "If they suspect you, they'll start looking at cameras near your apartment, and they'll spot that gas-guzzling boat you drive and see you weren't home when you said you were."

McIntyre said, "But why would anyone suspect us? We had no motive for killing that kid. Our screwups on the Berman case were already documented; we got suspended and got letters in our jackets saying what a couple of fuckups we are, and when it comes to us, that's the end of it. Why the hell would anyone think we killed her? I'm telling you, Patty, we're good here."

Patty closed her eyes. McGruder started to say something, but she said, "Shut up. I'm thinking."

She was thinking that as long as there was no physical evidence tying them to the girl's murder, maybe they were okay, because McIntyre was right: no one would think that they had any plausible, rational motive for killing her.

"Okay," she said, "I'm flying back to D.C. this afternoon, and I'll poke around as best I can to see if anyone is looking in your direction. But if anyone talks to you about the girl, you call me *immediately*. And don't you dare do another goddamn thing without talking to me first. You got that?"

"Hey, fuck you," McGruder said. "We're not as dumb as you think we are."

Yes, they were.

11

DeMarco and Emma walked down the Jetway, pulling their carry-on luggage behind them. Last night, Emma had read the file that Henry Cantor had given them. DeMarco skimmed the file on the flight to Miami.

DeMarco asked, "So, do we have a plan here?"

By "we" he meant "you." Whenever DeMarco worked with Emma, she was always the one in charge whether he liked it or not.

She said, "The first thing we're going to do is go see the sheriff in charge of the murder investigation. Henry thinks these two FBI agents might have murdered her, but there's no evidence to support that conclusion. So let's start with an open mind."

DeMarco shrugged. "Okay," he said.

As they walked through the terminal, Emma said, "I booked us rooms at a hotel near the FBI's Miami field office. I've stayed there before. It's adequate."

DeMarco had left all the travel arrangements to Emma because she was the one with the DOJ credit card. And her idea of *adequate* was certain to be good enough for him. Her standards tended to be higher than his.

"Now let's find the rental car place," she said. "We'll rent two cars in case we need to split up."

"Since DOJ's picking up the bill, I think I'll see if they've got a Mustang convertible."

"No, you will not. You will rent an economy car. It's bad enough that the taxpayers pay your salary without you bilking them for even more."

"I was just kidding," DeMarco said. He hadn't been. He really wanted to get a convertible. He was in Florida, and it was spring, after all.

They reached the main terminal, and DeMarco said, "I gotta go to baggage claim before we go to the rental car place."

"Why? How many clothes did you pack?"

"All my clothes are in my carry-on," DeMarco said. "I gotta pick up my golf clubs."

"You brought your golf clubs!" Emma shrieked.

"Hey, don't have a stroke. I don't know how long we're going to be down here or what our schedule's going to be. I just figured if I had any free time, I should be prepared."

"I swear, DeMarco, if you don't take this seriously, I'll —"

"I am taking it seriously. Just because I brought my clubs—"

"Shut up."

———◆◆◆———

They got their rental cars, DeMarco's so damn small his clubs barely fit in the trunk.

Emma said, "The sheriff's main office is located in Naples. That's about two hours from Miami. We'll be passing right by the place where Andie was killed, but we'll look at it after we've talked to the sheriff."

"We should stop on the way and get something to eat. I didn't have breakfast."

"We'll eat after we've seen the sheriff. If we have time."

Aw, Jesus. He could see that Emma was going to turn this trip into some sort of Bataan Death March. With her, it was never a walk in the park.

As he was following her to Naples, driving down Alligator Alley, DeMarco looked out at the Everglades. He'd seen commercials showing tourists riding through the saw grass of the swamp in those boats with a big fan on the back, the boat usually driven by some grinning Bubba wearing his baseball hat on backward. The commercials made it look as if the tourists were having a ball, but there was no way DeMarco was going into the Everglades.

DeMarco was terrified of alligators. He actually had nightmares about the creatures.

In one of the first jobs he'd done while working for Mahoney, he'd found himself in the Okefenokee Swamp in Georgia in a canoe being paddled by a psychopath who'd been planning to kill him. He'd intentionally tipped the canoe over to keep from getting killed, and the psycho was eaten by an enormous alligator. The jaws on that gator had opened wide enough to swallow a hog. Why the alligator had chosen to dine on the psycho instead of him, DeMarco would never know, but he'd ended up standing on the root ball of a cypress tree, clinging to the trunk for hours, surrounded by alligators, watching water moccasins slither through the water, until he was finally rescued.

There wasn't enough money on God's green earth to get him to go into another swamp.

The Collier County sheriff's main office was located in a sprawling white structure in Naples that also housed the county's jail. DeMarco followed Emma inside, where she asked a deputy for directions to the sheriff's office. They found it, and a young woman DeMarco assumed was the sheriff's secretary greeted them with a smile.

Emma didn't smile back. She produced the credentials Henry had given her and said, "Department of Justice Inspector General." She said this like she was *the* inspector general. She jerked a thumb at DeMarco standing behind her and said, "He's a special investigator from Congress. I want to see the sheriff. Immediately."

The young woman sprung up from her chair and said, "Yes, ma'am." When Emma gave an order, people tended to leap to attention. They just couldn't help themselves.

The Collier County sheriff was a medium-size fellow with soft white hair, a deep tan, and teeth so white they were blinding. He was wearing a uniform consisting of gray pants, a gray shirt, and a black tie. There were black epaulettes on the shoulders of the shirt, and a five-pointed star was pinned to his chest. In spite of the uniform, he struck DeMarco as more of a politician than a cop: there was a politician's oily slickness about him. He barely glanced at Emma's credentials.

"What can I do for you folks?" he said. "Always happy to help our federal government."

DeMarco stopped himself from making a raspberry sound.

"We're here about the murder of Andrea Moore," Emma said. "Not only was she a DOJ employee, but her parents are friends with some very powerful people in Washington. Which is the reason we're here. I'd like to see what you have on the case, and hopefully I'll be able to report back to the attorney general that you're doing everything that can be done."

DeMarco thought that was a nice touch, Emma not only lying about the influence of Andie's parents but also implying that she was communicating directly with the attorney general of the United States.

"Be happy to show you what we got," the sheriff said. "Transparency is my middle name." Then he laughed and added, "Well, not really. My middle name is Homer, after my grandfather, but you get what I mean."

When Emma's only reaction was to stare at him, the sheriff said, "Uh, yeah, let me get Hal Fisher in here. He's the lead detective on the case."

———◆◆◆———

Fisher was black, in his fifties, a serious-looking, heavyset man with sharp, suspicious eyes. Naturally he was suspicious; he was talking to people from Washington. He spoke with a heavy Southern accent, and unlike the sheriff, he wasn't wearing a uniform. He had on a blue polo shirt and wrinkled khaki pants.

He started by saying, "We got nothing, so far."

The sheriff interrupted to say, "But, by God, we're doing everything we can."

Everyone ignored the sheriff.

Fisher went through the sequence of a person making a 911 call to report the murder, law enforcement arriving at the scene, and eventually identifying Andie thanks to the rental car papers, at which point the FBI was notified. He said they found her behind the wheel of her car, the driver's-side window down, and two evident gunshot wounds in her chest. He said the blood splatter was consistent with her being shot while sitting in her car by someone shooting her through the driver's-side window.

Fisher said, "Whoever did it rifled her car, looking, I guess, for things to steal, but he didn't leave any evidence behind like shell casings. My fingerprint guy said someone had wiped down the car and he'd been wearing gloves when he opened the glove box. The most likely suspect is some poor, dumb cracker who was camped out at the rest stop and decided to rob her. The only thing wrong with that theory is that most dumb crackers wouldn't have a pair of gloves to wear. This is Florida, after all. The other thing that bothers me about the dumb cracker theory is that he shot her. I can see a guy using a gun to get her to hand over her purse, but most folks would have probably just taken her phone so she couldn't call the cops and run off afterward. So right now, I've got more questions than answers."

"There were no cameras at this rest stop?" DeMarco said.

"Yeah, there are two, one pointed in the direction of where Ms. Moore was parked. The cameras are pieces of crap to begin with, and the fact that they had bird shit smeared on the lenses didn't help. Anyway, the rest stop lights are turned off at nine p.m., and all the camera video showed were two flashes of light, probably gunshots, at about one a.m. One a.m. is also consistent with the ME's guess as to when she was killed."

Emma said, "Didn't the cameras show Andie's headlights when she drove into the rest stop?"

"Nope, which is another weird thing. She must have turned off her lights when she drove in, but I have no idea why she would have done that."

"Any other anomalies?" Emma asked.

"Yeah. Her hands were dirty, her shoes were muddy, and her clothes were soiled. If I had to guess, I'd say she fell somewhere before she was shot. But like I said, she was definitely shot in her car."

"So what are you doing now?" Emma asked.

"A couple of things. There's a bunch of old farts who volunteer at the rest stop, passing out coffee and tourist brochures. We're tracking down all of them—different ones go there on different days—and asking them if they'd seen anybody who looked strange hanging around the rest stop, anybody who tended to camp out there at night. That sort of thing. We're also visiting pawnshops all over the county. I talked to the girl's mother, that poor woman, and she said Andie had a semi-expensive watch they gave her when she graduated college and a laptop she always carried with her in a nice leather case, also a present from her folks. She wasn't wearing a watch, so whoever killed her most likely stole it. So I got photos of the kind of watch she had, and we're talking with pawnshop owners. We're also asking if anyone pawned a laptop, a fancy laptop case, or a phone. We didn't find either a phone or a laptop in her car. The problem with electronics these days, like phones and laptops, is they're all password protected and not much use to anyone who steals them, and the thief might have just chucked them into the swamp. I figure we're more likely to find the watch."

"Are you trying to locate the phone?" DeMarco asked. "You know, pinging it or whatever you call it."

"Yeah, we'll be doing that sometime today. We would have done it yesterday, but my guy that does that sort of stuff had to leave early because one of his kids broke an arm falling off his bike. Today, we'll get a warrant, although I don't know why we need one, but that's what the lawyer said, then we'll get Verizon to help us try to find the phone."

Fisher took a breath and said, "Anyway, that's where things stand right now. We're talking to old farts hoping to get a lead on a suspect and talking to pawnshop owners that are just as likely to lie to us as not. If you got any other ideas, I'm all ears."

DeMarco waited for Emma to say something—he could tell she was mulling something over in that big brain of hers—and when she didn't speak, he asked, "Are you looking to see if her death might be connected to the work she was doing here in Florida?"

Fisher said, "I'm not. The FBI's handling that end of things, an agent named Atkins out of the Miami office. But based on what Atkins told me, it doesn't sound like her getting killed would have been related to her work."

"Why's that?" DeMarco asked.

"Atkins told me Ms. Moore was doing a review of some case the FBI screwed up. Apparently, a couple of agents failed to follow procedures on some Medicare fraud case, and they messed up so badly that the crooks involved were never convicted. According to Atkins, Moore was looking into agent training and standard operating procedures and supervision issues. Stuff like that. She wasn't investigating actual criminals, and Atkins thought it pretty unlikely that anyone would have killed her based on what she was doing. What nobody can figure out is why she was at the rest stop. One agent heard she might have gone to visit a friend in Naples, but according to her mom she didn't have any friends in Naples, so we have no idea why she would have pulled into that rest stop at one in the morning. I'd suggest if you got questions related to her job, you talk to Atkins or her boss back in D.C."

Emma sat for a moment, then stood up and said, "I'll do that, Deputy. And, Sheriff, thank you for your time."

As they were leaving the building, DeMarco said, "Fisher seems like a good guy."

"Yes," Emma said, "and if he's right about Andie being the victim of some random robbery that turned into a murder, he'll most likely never catch the person who did it. We're going to proceed on the basis that her death was related to her job, as Henry thinks."

12

"Now can we go get some lunch before I pass out?" DeMarco said.

"No. I need to do something first."

"What's that?" DeMarco said.

Emma ignored him and took out her phone. She made a call but then muttered, "Damn it, where is he?" Into her phone, she said, "Neil, call me. Right away."

"Why are you calling Neil?"

"Because I want him to see if he can locate Andie's cell phone before the sheriff does."

"You gotta be kidding me," DeMarco said.

"You heard what Henry said, that the FBI is assisting the sheriff and we can't trust the FBI."

DeMarco wasn't sure he was buying that explanation. A more likely one was that Emma wanted to solve Andie's murder before anyone else did. Emma had a competitive streak wider than an eight-lane freeway.

He said, "Well, can we at least go eat while you're waiting for Neil to call you back?"

"Oh, for Christ's sake," Emma said.

They found a place with outdoor seating near Naples Beach with a view of the Gulf of Mexico. There were pleasure boats cruising around, more than a few of them containing young ladies clad in brightly colored bikinis. DeMarco would have been content to sit there for a couple of hours sipping beer and enjoying the view, but he knew that wasn't going to happen.

As they were eating lunch—DeMarco wolfing down a Reuben, while Emma picked at a salad—Neil returned Emma's call.

"What took you so damn long to get back to me?" Emma asked him. Before Neil could respond, Emma said, "I want you to locate a cell phone belonging to a woman who was killed in Florida. There's a good chance the battery's dead or the phone has been destroyed, but I want you to search for it anyway. The woman's name is Andrea Moore."

Emma flipped through the file Henry had given her, found Andie's number, and rattled it off to Neil.

Emma said, "I want this done immediately." She hung up, having no doubt that Neil would do as he was told.

Neil was a mostly harmless criminal whom Emma and DeMarco had both used before. He called himself an "information broker," a benign euphemism for someone who hacked into databases or bribed people who had access to those databases, then sold the information to those who desired it. Politicians found him useful in getting a leg up on the competition; the lawyers of women divorcing wealthy husbands used him to make sure their clients got all they deserved; corporations plotting takeovers of their rivals found him helpful. To his credit, Neil didn't use his skills to steal; he wasn't a thief, unless you considered stealing confidential information theft.

When DeMarco used his services, he paid Neil exorbitant amounts. Well, actually the taxpayer footed the bill. When Emma wanted something, however, he never charged her a cent. DeMarco had no idea what hold Emma had over Neil because they both refused to tell him, but he knew, based on something Neil had once said, that had it not been for Emma, Neil would currently be residing in a federal prison and most likely as the corpulent bride of some muscle-bound, tattooed inmate.

DeMarco said, "You think whoever killed her would be dumb enough to still have her cell phone?"

"It rarely pays to overestimate the intelligence of criminals. Now hurry up and finish eating. I want to talk to that FBI agent, Atkins, who's working with the sheriff on the murder. And before we go see him, I want to see the place where Andie was killed."

An hour later they pulled into the rest stop on Alligator Alley. It was half filled with cars and trucks; people were walking to the restrooms and eating at picnic tables. DeMarco saw a kid with a dachshund on a leash, the wiener dog barking frantically at something on the other side of a chain-link fence—the fence designed to keep the alligators in the swamp and prevent them from eating the tourists and their dogs. DeMarco couldn't see what the dog was barking at but had no doubt it was a fucking gator. It wouldn't bother DeMarco if all the alligators in the world were turned into shoes and belts. Some species deserved to be extinct.

Emma walked over to the building containing the restrooms and glanced up at the camera on the roof pointing east. From there they walked down to the east end of the parking lot, to the spot where Andie's car had been parked the night she was killed. The car had been towed away, but Henry's file had contained a photo of the car with Andie still sitting in it and a sketch showing the location of the car in the parking lot. A big Harley-Davidson motorcycle was currently parked in the spot, the Harley's fat, bearded driver sitting on the machine, talking on a cell phone. A scrap of yellow crime scene tape dangling from a nearby bush was the only evidence remaining of a young woman who had died a violent death.

"What in the hell could have made her come here at one in the morning?" DeMarco asked.

"I don't think she would have," Emma said. "At least not voluntarily."

They stood there for a moment, both thinking of the terrifying final moments of Andie Moore's life. Fisher had said she'd been shot through the driver's-side window. She'd no doubt seen the person who killed her and had been helpless to prevent her own death.

Emma said, "Let's go talk to the FBI."

13

For twenty-eight years the FBI's Miami field office was located in the North Beach area of Miami. But in 2015, FBI director James Comey—who later became famous for possibly causing Hillary Clinton to lose the 2020 presidential election—presided over a dedication ceremony for a grand new home for the bureau's Florida-based personnel. The building was called the Benjamin P. Grogan and Jerry L. Dove Federal Building—Grogan and Dove being two agents who were tragically killed in the line of duty—and it was located in the Miami suburb of Miramar.

The 383,000-square-foot office complex that now housed the FBI and other federal employees consisted of two connected glass towers advertised as being as green as green can be: it had arrays of solar panels on the roofs, systems to collect and reuse water, and it was near a carefully tended wetlands restoration area. More than a thousand employees worked in these environmentally friendly digs, which cost the taxpayers a mere one hundred and ninety million dollars.

As Agent Stan Atkins didn't have sufficient rank to rate an actual office, DeMarco and Emma met him in a small conference room near his cubicle. Looking through the conference room windows, you could see the Everglades. But DeMarco wasn't looking at the swamp. He asked Atkins, "What's the name of that golf course over there?"

Emma stabbed DeMarco with her eyes, but Atkins didn't notice. He said, "Flamingo Lakes."

Atkins was a bit on the stumpy side and had the jowly face of a bulldog; DeMarco thought he'd probably look like J. Edgar Hoover by the time he retired. Emma made it clear to Atkins—just as she'd made it clear to the Collier County sheriff—that there were political heavyweights behind their mission and any lack of cooperation on his part would not be good for his career.

Emma asked if Atkins was looking into Andie's murder being connected in any way to the case she'd been working on in Miami.

"Yeah," Atkins said, "but it seems pretty unlikely that her death had anything to do with her job. She was down here because a couple agents who work fraud screwed the pooch on a case. These knuckleheads did everything wrong that could possibly be done wrong, and the IG, rightfully so, wanted to know how they could have fucked it up so badly."

"We know *why* she was here," Emma said. "But what I want to know is if these agents could have felt threatened by her investigation."

Atkins laughed. "Threatened? McIntyre and McGruder are two old-timers just marking time until they retire. They've already been suspended without pay for screwing up the Berman case, and they know that nothing else is going to happen to them. I mean, if they'd been younger, and not so close to retirement, they'd have been fired, but since they've only got a few months to go, the powers that be decided to let them finish their careers, after which they'll be gone for good. So why would they have felt threatened? There wasn't anything Moore would have been able to do that would have affected them personally, plus she wasn't supposed to even be looking at them directly. Her job, which I think was a total waste of time, was to see if we needed to modify training, like you can train people not to be lazy and stupid."

Switching tracks, Emma said, "Do you have any idea why Ms. Moore was at the rest stop where she was killed? Did you try to trace her movements?" Then she quickly added, "I know the sheriff is trying to locate her cell phone, but I was wondering if you were doing anything else to explain why she would have gone there."

Atkins said, "I asked people at the hotel where she was staying if they knew anything, like if she'd asked for directions to someplace or information about the Everglades or anything like that. They said she hadn't. And there wasn't anything about her assignment that would have taken her out of Miami. Everything she needed to look at and everyone she needed to talk to was here in this building. But I did hear one plausible theory. McIntyre told one of my guys that she had a friend in Naples that she was thinking about visiting. So maybe she went to Naples and, when she was driving back to Miami that night, decided to stop at the rest stop."

"You're saying that McIntyre volunteered this information?" Emma said.

"Yeah. Naturally, the girl talked to him and McGruder about the case and how they'd screwed it up. I guess after she finished interviewing them, she mentioned this friend of hers."

DeMarco thought that sounded completely wrong, that she'd tell the two guys she was investigating what she was planning to do in her free time. Then there was the fact that Andie's mother had said that she didn't have any friends in Naples.

Emma said, "Did you ask McIntyre and McGruder where they were the night she was killed?"

Atkins said, "No, why would I? Like I already said, I don't consider them suspects."

Emma said, "Well, I want you to ask them where they were that night. Then, no matter what they tell you, I want you to check their phones and their credit cards to see if they match their stories."

"I'll need a warrant to check their credit cards and phones."

"No, you won't," DeMarco said. "Just call them and tell them we're busting your ass about where they were that night and ask their permission to look at their records. If they don't have anything to hide, they shouldn't have a problem with that. And if they do have a problem, well, then, maybe you ought to get a warrant."

Atkins mulled that over for a moment. "Fine. I'll do that. I'll ask."

Emma said, "So ask them."

Atkins said, "You mean right now?"

"Yes. Right now," Emma said. "Put your phone on speaker mode and call them. Don't tell them we're listening."

Atkins stared for a beat into Emma's frosty blue eyes, then, having no other recourse, took out his phone and punched in McIntyre's number.

McIntyre answered, saying, "Yeah, hello."

"Mac, it's Stan Atkins."

"Hey, I'm glad you called," McIntyre said. "I was planning on calling you later and asking if you got anything on that poor kid's murder."

"No, nothing new." Before McIntyre could say anything else, Atkins said, "Hey, there's a couple of people here from D.C. looking into the girl's death. A lady from the IG's office and a guy from Congress."

"Congress?"

"Yeah. Apparently, Moore's family knows people. Anyway, they want to know where you and McGruder were the night Moore was killed."

"I was in my apartment, watching a game. And as far as I know, McGruder didn't go anywhere that night either."

"Yeah, well, they want more than your word on that."

"You're shittin' me," McIntyre said.

"No. They want me to look at your credit card and phone records to see if they might show you *weren't* at home. I told them that would take a warrant but that I was pretty sure you wouldn't have any objection."

There was a moment of silence, then McIntyre said, "I'll get a hold of McGruder and we'll swing by your office, bring our phones and our credit cards with us. We'll get on the line with you, call the credit card companies and have them read off the recent transactions. Same with the phones. You can look at the recent calls directory in the phones, and if you want, we'll give you all the info, passwords and shit, so you can talk to Verizon. I gotta tell you, though, it really pisses me off that someone says we have to prove where we were. I'm so glad I'm retiring from this chickenshit outfit."

McIntyre hung up, and Atkins said to Emma, "Okay. You happy now?"

Emma said, "Call me after you've looked at the records."

"Yes, ma'am," Atkins said. He said this as if he was trying to be sarcastic but couldn't quite pull it off.

14

When Atkins called McIntyre, he and McGruder had been sitting on the patio of a restaurant with a view of a beach sprinkled with frolicking coeds from the nearby University of Miami, both of them wishing they weren't so old and fat. Neither of them could remember the last time a woman younger than fifty had taken an interest in them.

McGruder had heard McIntyre's side of the conversation with Atkins. He said, "What's going on?"

"Apparently there's a couple of heavy hitters from D.C. down here pushing Atkins on the kid's murder."

"Who are they?"

"I don't know. He didn't tell me their names. We'll find out when we go see him."

"Well, all I can say is thank God we did what Patty told us."

Patty had told them not to take their personal phones with them when they killed the Bermans because, thanks to fucking Google, there would be a digital map of where they'd been. She'd also told them not to use a credit card to pay for anything. Fortunately, as McGruder had said, they'd followed her directions.

A waitress wearing shorts so tight they looked as if they'd been painted on passed by their table, and McIntyre said, "Hey, honey, bring us a couple more beers."

McGruder said, "You think it's a good idea going to see Atkins smelling like the inside of a keg?"

"Who gives a shit what Atkins thinks? He's lucky we're cooperating at all."

McGruder said, "We need to call Patty and tell her about these folks from D.C."

"Yeah, I know," McIntyre said. "And I'm sure she'll have all kinds of advice for us we don't need."

"If she has any advice, I'm taking it," McGruder said. "She's the smartest person we know. Plus, we need her to find out about these people bugging Atkins."

"We'll call her as soon as we get the names from him," McIntyre said.

Pointing at a blonde on the beach in an orange bikini, McGruder said, "Jesus, will you look at her. She looks just like Pamela Anderson."

"You realize Anderson's almost our age now."

"Now why did you have to go and tell me that?"

15

As they were walking toward their rental cars in the lot outside the federal building, Emma pulled out her phone and called Neil. She said, "Where's the girl's phone, Neil?"

"I'm working on it," Neil said, "but I'm having a problem because—"

"I don't want to hear any excuses," Emma said. "Find that damn phone." Emma stabbed her phone with a finger to disconnect the call.

DeMarco said, "If Neil is having a problem finding the phone, the sheriff is probably having one, too."

DeMarco wasn't enamored with the idea of beating the sheriff to Andie's cell phone, because if they did, they'd most likely be tampering with evidence in a homicide investigation. He was sort of hoping the sheriff would win the race but doubted the sheriff's technicians were as good as Neil. Knowing he wouldn't be able to change Emma's mind when it came to the phone, all he said was: "Where to next?"

It was close to six, and they'd been going ever since they'd gotten off the plane that morning, and he was hoping that Emma would decide it was time to knock off for the day. He was also thinking that since it wouldn't get dark until eight or so, maybe he could squeeze in nine holes at the golf course he'd seen from the FBI's conference room. In fact, maybe it would have some kind of twilight rate.

Emma said, "I want to go see the Bermans. Andie was convinced that they conspired with McIntyre and McGruder. I want to get a sense of them, and maybe threaten them and see how they respond."

"Threaten them with what?" DeMarco said.

"I'm going to tell them that Andie Moore was a brilliant investigator, and thanks to new evidence she uncovered, we can now prove conclusively that they conspired with McGruder and McIntyre to keep from getting convicted. I might also tell them that we suspect that they were involved in Andie's murder, and that if they don't come clean with us, they're not going to be charged with some white-collar crime where they spend five or six years in a medium-security prison. They're going to be convicted of accessory to murder and spend the next thirty years in a federal supermax."

"You think you can bluff them that easily?"

"Probably not," Emma said, "but I want to see how they react."

DeMarco doubted that confronting the Bermans would result in anything useful, but all he said was: "You want to go see them tonight? It's getting late."

"It's not *late*. It's only six o'clock. Their address is in the file Henry gave us. Just follow me when I leave the lot."

Before they reached their rental cars, DeMarco now beginning to wonder why they'd bothered to get two cars, he said, "One thing that's bugging me. From everything we've heard about McIntyre and McGruder, they don't sound smart enough to have pulled something like this off."

"They're FBI agents. They'd know how to kill someone and not get caught. As for intentionally screwing up the Bermans' conviction, I'm inclined to agree with you. But all that means is that someone smarter than they are was working with them, which is what Henry also thought. But we'll worry about them having a partner later. Right now, let's go squeeze the Bermans."

DeMarco could tell by the expression on Emma's face—she made him think of a blue-eyed lioness stalking her prey—that she was looking forward to meeting the Bermans. He almost felt sorry for them.

———◆———

DeMarco followed Emma into a Miami suburb known as Coral Gables.

The Bermans' house was a low ranch-style home with a red tile roof and an attached two-car garage on a street called Alhambra Circle. Hedges and large plants provided privacy from their neighbors. They parked in the driveway leading to the garage and walked up to the front door.

Emma rang the bell, waited a moment, then rang it again. When no one answered, she leaned on the bell while simultaneously hammering on the front door with her right fist. "I guess they're not home."

She went back to her car, got the file Henry had provided, placed it on the hood of her car, and found the Bermans' cell phone numbers. She called Lenny Berman, then Estelle Berman, and both calls went immediately to voice mail.

As they were standing next to their cars—DeMarco hoping they were through for the day—a little old lady with a yappy terrier on a leash walked by them, then turned back and said, "Are you looking for Lenny and Estelle?"

"Yes," Emma said.

"I don't think they're home. I think they might have taken a trip or something."

"Why do you think that?" Emma said.

"'Cause I see Estelle walking every morning, about six or so, while I'm having my coffee. She's one of them fast walkers, wears a fancy watch that counts the steps and measures her heart rate. But I haven't seen her the last couple of days. And last night, when I got back from playing bunco, I noticed their lights weren't on." Then, as if she realized she was giving too much information to a couple of strangers, she said, "Who are you?"

"I'm an old friend of Estelle's," Emma said. "I worked with her when she and Lenny ran an assisted living place in Orlando. I called her a week ago and said I'd be in Miami today, but maybe she forgot I was coming."

The woman said, "Well, if I see Estelle, I'll tell her you dropped by. What's your name?"

"Emma," Emma said. "This is my nephew," she added, jerking a thumb at DeMarco.

The woman left, tugging her dog, who it appeared wasn't in the mood for walking. She was practically dragging the little beast.

DeMarco said, "Where to now, Aunt Emma?"

"We'll go check into the hotel and have some dinner," Emma said.

Thank God.

"Then we're going to come back here after it gets dark and break into their house."

Aw, Jesus.

16

While at work that day, Patty McHugh took the time to make a few phone calls not related to her current assignments, which had to do with half a dozen cases involving money laundering and tax evasion. She called the Collier County sheriff and identified herself as a DOJ lawyer. She said if the sheriff doubted who she was, he could look up the DOJ number in D.C. and call back and ask for her.

The sheriff said, "Naw, I believe you. What can I do for you?"

McHugh said, "I'm one of the attorneys working with the FBI on the Andrea Moore case and just wanted to get an update from you."

"Geez, how many people do they have working that girl's murder? Today I had someone from your inspector general's office and some guy from Congress come and see me."

What the hell? McHugh thought, but she couldn't ask whom the sheriff was talking about as she was supposed to be involved in the case. She said, "Yes, I know, but I haven't had a chance to talk to them. Anyway, can you fill me in on the status of the case?"

The sheriff was happy to oblige her, and when he finished, she concluded he didn't have zip. After that she called a lawyer she knew in the FBI's Miami field office, chatted with her briefly about a case she was working on involving a guy who used to be a criminal in Cuba and was now a criminal in the United States, then said, "Oh, hey, what's going on with that poor girl from the inspector general's office who was killed down there? I never met her, but I heard she was really sweet."

Her pal in Florida informed her that, as far as she knew from the office grapevine, the FBI didn't know shit from Shinola regarding what had happened to Moore. The Miami lawyer said that everyone figured it was some alligator-poaching redneck who did it, but no one knew for sure.

When Patty got home, she took off the suit she'd worn to work and put on a pair of shorts, a tank top, and flip-flops and made a margarita. As she was making the drink, she glanced around her apartment. It was a decent-sized two-bedroom unit; the furniture was acceptable, and she wasn't embarrassed to invite her friends over—but God was she sick of the place. She could hardly wait to go hunting for real estate in Sedona. She said a silent prayer: *Please, please, Lord, don't let McIntyre and McGruder fuck everything up.*

She took her drink and went to sit on her balcony, one just big enough to hold a couple of lawn chairs, and looked out at her view: the apartment building across the street—not the red hills surrounding Sedona. She lit a cigarette. She didn't normally smoke, but she did occasionally when she was under stress—and she was definitely feeling stressed.

She was fairly certain McIntyre and McGruder wouldn't be caught for killing the Bermans. For one thing, nobody knew the Bermans were dead, and the bodies would never be found. The Everglades was the perfect place to dispose of a corpse, thanks to the alligators. More important, she'd created the plan for killing them, was certain she'd thought of everything, and McIntyre and McGruder had followed her plan to the letter—except for killing the damn girl.

She thought about what the sheriff had told her, about two people from D.C., one from the IG's office and one from Congress, being down in Florida. As she thought about that, even though she didn't know who they were, she decided they probably weren't worth worrying about. They weren't trained investigators. They weren't cops. They'd probably just been sent to Florida to put some pressure on the people working the murder. No, she wasn't too worried about this pair from D.C. What she was worried about was McGruder and McIntyre. They'd gotten old, fat, and sloppy, and God knows what kind of mistakes they might make in the future or what mistakes they'd made when they killed the girl.

They were like bookends, virtually interchangeable. As they'd gotten older, they'd even started to look alike, both of them overweight, their dark hair thinning, identical double chins. Their given names were Andrew and Michael, but they called each other Mac and everyone they knew called them Mac. McIntyre's wives had been chubby blondes; McGruder's had been slender brunettes, one Latina, one Asian, but other than their taste in women, she could hardly think of anything that distinguished them. McIntyre tended to dress a bit better than McGruder; McGruder liked to gamble whereas McIntyre didn't. McGruder had the shorter temper, while McIntyre tended to be a bit of a whiner, but they could have been cloned from the same egg. They'd even been pretty much alike in bed, the one time she'd gone to bed with each of them. The main thing was that, although she trusted them, neither would ever have been admitted to Mensa, and she could just see them doing something stupid that might come back to bite her.

Just as she had this thought, her burner phone rang. It was McIntyre. "What?" she said—and that's when he told her about Atkins asking them to produce phone and credit card records to prove they weren't lying about where they were the night the girl was killed.

"Goddamnit!" she shrieked. "Is he suspicious of you?"

"No, and calm down. He's not suspicious of us at all. The only reason he asked us to prove we were home that night was because of this guy and gal from D.C."

"Who are they? I know one's from the inspector general's office and one's from Congress, but I don't have their names."

"How did you find out about them?" McIntyre said.

"Never mind how I found out. What are their names?"

"The guy from Congress, his name is DeMarco. I remember that because I knew a guy named DeMarco when I was stationed in Phoenix. The woman's name is Emma something."

"Emma *something*? What's her last name?"

"I don't know. Atkins said her name so fast I didn't really hear it. And it's not like I was in a position to take notes or ask him to repeat it. I had to act as if I didn't give a shit."

"What are they doing down there?"

"According to Atkins, they've been sent to make sure everyone is doing their job. He said Moore's family is politically connected and is pushing folks to make sure they find out who killed her."

That's what Patty had thought. But it would be nice to find out more about them. She said, "So is anything breaking when it comes to her murder?"

"No. And as far as I know, no one is asking about the Bermans either. Why would they?"

"Have these people from D.C. talked to you and McGruder?"

"No. But I wouldn't be surprised if they did."

Patty lit another cigarette, thought for a second, then said, "If they do ask you about the girl, what are you going to say?"

"I'll say she talked to us about how we'd fucked up the Berman case the way we did, and we cooperated with her, answered all her questions, and she went on her merry way." McIntyre paused, then said, "And I think what I'll do is get pissed. That would be a natural reaction. I'll say I'm sorry we screwed up, but that I'm getting goddamn sick and tired of everybody bugging us about it. And I'll say that I'm *really* pissed that anyone would think we would have anything to do with that kid's death."

Patty thought over what he said and concluded she didn't want them talking to anyone. She said, "What I want you to do is get the hell out of Miami. Tell your boss you want a couple of days off and then disappear. Don't tell anyone where you're going. Can you do that?"

"Yeah, I guess. No one's told us we have to stay here, and our boss definitely won't give a shit if we take some time off. She hates us."

"So do that. Get out of Miami, and maybe in a few days this pair will head back to D.C."

17

They had dinner at the hotel where they were staying. As they were eating, DeMarco said, "You want to tell me why it's necessary for us to break into the Bermans' house? I'd just as soon not get arrested. I mean, this is Florida. They probably still have chain gangs down here." Then, for no good reason, he lowered his voice an octave and quoted the line from *Cool Hand Luke*: "What we've got here is a failure to communicate."

Emma said, "I want to see if we can find anything tying them directly to conspiring with McIntyre and McGruder. Andie thought they did, but there's no proof they did, and maybe we can find something."

"Like what?"

"I don't know. Maybe documents to show they've been communicating with McIntyre and McGruder after the case was settled. And Henry thought a lawyer helped them blow the case, so maybe we'll find something to ID the lawyer. Or maybe something that points to an offshore bank where they stashed the money. I don't know."

"Yeah, maybe," DeMarco said, doubting that the Bermans would be dumb enough to leave a statement lying around showing that they'd stashed fifteen million bucks in the National Bank of Panama.

DeMarco knew that Emma was committed to catching Andie Moore's killer because she wanted to give Henry some sense of closure and because she wanted to see justice done. But she also had a less noble motive: boredom. She'd spent a career at the DIA involved in high-stakes, life-and-death operations—operations involving spies and terrorists and black helicopters flying below the radar. Now she spent her days exercising, tending to her yard, and volunteering for various charitable and civic organizations—and none of those activities gave her the adrenaline rush of what she used to do. Which was one of the reasons she'd helped DeMarco several times over the years. Helping him had occasionally put her in situations that gave her a chance to use some of her old skills. Skills like breaking into people's houses.

It wasn't that DeMarco had a moral objection to breaking into the Bermans' house. The Bermans were a pair of thieves. And last year, he had broken into the home of a guy in Wyoming to get evidence related to a woman who'd been killed. But in that case, he'd been willing to take the risk because the woman had at one time been his lover. So although he, too, wanted justice for Andie Moore, he wasn't anxious to put himself in a position where he might end up in jail.

If they were nabbed breaking into the Bermans' home, he supposed that Emma could wave the credentials that Henry had given her, deputizing her as a member of his staff, and try to bluff her way out of being arrested. That might work, but only if the cops weren't terribly bright. And if they were caught, the penalty was admittedly low; they wouldn't be arrested for theft or property damage, only for trespassing, which was a misdemeanor. But there'd still be the hassle of court appearances and lawyers' fees and maybe a fine. So, should he help her or not?

The smart thing would be to sit in the car and play lookout.

But he already knew he wasn't going to do the smart thing.

They finished dinner and Emma paid the bill. As it was only seven thirty and still light outside, she said, "Meet me here in the lobby at nine. Oh, and put on some dark clothes."

"You mean, like something a cat burglar would wear? Should I go out and buy us a couple of ski masks?"

Emma walked away without responding.

DeMarco went up to his room, set the alarm on his phone to go off at eight thirty, and lay down on the bed to take a nap—but then he couldn't sleep, thinking about how he might end up spending the night in a cell if he and Emma were caught.

He hadn't forgotten about the assignment Mahoney had given him regarding the rogue congressman, Stanley Freeman, the guy who'd voted with the Republicans on a bill involving wetlands. So having nothing better to do, he googled Freeman, refining the search to include the words "wetlands," "marshes," and "swamps." The all-knowing Internet revealed nothing.

DeMarco figured someone must know why in the hell Freeman voted the way he did, and one obvious person occurred to him, although he imagined Mahoney would have already spoken to the man. The other congressman from Rhode Island—the state had only two—was a guy who seemed to have been in Washington since the Capitol was built. His name was Roland Price, he was almost ninety, and he had to be wheeled into the chamber by an aide to cast his votes. Price had mentored Freeman when Freeman first arrived in Congress, and DeMarco imagined that the state's only two congressmen would have some kind of personal relationship.

He had Price's cell phone number in his contacts list because he'd dealt with him before in connection to some scheme that he and Mahoney had hatched. After he identified himself and said he was calling on behalf of Mahoney, he said, "Congressman, you got any idea why Freeman would vote with the Republicans on that wetlands bill? You know, the one that passed a week ago? It's driving Mahoney crazy."

"No," Price said, "and Mahoney already asked me that. But there's something tickling the back of my brain, something Freeman once said, something having to do with his sister."

"His sister?"

"Yeah, but for the life of me I can't remember what it was. At my age, I'm lucky if I can remember what I had for dinner."

No shit, DeMarco thought. *Which is another reason for term limits.*

"Anyway," Price said, "I have no idea why he voted the way he did. He's always been a team player, so I don't know what got into him and he wouldn't tell me. If I can dredge up what I'm trying to remember, I'll give you or John a call."

DeMarco thanked him, hung up, and googled Freeman's sister and then used one of those online search engines to do a records search. It cost him only $9.95 to invade Margret Freeman's privacy. He learned that she was divorced and that Stanley was her only brother. He also learned that she owned a lot of commercial real estate in Providence and probably earned ten times what her brother made as a public servant. She owned an apartment building, a strip mall, two small office buildings, and four parking lots. She also had a residence near the town of Sprague, Connecticut, which was about an hour from Providence. That one stuck out because it wasn't located in Rhode Island and it wasn't a commercial property; it was just a small house.

He googled Sprague, Connecticut, and learned it had a population of about three thousand and that the Shetucket River flowed right past the town. There were nearby wetlands, and the town even had a commission called the Inland Wetlands and Watercourses Commission — and DeMarco thought, *Hmm.* Maybe Freeman was doing something to assist his sister; maybe she was planning to turn a marsh into a parking lot. Back to Google again. This time he put "Stanley Freeman" and "Sprague, CT" into the search engine.

Up popped a single article posted by an online newspaper called the *Sprague Journal,* which came out daily and limited itself to hometown

news: what was happening at the high school, what stores were clos-
ing, whose kid just got an award, who'd died since the last edition. The
article that included Stanley Freeman's name was a small column about
who'd been in trouble with the law recently: Junior Talbot got his third
DUI. Marty Hansen was arrested for domestic violence; she'd taken a
skillet to her husband's head. And then there was Stanley Freeman, who
was fined two hundred dollars for the unlawful discharge of a firearm.

A firearm? What the hell?

The article didn't mention that Stanley Freeman was a U.S. congressman. Maybe no one in Sprague knew what Freeman did for a
living. Half the people in the country can't identify their own congressman, much less one who represents another state. If Freeman had done
something sexual, like getting nabbed for paying for sex or dating a
seventeen-year-old, someone, like whatever Republican was planning
to run against him in Rhode Island, might have noticed, but a two-
sentence article about the unlawful discharge of a firearm seemed to
have flown below everyone's radar. DeMarco looked for similar articles
tying Freeman or his sister to the little town of Sprague, but all he found
was the one article.

He looked at his watch. It was time to go meet Emma. He'd have
to get back to Gunslinger Freeman later, although he couldn't see how
illegally discharging a firearm could be related to his vote on the wetlands bill.

18

DeMarco took off the clothes he'd worn that day— khakis and a white golf shirt and Top-Siders—and put on jeans, a dark blue golf shirt, and tennis shoes. He figured the tennis shoes, although white, would be better than the Top-Siders if he had to run from the cops.

At nine he met Emma in the lobby. She was dressed in black jeans and a black T-shirt, and he wondered if she'd packed the clothes knowing in advance that she planned to commit a crime.

As they were driving, DeMarco asked, "Did Atkins ever get back to you about McIntyre's and McGruder's phone and credit card records?"

"No, but I called him after we had dinner. He said he forgot to call me. Anyway, he said he didn't see anything to *disprove* that they weren't at home that night like they said they were. They didn't call anyone, and they didn't use their credit cards."

"But that doesn't really prove they were home, does it?"

"No, it does not."

They got to the Bermans' house at about nine thirty and parked on the street in front of it. The house was dark, and thanks to the plants surrounding it, it wasn't visible to the next-door neighbors, but the neighbors across the street would be able to see them walking up to the Bermans' door.

Emma, while sitting in the car, looked at the house directly across the street and said, "The lights are on, so they're up, but the blinds are closed. They're probably watching TV or something. We'll just have to take the chance."

DeMarco wanted to scream, *No, we don't have to take the chance!*

Emma said, "We'll walk up to the front door and pretend to knock. Try not to look sneaky. As soon as we're inside, we'll turn on the lights."

"Turn on the lights?" DeMarco said.

"Yes, lights on in a house at night look normal. A couple of flash-lights bouncing around in the dark don't."

"How are we going to get in? Break a window?"

"Don't be stupid. I have a set of lockpicks."

"Do you always pack your lockpicks when you travel?"

Instead of answering the question, Emma said, "When we were here earlier, I didn't see any signs that they have a security system. If they have one, and an alarm goes off, we'll leave. As for the front door lock, it won't be a problem. It's an expensive house, but the locks aren't any-thing special."

DeMarco stood behind her as she picked the front door lock, which she did in less than a minute. But a minute can seem like a long time when you're expecting someone to yell out, *Hey! What in the hell do you think you're doing?*

Once the lock was picked, Emma opened the door a couple of inches and listened for the beeping sound of a security system. When she didn't hear anything, she and DeMarco stepped inside the house. Emma closed the door and groped until she found a light switch. The first thing DeMarco noticed was an alarm panel on the wall near the front door. Emma said, "That's odd. If they were taking a trip, why didn't they set the alarm?"

"I don't know," DeMarco said, just thankful that they hadn't.

Emma said, "I'm going to find their home office and look at their files. You just look around for, hell, I don't know. Clues. Anything connected to where they might have gone, anything related to McIntyre and McGruder."

DeMarco went to the kitchen first, just because it was close to the living room. He opened a few drawers and found nothing but silverware and cooking utensils. For no good reason, he opened the refrigerator and noticed there was a carton of milk and a few things covered with Saran wrap that looked like leftovers. It occurred to him that they must not be planning to be gone for long since they hadn't bothered to get rid of things in the refrigerator that might spoil.

He opened a closet near the front door and, under a blanket, found a fireproof lockbox. He had one just like it at his home in Georgetown. In his box, he kept documents like his passport, birth certificate, insurance papers, and a couple of grand in rainy-day cash. He never locked the box, because if somebody wanted to steal what was in it and it was locked, they'd just haul the box away and break into it later. The purpose of the box wasn't to prevent theft; it was to prevent important documents from being destroyed in a fire.

He knelt and pushed down on the latch holding the box closed, and it opened. Inside it he found the deed to the house, insurance papers, birth certificates, Social Security cards, and a bunch of old photos of people who might have been the Bermans' parents or grandparents. He didn't see their passports, nor did he see anything that looked like bank statements. He went back to the kitchen and opened a drawer where he'd seen a pad of paper and a bunch of pens. He took the pad and a pen and went back to the lockbox and wrote down the Bermans' Social Security numbers and birthdates. The numbers and dates might be useful if they needed Neil to trace something online.

Next he wandered into the master bedroom, and the first thing he saw was a suitcase lying on the bed. The door to the walk-in closet was open, and there were a lot of empty hangers and spaces where clothes were missing. He opened drawers in the bedroom, found nothing useful or interesting, then walked into the master bathroom. He glanced at his watch. They'd been in the house ten minutes. He wished Emma would hurry up; he wanted to get the hell out of there before the cops showed up. He didn't really think Florida still had chain gangs, but he didn't want to find out if it did.

In the bathroom he opened a cabinet door, and the first thing he noticed were two electric toothbrushes in charging stands. He thought, *Hmm?* On a shelf he saw a circular plastic container and opened it: birth control pills. Also on the shelf was a vial for a prescription medication. The label on the bottle said it was for Lenny Berman and contained lisinopril, which DeMarco knew was used to treat high blood pressure. The label said it should be taken daily.

He went to find Emma. She was kneeling on the floor next to a two-drawer metal file cabinet, flipping through file folders. He said, "You find anything?"

"No," she said, without looking at him.

He said, "Well, come with me. I want to show you something."

She stood up and followed him into the master bedroom. He pointed at the closet and said, "It looks like a bunch of clothes are missing, and with the suitcase on the bed, it looks like they might have taken a trip like that old lady said. But they didn't clean the perishable stuff out of the refrigerator, and in the bathroom are electric toothbrushes, birth control pills, and prescription medications."

Emma went into the bathroom and took a look and said, "There's also a lot of Estelle's makeup in here, and the air conditioner is running full blast. Usually when you take a trip, you either turn off the air conditioner or set the temperature higher so you don't waste so much energy. And the alarm wasn't set, which you'd definitely do if you were taking a trip. It's starting to look like somebody wants us to *think* the Bermans took a trip."

"Or they just forgot to set the alarm and turn off the air conditioner," DeMarco said. "I also found a lockbox that had a bunch of papers in it like insurance papers and birth certificates, but no banking information. I wrote down their Social Security numbers and their birthdates in case we might need them later. Now I think we ought to get out of here before we're arrested."

"We're not going to get arrested. If someone had seen us break in, they would have called the cops and the cops would have gotten here by now. Just keep looking. Go look in the garage. Guys tend to hide things in garages."

"Yeah, all right," DeMarco said. "But I swear to God, if I get arrested—"

Emma's cell phone rang—and DeMarco almost had a heart attack. He said, "Jesus Christ, answer that thing before it rings again." He wondered why a master burglar like Emma hadn't set the damn phone on vibrate, although he hadn't remembered to silence the ringtone on his phone either.

Emma said, "It's Neil." She answered the phone before it could ring a second time, saying, "Yes."

She listened for several seconds, then she said to DeMarco, "Go get me a piece of paper and a pen." DeMarco did, and he heard Emma say to Neil, "Okay. Give them to me." She jotted down some numbers on the paper, then said, "Good work, Neil," and hung up.

To DeMarco, she said, "Let's get out of here."

"Hell, yes," DeMarco said.

"Neil located Andie's cell phone. We're going to go get it."

They left the house, Emma locking the front door by pushing down the button on the doorknob, and they got back into Emma's rental car. She started the car and took off.

DeMarco said, "So where's the phone? And how do you know it's not with whoever killed her?"

"It's in the Everglades. It's been in the same location for over twenty-four hours."

"The Everglades?"

"Yeah, close to the Everglades Parkway."

"You mean Alligator Alley."

"Neil said we got lucky. Andie owned the latest model iPhone, and the battery will go days without needing to be recharged, but who knows the last time she charged it?"

"How are we supposed to find it at night in a damn swamp?"

"Neil gave me the GPS coordinates. The coordinates will put us within ten yards of the phone."

"And like I said, maybe whoever killed her has it." DeMarco was thinking that Deputy Fisher might have been right about some Florida cracker killing Andie, like some poacher, sitting in his swamp shack, armed to the teeth, drinking moonshine while skinning dead reptiles. "Or it could be like the clock in the Peter Pan story, and it's been swallowed by a fucking alligator."

"That was a crocodile, not an alligator," Emma said. "And I don't care where it is, we're going to get it."

19

They passed the rest stop where Andie had been murdered, Emma driving about ninety.

DeMarco had been thinking that the phone might be at the rest stop, but the GPS coordinates had it someplace two or three miles to the west.

Emma eventually slowed down, the car now moving about five miles an hour, as she looked at the screen of her phone. Finally, she stopped the car. "It's within a hundred yards of here," she said.

Emma and DeMarco got out of the car. It was just past midnight and pitch-black outside. DeMarco could hear sounds coming from the swamp—crickets, frogs, and God knows what else. He wondered if there were still panthers roaming the Everglades. He knew that at one time there had been. He said, "We ought to come back in the morning and look for it."

"No, this is better," Emma said. "For one thing, it will be easier to hear the phone ring at night without the noise of cars passing on the highway. And it will be easier to see the phone when it rings. My phone lights up when someone calls. But the main thing is, we need to find it before the battery dies."

"Why would her phone be here? I could understand if it was at the rest stop, but why here?"

"I don't know. We'll think about that later."

Emma rolled up her pant legs and took off her shoes and tossed them into the car.

DeMarco said, "You're taking your shoes off? Are you nuts?"

"It's just grass, mud, and water. And they're expensive shoes."

There was no fucking way DeMarco was taking off his shoes. There were probably leaches in the water, or some parasite that would tunnel its way into your bloodstream through the soles of your feet and eventually kill you. And he wasn't going to roll up his jeans either. The jeans and the shoes would provide some protection from the water moccasin that was bound to sink its fangs into him. But what he was really worried about were the goddamn alligators, and he said so.

"What about the damn alligators?"

"Don't worry about them. Alligators don't normally attack a full-grown human being. They might attack a child standing near the water, like that poor kid killed at Disney World, or a dog, but they usually won't attack a man."

To DeMarco, the two important words she'd used were "normally" and "usually." He said, "Emma, I saw a guy get eaten alive by an alligator."

Emma was aware of what had happened in the Okefenokee Swamp because that was the first time she'd assisted him when he was doing a job for Mahoney, a case involving the Secret Service that he'd never forget.

She said, "Well, he was in the water, not walking on dry land." Before DeMarco could ask what difference *that* made, she said, "Let's go. Turn on the light on your phone to guide us. I'll start calling Andie's number on mine. Listen for the sound, but also see if you can spot the light on her phone. It should be about fifty paces from here."

They walked toward the swamp. At first the ground under their feet was solid, but before he'd taken twenty steps, DeMarco was ankle-deep, then calf-deep, in muck and water. Emma kept hitting Andie's number, but he couldn't hear a thing.

Emma muttered, "It ought to be right about here."

DeMarco heard a sound to his right. He swung his phone's light in that direction and there was an alligator. The bastard looked about ten feet long, and its satanic eyes were staring right at him. "Jesus Christ!" he yelled.

Emma glanced over at where he was shining the light, raised her arms, and yelled, "Scoot!" The alligator whipped around—it was incredibly fast—and slithered back into the swamp.

Emma said, "Turn off the light on your phone."

"Turn off the light? Are you insane?"

"No. Turn it off. We should be standing right on top of her phone. We should be able to hear it ring, but maybe she had it set to vibrate."

"Or maybe the battery's dead. Or maybe an alligator ate it." DeMarco really believed his Peter Pan clock-in-the-croc theory was possible.

"Turn off the light," Emma repeated.

DeMarco turned off the light on his phone. Emma dialed Andie's number again—and there, under the water, about a foot from where they were standing, was the phone. It was vibrating and the face was lit up.

Emma reached down and picked it up, looked at it briefly, then said, "We have to get back to the car fast. The battery's down to five percent. If it dies, we'll never be able to open it."

DeMarco was about to ask how she planned to open the phone even if the battery was charged, as that would require a fingerprint or a password, but before he had a chance to speak, Emma turned and sprinted—barefoot—back to her car. DeMarco didn't run, figuring a running person was more likely to attract a man-eating gator, but he walked quickly, using the light on his phone to spot any lurking monsters.

Back in the car, Emma quickly started the engine and reached into the glove compartment for a car phone charger. She said to DeMarco,

"I always bring my car charger with me, but I don't know if it will fit this model iPhone. It's newer than mine."

She plugged one end of the charger cord into the port under the dash, then carefully attempted to plug the other end into Andie's phone. It went in, and Emma muttered, "Thank God."

Leaving the engine running, she pulled a handkerchief from the back pocket of her jeans and wiped off her feet and lower legs. DeMarco looked down at his mud-covered, water-soaked jeans and tennis shoes and shook his head. The tennis shoes would never be white again.

As Emma was putting on her shoes, she said, "It's a good thing she had one of the new phones. They're supposed to be watertight in up to ten feet of water. Let's just hope that's true."

"But how are we going to get into the phone without a password?" DeMarco said.

"I have an idea," Emma said.

Of course she did.

She put the car in gear and took off, heading west.

"Where are we going?" DeMarco said.

"Naples," she said.

The only thing in Naples that DeMarco could think of was the sheriff.

At two a.m., Emma parked in front of the building housing the Naples morgue and the medical examiner's office.

She checked the battery level of Andie's phone and then used her own phone to call Neil. She didn't care that it was two a.m. and that she'd be waking Neil up.

She said, "I got the girl's phone. I need to know how to change the password on it."

Neil said, "Geez, Emma, it's so early I can barely breathe."

"Neil!" she snapped.

"You go to Settings, tap the button that says Face ID and Passcode, then you enter the old password and then type in the new one."

"I don't have the old password," Emma said.

"Then you're screwed," Neil said.

Emma thought for a moment, then asked, "How do I keep the phone from going to sleep? I mean, so I don't have to keep entering the password?"

Neil said, "You go to Settings, tap Display and Brightness, tap Auto-Lock, then set it to Never. That'll keep you from having to enter the password. But you have to be able to open the phone in the first place, which means you need the password or a fingerprint."

"Thanks, Neil. Go back to sleep."

Emma reached behind her and grabbed the folder containing the file Henry had given her off the back seat. She flipped through it until she found the card that Deputy Hal Fisher had given her. She called his number, and when he answered, Emma identified herself and said, "I'm really, really sorry to bother you at such an awful hour, Deputy, but I have to see Andie Moore's body. I have to see it right away. Is it still at the morgue?"

"At this time of night? This can't wait until tomorrow?"

"No. You see, Andie's mother called me tonight. I didn't tell you this, but I know her personally. She's a friend. Well, she refuses to believe the girl who was killed is her daughter even though a positive identification was made. The poor woman is obviously distraught and she's not thinking rationally. Anyway, she lives two hours from an airport, and in an hour, she's going to leave home to catch a flight to Miami and then drive to Naples, and she's in no condition to be going anywhere. So I told her to wait and that I would *personally* verify it's Andie and I would take a photo, although I have no intention of showing it to her. Like I said, I really apologize for this but . . ."

DeMarco couldn't remember the last time he'd heard Emma apologize for anything.

". . . but if I can get in to see the body right away, I may be able to stop her mother from coming down here. So is her body still at the morgue?"

"Yeah, it's still there. They completed the autopsy, but I didn't want to release it so early in the investigation."

"Deputy, I'm parked outside the medical examiner's building. All I want you to do is call the morgue—I'm sure they must have a night attendant—and tell him to allow me to look at the body."

Fisher was silent. He was a bright guy and probably smelled something off. Then he most likely decided that it wasn't worth bucking a power hitter from D.C. who maybe had enough clout to wake up the governor. "Okay," he said. "I'll call the morgue right now and tell them to let you in. Wait about ten minutes."

"Thank you, Deputy," Emma said. "And again, I apologize for waking you."

Emma and DeMarco walked up to the main door of the building and peered inside, able to see nothing but an unlit entry area. Emma hammered on the door, and a moment later a guy wearing a white lab coat appeared. He was tall and skinny, with dark hair shaved close on the sides and skin so pale it looked as if he'd never been exposed to sunlight. DeMarco thought he was creepy looking and perfectly fit his image of a guy who spent his nights with corpses.

He opened the door and said, "You Emma?"

"Yes," Emma said.

"Come with me," he said. DeMarco had expected him to have some sort of Transylvanian accent, like Dracula, but he sounded like an ordinary Florida native.

He led them to a room that looked like the morgues DeMarco had seen on TV: a wall filled with small, refrigerator-like stainless steel doors and a couple of examining tables. The temperature in the room felt like it was about fifty degrees. On one of the examining tables, apparently waiting for an autopsy, was the nude body of a guy who looked like he might weigh four hundred pounds. Not a pleasant sight.

The morgue attendant walked over to one of the doors, opened it, and slid out a long tray on which there was a body covered by a white sheet. He started to pull back the sheet, but Emma said, "I'm sorry, but would you mind leaving me alone with her for a moment? I knew her quite well, and this is very emotional for me." Emma, one of the least emotional people DeMarco knew, and apparently a better actress than he had ever imagined, sounded as if she were about to cry.

"Yeah, sure," the morgue attendant said. "I'll be there in the office. Tell me when you're finished."

"Thank you," Emma said.

When the morgue attendant was seated in his office, she said to DeMarco, who was standing next to her, "Stand on the other side to block his view."

DeMarco moved to the other side of the body as instructed, and Emma pulled down the sheet covering Andie's face. Her face was waxy and had a bluish tinge; her eyes were half open. She didn't look peaceful—she looked dead. She had small features: a button nose and a mouth with Cupid's bow lips. She looked even younger than her twenty-three years, and the sight of her broke DeMarco's heart.

Emma didn't pull the sheet covering the body all the way down. She just exposed Andie's right arm and then reached into her pocket and pressed Andie's right thumb against the cell phone. The phone was now fully charged and immediately came to life. Emma quickly went through the procedure that Neil had told her to follow to keep the phone from going back into sleep mode.

That done, she looked down at the girl's face for a moment, then whispered, almost like a prayer, "I'm going to get the bastards, Andie."

She covered Andie's arm and face and walked over to the office, where the morgue attendant was busy typing something into a computer. She said, "Thank you again for allowing me to see her. I'm hoping now that her mother can move on."

"Yeah, uh, I hope so," the morgue attendant said. "Can you find your way out?"

"Yes," Emma said.

20

———◆———

Back in the car, the first thing Emma did was go to the privacy settings on Andie's phone and turn off the location tracker.

DeMarco said, "You know the sheriff's guy might be able to trace her phone to this morgue, and it will show it was here when we looked at her body."

Emma shrugged. "We'll cross that bridge when we come to it."

Emma had yet to encounter a bridge she couldn't cross.

She looked at the recent calls directory in Andie's phone. She told DeMarco, "It looks like the only person she called the day she was killed was Henry. She called him that morning. Remember he told us she called, and he told her to come home, but then she didn't." Emma paused then said, "Now this is strange. Somebody called her twenty-four times, one call right after another, in a twenty-minute period. It looks like someone was desperate to reach her."

"When were the calls made?" DeMarco asked.

"After her body was found," Emma said.

"Did whoever called leave a voice mail?" DeMarco asked.

"No. And the caller isn't identified. It's just a number with a Florida area code. Neil will have to find out who the number belongs to."

Emma looked at the text messages in the phone next. The only one Andie had sent while she was in Florida was to her mom. Emma read it out loud. "My plane just landed in Florida. The weather's beautiful. Mom, I love my job."

"Ah, Christ," DeMarco said.

Looking at the map app, she said, "There's nothing here to show she was going to Naples. So that thing about her going there to visit a friend sounds like bullshit. She put in the address for the FBI field office in Miramar, the address for the Bermans' house, and two addresses that, if I remember correctly, are McIntyre's and McGruder's home addresses. There are two more Miami addresses. We'll have to look them up. I'm guessing one is for the hotel where she was staying."

Emma went on to the Safari app and looked at the search history. She muttered, "Nothing useful here that I can see." On to the calendar app. She said, "She put down only one appointment on the day she was killed. One with McIntyre and McGruder. Shit, I need a password to get into her e-mail."

"Look at the photos," DeMarco said.

"Why?" Emma said. "She wasn't here as a tourist."

But then Emma did as DeMarco suggested and tapped the Photos app. She said, "I'll be damned. The last photo she took is of McIntyre and McGruder with the Bermans. The date/time stamp shows it was taken on the night Andie was killed, a little after ten p.m."

She showed the photo to DeMarco. It had been taken at night, but there must have been a streetlight nearby because he could see the people in the photo clearly. The Bermans were walking ahead of McIntyre and McGruder. Henry's comprehensive file had contained photos of all of them.

"Can you tell where it was taken?" DeMarco asked.

Emma said, "I'm not positive, but it looks like the Bermans' house. You can't see the house in the photo, but you can see a small palm tree, and I remember a tree like that near the Bermans' driveway."

DeMarco said, "The only thing that photo proves is that McIntyre and McGruder were with the Bermans. That's not a crime."

"It proves more than that," Emma said. "It proves they lied to Atkins about where they were the night Andie was killed. They told him they spent the night in their apartments, which they obviously didn't. And why would they be visiting the Bermans? The case against the Bermans was already closed."

Emma looked down at Andie's phone again. "There's a video here that was taken about half an hour before Andie was killed."

Emma hit the PLAY button, and she and DeMarco watched the video together. DeMarco couldn't see anything. The screen was completely dark except for a couple of blurry shapes that might be people. And the video was bouncing all over the place, like Andie had been walking with the phone in her hand as she'd made it. Then DeMarco heard four pops and saw four quick flashes of light.

"Those were gunshots," Emma said.

The video stopped a couple of seconds after that.

Neither of them said anything for a moment.

Emma said, "I think that video shows McIntyre and McGruder killing the Bermans. Andie must have followed them after she took the photo of them with the Bermans and then videoed them killing the Bermans, but they caught her. Deputy Fisher said she had mud on her clothes. I think they spotted her, chased her, and she fell, and that's when she dropped the phone where we found it. Then they took her to the rest stop where they killed her. At some point, before or after that, they went to the Bermans' house and made it look as if the Bermans had taken a trip somewhere."

"You might be right about all that, but the video doesn't prove anything because it doesn't show anything other than a couple flashes of light."

"But we know they lied about where they were the night Andie died."

"The fact that they lied still doesn't prove they murdered anyone. Emma, we need to turn that phone over to the sheriff or the FBI. If we show them the video and tell them where we found the phone, we can probably convince them to go into the swamp and look for the Bermans' bodies. And, by the way, there's no way in hell *I'm* going into the swamp to look for the bodies."

"They won't find the bodies," Emma said. "The alligators would have hauled them off, and what they didn't digest would be scattered all over the swamp."

"We should turn over the phone, Emma," DeMarco said. "We're withholding evidence."

"Not yet. I'm going to call Neil and tell him to get his ass down here and see if he can enhance the video so we can actually see something."

Before DeMarco could object, Emma called Neil, woke him up again, and said, "I want you on the first plane to Miami in the morning. Text me your flight number and arrival time." She hung up before Neil could respond.

DeMarco said, "Now can we go get some sleep?"

Emma paused before saying, "Yes. I can't think of anything else to do tonight."

"Thank God," DeMarco said.

21

At nine the next morning, DeMarco and Emma were waiting in the baggage claim area of Miami International Airport. DeMarco was slumped in a chair with his eyes closed; Emma was on her feet, pacing, waiting impatiently for Neil to appear.

DeMarco was exhausted. Last night, by the time they arrived back at their hotel in Miami after finding Andie's cell phone, it was five a.m. Then he got only three hours of sleep before Emma woke him up at eight saying they needed to pick up Neil at the airport. DeMarco's first question was: *Why did they both have to go to pick up Neil?* His second question was: *Why couldn't Neil take a cab to the hotel?* The answer to both questions was: "Get moving, I don't have time to argue with you. Meet me in the lobby."

He heard Emma say, "Finally. There he is. He must have been the last person to get off the plane."

DeMarco opened his eyes and saw Neil coming toward them. He moved with all the enthusiasm of a man ascending the steps of a gallows.

Neil was an overweight white man who tied his thinning blond hair into a short ponytail. He was pulling a carry-on bag and had a laptop case slung over his shoulder. Considering what Neil did for a living, DeMarco had always thought that Neil's laptop should have been registered as a weapon. And he was dressed as he almost always was, in a voluminous, brightly colored Hawaiian shirt, shorts, and sandals. The clothes were appropriate for Miami in the spring, but even in the winter, Neil wore short-sleeved shirts and shorts, although he might put on boots if there was snow outside. But as Neil was almost always indoors, his stubby fingers within reach of a keyboard, his lightweight attire was normally adequate.

Had DeMarco asked Neil to fly to Miami on a moment's notice and without being given an explanation, Neil would have refused. Or he would have charged DeMarco an exorbitant amount and then still whined about the inconvenience. With Emma all he said was: "Okay, I'm here. What's going on?" DeMarco would give anything to know what Emma had on him.

Emma handed him Andie's phone. She said, "There's a video on that phone, the last one taken. It was shot in the dark and I can't see a thing on it. I want you to see if you can enhance it. Do not let the battery on that phone die because I won't be able to open it again. I opened it the first time using a dead girl's fingerprint."

"You what?" Neil said.

"Let's go," Emma said. "We'll drop you off at the hotel, and you can work from there. I'll explain everything to you on the way."

Which Emma did, telling Neil everything they'd done and learned while they'd been in Florida, including the fact that he was now in possession of evidence that should have been turned over to the cops. Neil was extremely bright, possibly even a genius, and Emma figured the more he knew about what they were doing, the more he'd be able to help. And she wasn't worried about him talking about what she told him. Neil feared Emma more than he did anyone in law enforcement.

She told him that after he'd enhanced the video—assuming he could enhance it—she wanted him to identify the people associated with all the addresses in the map app and identify the people Andie had called during the time she'd been in Miami. Emma said, "Also someone called her about twenty times the day her body was found, but the caller isn't identified. Figure out who it is."

When they reached the hotel, she told Neil she'd reserved a room for him, and as soon as he'd enhanced the video he was to call her. Neil trudged into the hotel looking like a man who knew he no longer had control over his own destiny—the way DeMarco usually looked when he was with Emma.

After Neil disappeared into the hotel, DeMarco asked, "Where are we going?"

Emma said, "I want to talk to McIntyre and McGruder."

"About what? Are you going to tell them that we know they lied about where they were the night she was killed?"

"No, I don't think so. I just want to meet them. I want to get a sense of how intelligent they are. I want to read their body language. They think we're a couple of heavyweights from Washington down here following up on Andie's murder, and I want to see how they react to us. Anyway, we'll see what happens."

In other words, she didn't have a plan and was going to wing it.

They arrived at the federal building in Miramar and, fifteen minutes later, learned from an agent who had a cubicle near theirs that McIntyre and McGruder had taken some time off and he didn't know where they were.

"Where's their supervisor?" Emma asked.

They found McIntyre and McGruder's supervisor in her office. Her name was Linda Brooks.

Brooks was a thin woman in her forties with an ash-gray complexion and no eyebrows. There were dark half-circles under her eyes that looked like bruises, and she had a brown-and-green scarf covering her head, which DeMarco suspected was hairless from chemotherapy.

Emma said she was from the IG's office and showed Brooks the credentials that Henry had given her, and Brooks said, "Yeah, I'd heard that you were down here looking into the death of that young woman. But you need to talk to Stan Atkins about that. He's the guy handling the investigation for the bureau."

"We're trying to find McIntyre and McGruder," Emma said. "One of your agents said they were on leave."

"Yeah," Brooks said. "They asked me if they could take a few days off, and I was happy to let them. The likelihood of them screwing something up is a lot less if they're not working."

"Do you know where they are?"

"No. I imagine if they're not home, they're fishing, but I couldn't tell you where."

"I see," Emma said. "I'm going to ask you the same question I asked Atkins. Do you think they could have had anything to do with Andie Moore's death?"

"No," Brooks said, and then basically gave the same explanation that Atkins had, that McIntyre and McGruder would have had nothing to fear from Moore's investigation. She added, "The only one who might have been hurt is me."

"What do you mean?" Emma said.

"My career has pretty much been destroyed by my failure to properly supervise McIntyre and McGruder when it came to the Berman case. I'm not going to rise any higher than I currently am. But I suppose that Moore could have written up something that hasn't already been written that might have caused me to get demoted. Not that I really care at this point."

Emma, in a softer voice, said, "What type of cancer do you have?"

"Ovarian. And right now the prognosis when it comes to me surviving is about fifty-fifty. So you can probably understand why my career, or what's left of it, is the last thing on my mind."

Emma nodded.

"And in case you're wondering, I got the diagnosis during the middle of the Berman case and was spending a lot of time with doctors, getting various treatments, and then, the icing on the cake, my husband decided to have an affair. So, like I've told everyone, my mind wasn't on my job as it should have been. Nonetheless, I accept that I'm responsible for everything that went wrong. Now I need to excuse myself because I'm about to throw up."

22

McIntyre and McGruder were in Key West, living the life they wanted to live every day after they retired.

They were on a fifty-foot charter boat with only two other people: the boat's captain and the kid who baited the hooks, brought them drinks, and would clean any fish they caught. They were fishing for trophy fish—sailfish, swordfish, and marlin—but if they caught a big shark, that could be fun, too. McIntyre had caught a good-size tuna. McGruder hadn't caught anything yet, but he had hooked a marlin and then lost it before he could land it.

The charter boat captain, by the way, was a gal in her thirties from Jamaica—or maybe it was Barbados—and she wore cutoff jean shorts and a halter top. Just watching her move about the boat was worth the price of the charter, whether they caught fish or not.

They figured they'd get back to the dock about one or two, and if they weren't too tired or too drunk, they'd go look at fishing boats. They knew they couldn't buy one yet—that was a year away—but they wanted to narrow down the kind of boat they wanted. Come dinnertime, they'd go to a place on the waterfront where they could get drunk, eat bloody rare steaks, and enjoy the sunset.

Tomorrow they'd go fishing again and maybe go look at condos. They knew they were going to spend a chunk of the Bermans' money on a fishing boat but hadn't decided how much they wanted to spend on their condos. They wanted nice places with a pool and an ocean view, and within walking distance of bars on the beach, but didn't see any reason to go overboard.

They figured they'd spend three days in Key West, and by the time they got back to Miami, those people from D.C. would have gone home. They couldn't hang around forever. They wanted to call and see how the investigation into the kid's death was going but decided it wouldn't be smart to show much interest in that. Plus, there was nothing they could do at this point. Either they'd get caught or they wouldn't—but they figured they wouldn't. They'd gone over everything they'd done a dozen times and couldn't think of anything they'd missed. The guns they'd used to kill the Bermans and the girl were weapons that McGruder had bought a couple of years ago at an estate sale after some gun nut had died, and they were now rusting in the Everglades, along with the laptop and the purse they'd taken from Moore's car. They'd left no fingerprints. There'd been no witnesses. No camera had spotted them. The only thing that nagged at them was that they hadn't been able to find the damn girl's phone.

———◆———

The boat was moving over the blue water at trolling speed, and McGruder had been watching his pole, hoping to see it bend in half like when a big fish struck, when, for whatever reason, his mind flashed back on Andie Moore sitting in the front seat of her car, her dead eyes staring at him. That had happened a couple of times, and it really shook him when it did. He turned to the bait boy and yelled, "Hey, bring me another drink."

He and McIntyre had never talked—nor would they ever—about how they *felt* about the girl's death. The only thing they'd vocalized was that it had been her own damn fault for having followed them the way she had. But the truth was that even though it was McIntyre who had pulled the trigger, McGruder felt terrible that they'd killed her, and he suspected that McIntyre did, too.

Stealing the Bermans' money didn't bother him a bit; that was something he could easily rationalize. He'd stolen from a couple of thieves and the U.S. government. The thieves deserved to lose their ill-gotten gains, and the government could certainly afford the loss. He hadn't taken food out of the mouths of widows and orphans.

But he'd never killed before, not even in the line of duty, and he hadn't really wanted to kill the Bermans. For one thing, if he was caught for stealing the Bermans' money, he could expect to spend maybe ten years in prison; for murder he could expect to spend the rest of his life. But it wasn't just a fear of prison time; it was more than that. Something deeper than that. He had been raised Catholic, and although he wasn't the least bit religious, he knew in his heart that killing another human being was more than a crime. It was a mortal sin. It was evil. A murder would leave an indelible stain on his soul and change him in some fundamental, irreversible way; he knew he was no longer the person he'd once been.

Yet, in the end, he helped McIntyre kill them. He shot Lenny while McIntyre killed Estelle. They killed them because Patty had insisted. She'd told them if they were going to steal the money, they had to be willing to go all the way or not go at all. She said there was no way they could allow the Bermans to live, because if they were ever caught for any other crime, they'd give up McIntyre and McGruder in a heartbeat. They wouldn't be able to give her up because they had no idea who Patty was; she'd just been a voice on the phone. But Patty had said, "We obviously don't want to share the money with them, but the money isn't the big thing. The big thing is that they're a couple of weasels who can't be trusted and will rat us out." By "us" she meant *them*. She'd said, "So tell me you're willing to kill them, and if you're not, you can forget about me helping you."

They acquiesced. They knew Patty was right, so they sucked up their guts and killed them. And the fact was that killing them hadn't really bothered McGruder all that much, and once it was done, he didn't think about their deaths other than in terms of doing what they needed to do to avoid being caught. The Bermans hadn't been innocents; they'd been two thieving slimeballs.

The girl had been different. For one thing, she'd been so damn young. Killing two people who'd spent more than forty years on earth, a lot of that time committing fraud, was something he could live with. But a twenty-something kid who hadn't done a damn thing wrong . . . that was eating away at him.

But he wasn't going to talk about it, not even with McIntyre. He'd drown his guilt in alcohol, and over time it would fade away, and maybe he could eventually convince himself that it had never happened. At least he hoped that was the case, because he could still see the girl's lifeless brown eyes staring at him.

<hr />

McIntyre interrupted his gloomy reverie, and McGruder was thankful he did.

McIntyre said, "You know, we ought to go see Hemingway's house while we're down here."

They'd been to Sloppy Joe's before— the bar in Key West where Ernest Hemingway used to hang out and get drunk and get into fights—but had never seen the writer's house and the feral six-toed cats that roamed around the place.

"What for?" McGruder said.

"Because the guy wrote *The Old Man and the Sea*. Maybe the best fishing story ever written."

"Never read it," McGruder said. "Never saw the movie either."

"Well, you are one illiterate, uncultured motherfucker."

"And proud of it," McGruder said, and burped.

McIntyre's phone rang. He looked at the caller ID. "It's the bitch," he said.

Meaning their boss.

"Don't answer it," McGruder said.

"I'm not."

A moment later, McGruder's phone rang. He didn't answer his phone either; it was the bitch calling him. They listened to the voice mail she'd left for them. It said: "Call me. Those people from D.C. want to talk to you."

No fuckin' way were they going to call her back. If she asked why they didn't, they'd say they were out at sea when she called and didn't have a cell phone signal, that their phones' batteries had died and they didn't bring a charger. Whatever. She'd know they were lying and they didn't give a shit if she knew.

McGruder's pole bent and McIntyre screamed, "You got one!"

A marlin leaped out of the sea, its black-and-white body twisting in the air. "Big son of a bitch," McGruder said. "Gotta be ten feet long."

"Yeah, try not to lose this one, too," McIntyre said.

"Fuck you," McGruder said with a grunt, praying he'd have the strength to land the fish.

He lost the marlin when it was only ten yards from the boat. The line somehow snapped, something that had never happened to him before.

He couldn't help but wonder if there really was such a thing as karma.

23

Emma and DeMarco returned to their hotel. She called Neil and told him to meet them down at the pool for lunch and tell her what he'd learned. DeMarco and Neil both ordered cheeseburgers and French fries. DeMarco had a beer; Neil, who didn't drink alcohol, had a Coke. Emma ordered a shrimp salad and an iced tea. DeMarco bet the woman didn't ingest more than a thousand calories a day.

While waiting for their food to arrive, Emma said to Neil, "Well?"

"I can't do anything with the video. I fiddled around with the illumination a bit, and if you really strain to see it, and know what you're looking for, you can make out what looks like the backs of two men."

"Crap," Emma said.

"But if you want, I can enhance it another way," Neil said.

"What do you mean?" Emma said. DeMarco knew what Neil meant.

"You get me photos of these two guys taken from behind, their heads turned a bit, I'll put them in the video clear as a bell."

"No," Emma said.

DeMarco said, "Well, not yet, anyway."

Neil said, "As for the calls she made, she called Henry Cantor, she called the FBI field office a couple of times, called her mom once."

"What about the person who called her about twenty times after she was dead?" DeMarco asked.

Neil said, "I traced the number to a batch of prepaid phones sold to Walmart but couldn't identify a specific store or who purchased it. The phone's a flip phone and about the only thing you can do with it is make and receive calls. I called the number, but no one answered, and the voice mail hadn't been set up. But here's the interesting thing. I was able to track the phone, and it's in the Everglades and about hundred yards or so from where Moore's phone was located."

Neil paused. "It looks to me like someone was trying to find Andie's phone. He bought a prepaid phone, called her number a bunch of times, and when he couldn't locate it, he gave up and tossed the phone."

"It was McIntyre or McGruder," Emma said. "They caught her after she filmed them killing the Bermans, but she didn't have the phone on her because she'd dropped it. After they killed her, they realized her phone was missing, so they tried to find it."

"That'd be my guess too," Neil said. "Anyway, moving on, the map app on Andie's phone showed the addresses for the FBI field office, her hotel, the Bermans' house, McIntyre's and McGruder's apartments, and a couple of restaurants."

"That's what we figured," Emma said.

"I tracked her movements on her last day. She went to the FBI field office at one, then—"

"Her calendar showed she had an appointment with McIntyre and McGruder at the time," Emma said.

"Yeah, I know," Neil said, "but the odd thing is, after the appointment she spent the whole afternoon sitting in the field office parking lot. At six, she drives to an area where there are a lot of restaurants and retail stores, parks her car in a parking lot, but never leaves her car. At eight, she drives to a spot half a block from the Bermans' house and parks there for two hours. Around ten, she drives from Coral Gables to the place where her phone ended up in the Everglades."

Emma closed her eyes as she spoke, as if she was visualizing Andie's movements. She said, "She was following McIntyre and McGruder even though Henry had told her not to do that. She waited until they left work, waited while they had dinner, then followed them to the Bermans' place. I don't know why they were in the Bermans' house for so long. Maybe they were getting rid of evidence, or questioning them, or doing what they had to do to make it look as if the Bermans had taken a trip. Or maybe they were just waiting for it to get dark outside. Whatever the case, after it got dark, they left the Bermans' house with Lenny and Estelle—we know this because of the photo Andie took— and then she followed them to the place where they killed the Bermans and videoed the killing."

"Yeah, that sounds right," Neil said. "Now can I go back to D.C.?"

"No. I want you to locate McIntyre and McGruder," Emma said, and wrote down their cell phone numbers on a coaster.

After he finished eating, Neil left to go back to his room to perform whatever magic was required to find McIntyre and McGruder. He called Emma only twenty minutes later and said that their cell phones were near Key West, moving, and about five miles offshore, mean- ing they were most likely on a boat. DeMarco wondered why it had taken him so long to find Andie's phone—maybe the newer model phones were harder to locate—but he didn't bother to ask, knowing he wouldn't have understood Neil's high-tech explanation.

Emma told Neil to start calling motels and hotels in the Key West area and not to stop until he'd found the place where they were staying.

DeMarco said, "So now that we know where they are, what are we going to do?"

"Go talk to them like we discussed before. I want to put some pres- sure on them."

"You really think that's going to work?" DeMarco said.

"I don't know," Emma snapped, clearly frustrated. "But I'm not going to just sit here in Miami waiting for them to get back."

DeMarco was thinking that waiting in Miami wasn't necessarily a *bad* thing, as that would give him time to go play golf, but before he could come up with some reason that sounded better than that one, Emma said, "I'm going to give Henry a call. I'm sure he'd appreciate an update."

———◆◆———

DeMarco ordered another beer as soon as Emma was gone. While sipping his beer, he thought about ways to prove that McIntyre and McGruder had killed Andie, and an idea began to form—but his thought process was derailed when a woman sat down at the table next to his. The woman was about his age and quite attractive. She was wearing a cobalt-blue bikini top and a matching sarong that revealed one long bare leg, a leg that would look even better when it was tan. She smiled at DeMarco and said, "Hi."

"Hi yourself," DeMarco said.

The woman's name was Marcie, and she was a teacher from Vermont who'd recently gotten a divorce. She'd dumped her two kids with her cheating ex-husband and had flown to Florida to enjoy the rewards of being single and to have some fun in the sun. Had circumstances been different—meaning if Emma hadn't been around—DeMarco concluded that he might have had an opportunity to be part of the fun.

———◆◆———

Henry said, "Thank you for calling, Emma. I'd thought about calling you but figured you'd call me when you had something to report."

Emma told Henry what she and DeMarco had done and learned while in Miami. In part she shared the details with him hoping that by reciting them she'd get an idea for what to do next. She concluded by saying, "Henry, I know they killed Andie and I know they killed the Bermans. But I can't prove it."

Henry said, "I'm sure you've done your best, and I appreciate it."

Henry was always courteous; Emma doubted the man ever raised his voice. She could picture him sitting behind his desk, small, quiet, calm, and gray. She tried to picture that same man at twenty-two, standing in a rice paddy, fearlessly shooting a pistol at enemy soldiers as he bled from multiple wounds. She had no doubt that soldiering and killing hadn't come naturally to Henry, but sacrificing himself to save others was exactly the kind of thing he would always do. Which was why Andie's death haunted him: because he hadn't been able to save her.

Emma said, "Henry, I'm not leaving here until they're in handcuffs."

She was about to leave the room when her phone rang. The caller ID showed it was from the Collier County Sheriff's Office. She let the call go to voice mail.

She played the voice mail and heard: "This is Hal Fisher, from the sheriff's office. I need to talk to you. I'm confused about something having to do with that girl's cell phone. Call me back as soon as you can."

Fisher must have traced Andie's cell phone to the Naples morgue. Emma thought for a second and deleted the voice mail.

Should she tell DeMarco that the sheriff might be coming after them?

No. He'd just get upset.

———◆———

Emma returned to the poolside restaurant to find DeMarco still drinking beer and talking to a woman sitting at the table next to him.

He damn well better not be making a date for later.

She sat down and DeMarco said, "Marcie, this is Emma. We, uh, we work together."

Marcie said, "It's nice to meet you, Emma. Are you a lawyer, too?"

DeMarco had told Marcie that he was a lawyer who worked for Congress but hadn't elaborated on what he did.

Emma said, "Yes, I am a lawyer. I'm *his* lawyer. I'm trying to keep him from getting convicted for multiple counts of bigamy."

"She's kidding," DeMarco said.

Marcie said, "Well, uh, I need to go back to my room. I forgot my sunblock."

Both Emma and DeMarco appreciated the sway of Marcie's hips as she walked away.

DeMarco said, "I was thinking about McIntyre and McGruder while you were gone."

"Yeah, I could tell they were foremost in your mind."

Ignoring that, DeMarco said, "We're never going to get the evidence to convict them of Andie's murder based on what we have now. But there's another way."

"And what's that?" Emma said.

DeMarco told her what he had in mind.

Emma mulled his idea over for a bit, then said, "Maybe I'm the one who should approach them."

DeMarco snorted. "You'd never be able to pull it off. You just look too . . . too *righteous*. This is more up my alley than yours."

"You realize you could get killed."

"Yeah, well, I'm counting on you to make sure that doesn't happen."

24

———◆———

The next morning, they left Miami at about six. Had it been up to DeMarco they would have left three hours later, but early-bird, worm-catching Emma wouldn't allow that. They decided to take both rental cars to Key West, then had a debate about whom Neil would ride with. Neil got carsick and had to keep his window rolled down, and sometimes he would stick his head out the window like a dog to keep from vomiting. He also had a bladder the size of a teacup, which meant frequent stops. DeMarco argued that Neil should go with Emma, as she was the one who'd ordered him to Florida. Emma countered that she had to ride alone because she needed to think and because she had calls to make.

"Who do you have to call?" DeMarco said.

"He's riding with you," she said.

To reach Key West from Miami, they took Highway 1, also known as the Overseas Highway, one of the most scenic drives in the United States with its view of the Gulf of Mexico on one side of the roadway and the Atlantic Ocean on the other. The highway runs from Key Largo to Key West, is a little over a hundred miles long, and has about forty bridges connecting the picturesque islands that make up the Florida Keys archipelago. At times it seemed as if the car was riding *on* the water instead of over it, making DeMarco wonder what the drive would be like during one of Florida's spectacular hurricanes.

On the way to Key West, Neil searched Airbnb for the sort of house DeMarco would need. The main requirements were that it had to be fairly isolated and had to have Wi-Fi. Neil couldn't find a suitable place in Key West, but he found one on Geiger Key, about twelve miles from Key West. And because Neil was with him instead of Emma—Emma who had the DOJ credit card—Neil booked the place using DeMarco's credit card. The property manager told them where they could find the keys and said that inside the house was a notebook that provided everything they'd need to know, such as the Wi-Fi password and how to use the barbecue.

When they arrived at the house on Geiger Key, the first thing Emma did was make a tour of the exterior with Neil. After she deemed it suitable for an ambush, she told Neil she wanted him to take her rental car and find a place where he could purchase four cameras, the smallest ones he could find, and ones with infrared lenses. She told him where she wanted the cameras mounted on the exterior of the house, and they found a ladder in the garage, along with most of the tools he would need to install the cameras. She told him to buy whatever other tools he required.

While Neil went camera shopping, DeMarco checked out the barbecue grill and was pleased to see that it used propane and not charcoal—charcoal being a pain in the ass—then drove to a nearby store. He planned to be in the house for only two nights, but he bought coffee, a six-pack of beer, a six-pack of Coke, a bag of potato chips, and three ham sandwiches that he suspected, because of the wilting lettuce, had been on the shelf for about a week. He also bought a rib eye steak, a big Idaho potato, and a decent bottle of red wine. The sandwiches and chips he would share with Neil and Emma at lunchtime; the steak and wine would be reserved for his dinner that evening.

Neil returned with the cameras. After they had lunch—Emma and Neil both complaining about the quality of the sandwiches that DeMarco had purchased—DeMarco helped Neil install the cameras. In fact, DeMarco did most of the work mounting the cameras on the eaves of the house and the garage because Emma was afraid that overweight, uncoordinated Neil would fall off the ladder. She apparently didn't care if DeMarco fell. After the cameras were installed, Neil ensured that the live feed from the cameras would go to Emma's laptop, then they had DeMarco walk around outside the house to make sure the cameras were all working as intended.

Emma's phone rang as DeMarco was repositioning one of the cameras. Emma glanced at the caller ID and silenced the phone.

"Who was that?" DeMarco asked.

"Robocall," Emma said. DeMarco could tell she was lying and wondered why.

"You haven't heard from the sheriff, have you? I mean, about Andie's phone."

"Point that camera a little more to the left," Emma said.

Neil and Emma left at about seven p.m. to find a motel where they'd spend the night, Emma first giving DeMarco his marching orders for the next day. As soon as they left, DeMarco—happy to be rid of them—barbecued the steak he'd purchased earlier, then enjoyed it along with his baked potato and most of the bottle of wine as he watched the sun set on the waters off Geiger Key.

———◆◆◆———

At six the next morning, DeMarco was parked outside the motel where McIntyre and McGruder were staying. He knew Emma was parked someplace nearby, but he didn't see her. The next phase of the plan was for DeMarco to find an opportunity to talk to the FBI agents alone.

At seven, McIntyre and McGruder came out of the motel and walked to a Cadillac sedan. DeMarco recognized them from the photos in Henry's file as well as the photo that Andie had taken. They were both big guys with big guts and cheerful expressions on their sunburned faces. They were wearing loose-fitting sports shirts, cargo shorts, and tennis shoes without socks. On their heads were long-billed baseball caps. They looked as happy as a couple of kids playing hooky from school.

DeMarco was hoping they'd go someplace for breakfast, but they didn't. They drove to a marina, and he watched as they parked the Cadillac and walked into a small office on the pier. They were in the office for about ten minutes, then walked down the pier to a charter fishing boat with a dozen fishing poles stuck in the pole holders. At eight the charter boat left the marina with McIntyre and McGruder sitting in chairs on the back, drinking from tall glasses. The name of the boat was *Sea Breeze*.

DeMarco walked into the office where McIntyre and McGruder had gone. It was a place to sign up for various excursions, including fishing. DeMarco asked the sort of questions a would-be customer would ask and eventually learned that the *Sea Breeze* would be back at the pier at one in the afternoon.

He called Emma. "They'll be back in five hours and hopefully after that will go someplace where I can talk to them. Anyway, we have five hours to kill, and I'm going to go find a golf course and play nine holes."

"What?" Emma shrieked, as if he were a soldier deserting a combat post.

"Well, why not?" DeMarco said. "There's no point in just sitting here. I'll be back before the fishing boat docks."

He hung up before Emma could come up with some sadistic reason he shouldn't be allowed to enjoy himself. He was so glad he'd brought his golf clubs with him.

He drove over to the Key West Golf Club, only twenty minutes from the marina. He asked the guy in the pro shop if he could play nine holes by himself but was told he'd be paired up with another golfer, which DeMarco said was fine with him.

"Yeah, well," the pro shop guy said, "you may change your mind about that after you play with him."

"Why's that?" DeMarco said.

"You'll see."

When his name was called, he walked over to the first tee. A lanky kid with a mop of blond hair, wearing a sun-faded red golf shirt and baggy shorts, was standing there whipping his driver back and forth to warm up. He was seventeen or eighteen, about six two, and couldn't have weighed more than a hundred and fifty pounds—but when he swung the club, it sounded as if the club head were moving through the air at about the speed of Mach 1.

DeMarco drove first. With his upper body strength, he could drive the ball fairly well, and his ball went about 230 yards. On average, PGA pros drive a golf ball 280 to 320 yards, so for DeMarco, at his age, a 230-yard drive was pretty damn good, even if this one did end up a few feet in the rough. DeMarco was pleased and happy that he hadn't embarrassed himself.

Then the kid drove—and his ball flew more than three hundred yards. Easily more than three hundred yards. DeMarco didn't think the ball was ever going to come down.

"Jesus, that was a hell of a drive," DeMarco said.

The kid shrugged.

On the third hole, after the kid sank a twelve-foot putt for a birdie, DeMarco asked, "Where do you go to school?"

"Arizona State. I'm on spring break."

"You on the golf team?"

"Gonna be," the kid said.

Phil Mickelson had played golf for Arizona State. Top PGA earners like Jon Rahm and Paul Casey had also played there. Rahm was ranked the number one golfer in the world in 2021. Casey had won three PGA events and fifteen European tournaments. So if you played golf for Arizona State, it meant you had the potential to become a multimillionaire.

By the ninth hole, the kid was five strokes under par, and DeMarco was feeling humiliated that he'd slowed him down on every hole. The kid was nice enough about the whole thing, acting the way he probably would have if he'd been playing with his grandfather. For maybe the first time in his life, DeMarco was actually happy to leave a golf course. His only consolation was that he knew one of these days he'd be watching a tournament on TV and be able to say, *I played with that guy once.*

DeMarco was back at the marina before one, as he'd promised Emma, and watched McGruder and McIntyre as they disembarked from the *Sea Breeze* and then posed for photos next to two big fish hanging from hooks on the pier. One of the fish DeMarco recognized as a swordfish; he didn't know what species the other one was. They faced the camera looking triumphant, with broad smiles on their sunburned faces. They were thieves and murderers, but they didn't make him think of Jesse James and his brother, Frank.

In most ways, the two FBI agents were rather ordinary. They were lazy, unambitious, and indifferent to their jobs, a couple of guys who just liked to drink and fish. In some ways, they weren't a whole lot different from him. How on earth had they become cold-blooded killers? Fifteen million dollars was a hell of an incentive, but DeMarco sensed that McIntyre and McGruder probably had to be *pushed* into committing murder—and he wondered who it was that did the pushing.

The agents left the fish where they were hanging and walked off the pier and over to a nearby restaurant that had outdoor seating, DeMarco trailing along behind them. He made a quick call to Emma to tell her where they were, although he was pretty sure she already knew. They both agreed that it was unlikely that McIntyre and McGruder would try anything in a public setting, but DeMarco found some comfort in knowing that gun-toting Emma would be close by. As for Emma's gun, it was a Beretta. She brought it to Florida in her carry-on bag, something she was allowed to do as she had the paperwork to show she was permitted to take a firearm on an airplane. How a retired civil servant came to be in possession of such paperwork he didn't know.

DeMarco waited until McIntyre and McGruder had ordered beers, then walked over to their table and sat down.

McIntyre said, "We're having a private conversation here. Go sit somewhere else."

DeMarco smiled and said, "Guys, my name's DeMarco. I'm from Congress, and I'm one of the people sent down from D.C. to look into Andie Moore's murder."

Both men looked annoyed—not alarmed, just annoyed—and McGruder muttered, "Aw, shit."

McIntyre said, "Yeah, we heard you wanted to talk to us. Our boss called and told us. But we're on vacation, and you're going to have to wait until we're back at work. How did you find us, anyway? We didn't tell anyone where we were going."

"Oh, finding you was a piece of a cake. There's a guy back in D.C., he's ex-NSA, and he found you for me using your cell phones. The other thing he found was Andie Moore's cell phone." DeMarco thought about telling them that Neil had also located the flip phone they'd used to try to find Andie's cell phone but decided not to. The fact that he'd found her phone was the only thing that mattered.

They both tried to contain their reaction to hearing that Andie's phone had been found, but neither of them was able to pull it off. Poker-faced, they weren't.

DeMarco said, "I got your attention now?"

"What do you want?" McIntyre said.

A waitress stopped at the table and asked DeMarco if he wanted anything. He pointed at the bottles of Corona McIntyre and McGruder were drinking and said, "I'll have the same thing my friends are drinking."

"What do you want?" McIntyre asked again after the waitress left.

DeMarco said, "Let's wait until she brings me my beer so we're not interrupted again. In the meantime, I saw those fish you caught. They were impressive."

"You've been following us?" McGruder said.

"What I was wondering was, what's going to happen to the fish? You just left them hanging on the pier. Do they cut them into fillets and send them to you?"

"Hey, fuck the fish," McGruder said. "And fuck you, too."

The waitress brought DeMarco his beer. He thanked her, took a sip, and tipped the bottle to the agents. "Cheers," he said.

They didn't respond.

DeMarco said, "Okay. First, let me tell you where things stand. Me and that woman who was with me—you know, the lady who works for the IG—we talked to the sheriff and that guy, Atkins, about the girl's murder. Basically, they don't have zip. So the IG gal, she figures it's time to give up and head back home, but like I told you, I got the bright idea of having this NSA buddy of mine hunt for the girl's cell phone. Figured it would be a waste of time, but then, I'll be damned, he located it. You know where it was?"

The agents looked at him stone-faced.

"Well, it was right where you killed the Bermans."

McGruder stood up, pointed a finger at DeMarco's face, and said, "Hey! We didn't kill anyone."

"Jesus, sit down, McGruder," DeMarco said. "Do you want people to hear this?"

"Yeah, sit down," McIntyre said. "But he's right. You got a lot of fuckin' nerve accusing us of murder. And I think you're bullshitting us about finding her phone."

DeMarco said, "No bullshit. I went to the place where the phone was based on the GPS coordinates. I was surprised the battery hadn't died, but what do I know about cell phones? Anyway, I went there at night—I gotta tell you, the fucking alligators scared the shit out of me—but I called the number and the phone lit up. It had been set on vibrate. Well, guys, guess what was in the phone?"

McIntyre said, "Now I know you're full of shit. You couldn't get into her phone without a password."

"Or a fingerprint," DeMarco said.

"That's right, or a fingerprint."

DeMarco smiled. "I took the phone to the morgue where they were keeping Moore's body and pressed her little dead thumb against it, and, voilà, it opened right up. Now if you think I'm bullshitting you, call the Collier County ME and he'll tell you I visited the poor girl's corpse."

McIntyre, clearly the more thoughtful of the two, was looking at him skeptically. McGruder looked as if he was about to leap out of his chair and strangle him. DeMarco was glad neither man appeared to be carrying a gun.

DeMarco said, "Well, guys, let me tell you what was in the phone. There was a photo of you and the Bermans leaving the Bermans' house the night Moore was killed. And there was a video of you killing them."

Both men started to say something, but DeMarco raised his hand before either man could speak. "Now I know what you're thinking. You're thinking I'm *still* bullshitting you. But I sent the photo and the video from Moore's phone to mine, and you can see for yourself."

DeMarco took out his phone and showed the agents the photo of them with the Bermans.

"That doesn't prove shit," McGruder said. "So what if there's a photo of us with them."

"You're wrong about that, m'man. Look at the date/time stamp. It proves you lied when you said you were both home the night Moore was killed. And once the FBI knows you're lying, they'll do a bunch of razzle-dazzle shit to trace your movements that night using cameras and facial recognition software and God knows what else and place you at the crime scene. But then you'd know more about the FBI's capabilities than I would."

As both men sat there stunned, trying to decide what to say, DeMarco tapped his phone a couple of times. "Now here's the video of you killing the Bermans."

They squinted at the screen as he played the video. McIntyre said, "Play it again," so he did.

"You can't see a fuckin' thing," McGruder said.

DeMarco said, "Well, you can see a little. And you can hear four pops that are gunshots and see four flashes of light, and if you look really close, you can see the backs of you and your partner, but in general you're right. The video isn't conclusive. But you remember that NSA buddy of mine, the one who located her phone? Well, he's a fuckin' genius. I didn't send him the video—I'll tell you why in a minute—but he told me that with these new iPhones, he could make that video look like it had been shot at high noon."

DeMarco could tell that McIntyre was beginning to see where this discussion was going. His partner hadn't caught up yet.

McIntyre, now sounding less tense, said, "So why didn't you give the phone to the sheriff or the bureau?"

DeMarco said, "First, a little preamble. Oh, hey, do you guys want another beer?"

"Just get on with it," McIntyre said.

"Okay. Moore was convinced that you two intentionally screwed up the Berman case so they wouldn't get convicted, and the reason you did that was so you could get part of the money they stole. But then you had an even better idea. You decided if you killed them, you'd get *all* the money they stole, which folks are guessing is about fifteen million. Well, guys, I'm a GS-13 civil servant, and thanks to a divorce and a bunch of shitty investments, I'm practically broke and I'm tired of being broke. So I was thinking. Should I do the right thing and turn Moore's phone over to the bureau and let them build a case to arrest your murdering asses, or should I pick door number two? Door number two is I throw the kid's phone away and you give me a million bucks. Which still leaves you with fourteen million, which isn't bad."

"Fuck you," McGruder said.

"Don't be rude," DeMarco said. "Now I have no idea where you stashed the money, but I'm sure, if you wanted to, you could transfer some of it to me electronically. So the next time we meet, you need to bring a laptop and whatever else you need to move a million bucks into my bank account. Right now, what I want is an agreement in principle that you're going to pay me."

McIntyre started to say something, but DeMarco kept going. "Now I know what else you're thinking. You're thinking that this could be some kind of setup. Like maybe I'm wired, or maybe I'll wait until you move the money, then I'll whistle for the cops. Well, guys, look me up online. Check out who I am. I'm John Mahoney's fixer, and there's a bunch of articles that will prove it. Now I might be as honest as the day is long, but do you really think someone who works for a crook like Mahoney is honest? You may have heard on the news about the shit he pulled on the federal building in Boston, where he's being accused of getting kickbacks from all the contractors. Well, guess who it was that carried the money to him? Yep, that was me. Just something for you to think about."

Neither man said anything, McIntyre looking thoughtful, McGruder looking as if he was struggling to control his temper. McIntyre said,

"We're not admitting to anything and we're not agreeing to anything. Not yet. We need some time to think this over."

"That's reasonable," DeMarco said, sounding reasonable. "And you have until eight o'clock tonight. That'll give you enough time to check me out and see if you can figure out a way to stay out of jail if you don't pay me. But if I don't hear from you tonight, then I'm heading back to Miami tomorrow morning and giving the phone to the FBI. The real FBI."

"Where's the girl's phone?" McGruder said.

DeMarco laughed. "I sure as shit didn't bring it with me. You guys aren't in great shape, but I couldn't take the chance that you might try to take it from me. The phone's hidden where you'll never find it."

DeMarco grabbed a napkin sitting on the table, wrote his cell phone number on it, and handed the napkin to McIntyre. He stood up and said, "I'm not bluffing, guys. Call me tonight or I'm out of here and you go down for killing three people. I'm not going to hang around here for days so you can have a chance to take a crack at me. And if you do call and you want to meet to make the transfer, I'll pick the place and it will be somewhere public."

DeMarco dropped ten bucks on the table to pay for his beer and walked away.

25

"Son of a bitch!" McGruder said. "We need to—"

"Shut up. We'll talk about what to do about him later. Right now we have to follow him. We have to find out where he's staying."

They could see DeMarco strolling away from the restaurant as if he didn't have a worry in the world. McIntyre took off after him, walking on the opposite side of the street, hanging back about half a block. DeMarco stopped at a stand that sold fish tacos. He bought a couple of tacos, took a seat at a picnic table, and ate them slowly while looking out at the ocean. He never once looked in McIntyre's direction.

DeMarco finished his lunch, tossed a paper plate and a couple of napkins into a waste container, and ambled across the street to a parking lot.

McIntyre, half a block away, was partially hidden by a booth where you could buy tickets for Key West tours. McGruder was waiting in McIntyre's car near the bar where they'd been drinking. McIntyre called his partner, told him where he was, and said, "Bring the car up. He just headed into a parking lot, which I'm guessing is where he's parked."

"Roger that," McGruder said.

A couple of minutes later, McIntyre watched DeMarco pull out of the parking lot in a small blue sedan. McGruder pulled up in McIntyre's

Cadillac, and McIntyre joined McGruder in the car. He pointed and said, "That little blue Ford up there."

McGruder hit the gas and followed DeMarco.

Emma followed McIntyre and McGruder.

DeMarco surprised them. He didn't go to one of the Key West hotels. He got on Highway 1, the highway to Miami.

"Where the hell's he going?" McGruder said.

"How the hell would I know?" McIntyre said.

DeMarco stayed on Highway 1, heading north, and drove through Stock Island, past the Key West Naval Air Station and Rockland Key, and on to Big Coppitt Key, then made a right onto Boca Chica Road, the road that leads to Geiger Key and that runs parallel to the water. He eventually ended up on a street that had half a dozen older houses on it, houses that had somehow managed to survive God only knows how many hurricanes. Across the street from the houses was a beach. DeMarco pulled into the last house on the street, a small one-story structure with a screened-in porch and a detached one-car garage. DeMarco parked his car in front of the garage.

McGruder drove past the house while McIntyre punched the address into his phone. McGruder continued onward, looking for a place to turn around, and came to a park called Geiger Beach Park. A sign said the park was open until seven p.m.

McGruder pulled into the park's small parking lot and stopped.

"Why the hell's he staying out here? Why isn't he staying in Key West. There isn't anything out here."

"I don't know," McIntyre said. "Maybe the house belongs to a friend or a relative. Maybe he can't afford to stay in Key West. You heard him bitch about how broke he was. Who cares why he's staying here? Let's cruise by it again."

McGruder did, and they noticed that the house faced south, toward the beach and the ocean. On the west and north sides of the house were low-lying plants and trees. A tall bamboo hedge separated the house from its neighbor to the east.

McIntyre said, "I like the looks of this."

"What do you mean?"

"I mean the place is pretty isolated and probably dark as shit at night."

McGruder said, "So what do you want to do? We should just go in there and shoot his ass and take the girl's phone."

"Not yet. First, I want to talk to Patty."

Emma called DeMarco. "Okay, they followed you. It looks like they bought your story, and they just drove past the house a second time to check it out. I don't think they'll try anything while it's light out. I'll stick with them until I'm sure they're headed back to Key West, then I'll come back to the house."

Twenty minutes later, Emma arrived on foot. She'd parked her car about a block away. DeMarco was sitting in a rocking chair on the screened-in porch, drinking a beer, looking out at the ocean.

Emma took a seat next to him in the other rocking chair on the porch.

DeMarco said, "You want a beer?"

Emma hesitated, then said, "Sure."

DeMarco went into the house and got her a beer, and as he handed it to her, he asked, "Where's Neil?"

"I told him he could go home. There's no reason for him to be here at this point. I imagine he'll rent a car and catch a flight out of Miami this afternoon."

"So what's the plan?" DeMarco asked.

Meaning the plan to make sure McIntyre and McGruder didn't kill him.

26

The burner phone in Patty's purse rang. She looked at the screen and saw it was McIntyre calling from his burner.

Patty had insisted, after they'd decided to go after the Bermans' loot, that they would use only prepaid phones to talk to each other. She couldn't deny she'd been friends with them, but she wanted no records showing that they'd been communicating recently.

She answered the phone, saying, "What is it?"

McIntyre said, "We could be fucked."

Patty was in her office. She walked around her desk and shut her office door. She said, "What's going on?"

McIntyre said, "I told you about those two they sent down here from D.C. to look into Moore's death, some gal from the IG's office and a guy from Congress."

"Yeah," Patty said. "And I told you not to talk to them. I told you to disappear from Miami so you could avoid them."

"We did. But that guy, DeMarco, tracked us to Key West."

"How did he track you?"

"It doesn't matter. But let me tell you what that son of a bitch did and what he told us."

As McIntyre was telling her about DeMarco finding Andie Moore's cell phone and the video and DeMarco's demand, Patty's head began buzzing as if her skull were filled with angry hornets. She said, "You dumb bastards!" when she learned that McIntyre hadn't told her that the girl's cell phone hadn't been on her when they killed her and how they'd looked for it and failed to find it. She would have screamed at him but was afraid her secretary might hear her even though her door was closed.

McIntyre concluded by saying, "DeMarco told us if we don't call him back by eight tonight and agree to give him a million, he's leaving tomorrow and he's turning the phone over to the bureau. So we gotta deal with this asshole and we gotta deal with him tonight. We've talked it over, and we think—"

"Shut up, just shut up," Patty said. "I have to think. I'll call you back."

She told her secretary she'd be back in a bit.

Her secretary said, "You have a meeting that starts in fifteen minutes."

Patty ignored her.

She stepped outside the DOJ building, lit a cigarette, then, pacing in front of the building like some sort of marching lunatic, she thought about what McIntyre had said.

Ten minutes and another cigarette later, she made a decision.

She used her phone to check on flights to Miami, then went back to her office. She told her secretary, "Rita, cancel my appointments. I'm going home. I've got some kind of bug and I just threw up everything I ate. The way I'm feeling, I may be out tomorrow, too. I'll let you know in the morning."

Outside the building again, she called McIntyre back. She said, "I'm flying down there today. I'll probably be in Key West around midnight. And you're right, we gotta do something about DeMarco, but I want to be there to make sure there are no more mistakes. So call him tonight, wait until just before eight, and tell him you'll pay him and that you'll meet him tomorrow morning wherever he wants to meet. That'll give us some time. But I don't want you to do anything else until I get there. You got it?"

"Yeah, okay. Where do you want to meet us?"

"Someplace near where he's staying. When I get close to Key West, I'll call and you can give me an address."

She took a cab to her place. She normally used the Metro to commute to work, but there wasn't time for that. In her apartment, she tossed a change of clothes and some toiletries into a carry-on bag. Also, three pairs of latex gloves.

She went to the small wall safe in her home office. In the safe she kept important papers and her rainy-day cash. In the safe there was also a driver's license, a passport, and two credit cards made out to one Katherine Bowerman. She took the Bowerman documents and grabbed two grand in cash just in case she might need it.

During the five years Patty had been in the FBI, she was used once in an undercover role, a case involving some wiseguys in Chicago, where she'd played the part of a drug dealer's girlfriend in an FBI sting operation. The Bowerman ID documents were real, not forgeries, because the FBI was the organization who'd obtained them. She was supposed to have turned the documents in after the wiseguys were arrested, but she forgot, and nobody noticed that she'd forgotten. Then a couple of years later, she rediscovered the documents sitting in her desk, and because she was a bit paranoid, she decided to keep them up to date.

She renewed the driver's license and passport to keep them current, updated the photos as she'd aged, and, every once in a while, charged something to the credit cards and paid the bill with bank checks. It just made her feel good, having a backup ID she could use if she ever needed to, like if she was trying to get away from some maniac stalking her. Well, nobody ever stalked her, and she'd never had a reason to use the Bowerman ID—but then Andie Moore was killed. Sometimes it pays to be paranoid.

When she flew to Florida to talk to McIntyre and McGruder after they killed Moore, she'd used the Bowerman ID, and she was going to use it again to fly down to Florida today. She didn't want anyone to know she'd been anywhere near Miami. Records would show that the last time Patty McHugh had been in Miami was almost a year ago, the night she and McIntyre and McGruder got drunk together and launched the plot to steal the Bermans' money.

The last thing she did was put a disassembled .38 revolver in her carry-on bag. She was going to have to check the bag before she boarded the flight, as she wouldn't be able to walk it through security at the airport.

As for the revolver, it was untraceable.

Patty's dad had been a bit of a gun nut, and Patty became one, too. Her dad had taught her how to shoot a pistol when she was about twelve and took her deer hunting with him throughout her teens, so she was better than most of the guys in her class at Quantico with a handgun and a rifle. After she left the FBI for the DOJ, she would still go to a range every couple of months and fire off a few rounds to remain proficient. And just because she liked to shoot guns. In addition to the revolver, she had three other pistols: a 9 mm SIG Sauer she kept in the nightstand next to her bed and two small ones, a .32 and .25, she could put in a purse or a pocket. She also had a hunting rifle, one that had belonged to her dad and hadn't been fired in years. The three automatics were all properly registered; the .38 revolver wasn't. It was a vintage Colt Police Positive Special with a four-inch barrel, the type of gun used by cops and FBI agents before they started using automatics. She'd bought it at a gun show in Virginia on a whim ten years ago and never filled out any paperwork when she did.

All packed and ready to go, she booked a flight to Miami leaving from Dulles in ninety minutes. She used the Bowerman credit card to make the reservation and took a cab to the airport because she didn't want there to be a record of her car being parked at an airport parking lot. Before she went into the terminal, she put on a long-billed baseball cap and sunglasses and walked looking down at the ground as much as possible to make it harder for security cameras to capture a clear image of her. She really wished she had a wig to wear, but there hadn't been time to go shopping for one. As it turned out, when she passed through security, the TSA agent barely glanced at her and didn't tell her to take off her hat or sunglasses.

Before boarding the plane, she had a rum and Coke to settle her nerves a bit. She wanted to have more than one but didn't, as she needed to keep her head clear to deal with the DeMarco situation.

DeMarco. Who the hell was this guy? She pulled her phone from her purse and googled him. The first thing that popped up was a photo of him wearing an orange prison jumpsuit with his hands cuffed behind his back. He was a hard-looking SOB, dark hair, unshaven, scowling at the cameraman. She thought he looked like a Mafia hood.

The accompanying article described DeMarco being arrested for killing Congressman Lyle Canton and then later being released when it was proven he'd been framed for the crime. It also mentioned that he was John Mahoney's fixer and—really getting Patty's attention—that his father had been an honest-to-God hit man for the Mob in Queens. Yeah, DeMarco may not have killed Canton, but the apple didn't fall far from the tree, and he was exactly the kind of guy who might try to extort money from her and her partners.

Maybe. Or maybe it was all a setup—which would make DeMarco even more dangerous.

27

―――◆―――

"So what's the plan?" DeMarco asked.

Emma said, "Just hold on. I don't want to have to repeat myself."

"Repeat yourself to who?"

A red Mustang convertible with two men in it pulled into the driveway. The convertible was the type DeMarco would have rented if Emma had let him.

Emma called out in Spanish, saying something to the men that DeMarco didn't understand, then told him, "Move your rental car so they can put their car in the garage."

DeMarco's car was parked in front of the garage. Emma had told him to park there so if McIntyre and McGruder drove past the place they'd see he was there.

The guys in the Mustang sat there waiting patiently while DeMarco got his car out of the way, then pulled the Mustang into the garage. They came out of the garage a moment later, both of them holding duffel bags.

Emma said, "Let's go into the house."

Inside the house, Emma said to DeMarco, "This is Javier and Sergio."

Javier and Sergio were small, muscular, dark-haired men in their late forties or early fifties. Javier had a mustache; Sergio didn't. Neither man was more than five foot six, but they were a couple of hard-looking little bastards, like ex–featherweight boxers. DeMarco wouldn't have wanted to tangle with either of them.

Emma said, "I worked with Javier and Sergio when I was in the DIA."

Ah, now DeMarco got it. These two were probably ex–special forces, although maybe not American special forces.

She spoke to Javier and Sergio for a few minutes in Spanish, smiling and laughing occasionally. Emma liked to practice her Spanish whenever she could to remain fluent. DeMarco knew she also spoke Farsi but didn't know whom she spoke to to remain proficient in that language.

To DeMarco, she said in English, "You didn't think we were going to take on two armed FBI agents on our own, did you? For one thing, you don't even have a gun, and if you had one, you'd probably shoot me."

"Would not," DeMarco said.

Emma said, "Okay. Here's the plan. I want McIntyre and McGruder alive. I don't want to get into a gunfight with them and have to kill them."

It never even occurred to Emma that they might kill her.

"For the rest of the day, until it gets dark, we'll all stay inside the house and monitor the outside with the cameras Neil installed. Like I said earlier, I don't think they'll try anything while it's light out, but if they do, then we'll deal with it. Come nightfall, I'm going to hide in the garage, and Sergio and Javier are going to disappear into the brush behind the house. McIntyre and McGruder will never see them. At eleven, you'll turn off the lights to make it look like you've gone to bed. Then you'll belly crawl—and I mean *belly* crawl—from the house to the garage. The whole time, Sergio and Javier will be watching for them, and they'll be in contact with me. They have earbuds and mics and night vision goggles. I'll be in the garage, monitoring the feed from the cameras."

Emma continued: "They can't kill you until they have your and Andie's cell phones. Which means they're not going to drive by the house and spray it with a machine gun. They have to make sure you have her phone with you and can question you if you don't. What they might do is knock on the front door, hoping you'll answer it, and then push their way into the house. But I don't think they'll do that. I think they'll wait until you've gone to sleep, approach the house from the back side, then break in.

"And what we're going to do is let them break into the house, and as soon as they do, I'll call the cops. But I want to keep them in the house until the police arrive. If they try to leave, we'll fire a few rounds to drive them back inside. Then they'll be arrested once the cops get here. There may be some sort of standoff situation where the cops have to bring in SWAT and a negotiator, but eventually they'll give up."

"What will they be arrested for? Breaking and entering?" DeMarco said.

"Yes. But if they fire at us, attempted murder can probably be added to the indictment. Then we'll tell the cops and the FBI everything. We'll tell them about the photos on Andie's cell phone and the fact that the Bermans are missing and that McIntyre and McGruder lied about where they were the night Andie was killed. We'll tell them about the story you fed them, and the fact that they broke into the house to kill you will be additional proof that they killed Andie."

Emma concluded with: "So that's the plan."

DeMarco didn't say anything for a moment. "You know, I used my credit card to rent this place, so try not to shoot the hell out of it."

The remainder of the day passed slowly. Javier and Sergio examined the area behind the house through the windows. They opened their duffel bags, tested the communication gear to make sure it was working, and checked their weapons. DeMarco watched the Golf Channel on TV, while Emma kept her eye on her laptop, which showed the feed from the surveillance cameras. A lot of the time Emma spent speaking in Spanish to Sergio and Javier, probably reliving the bad old days when they'd worked with her while she was still at the DIA.

At ten minutes before eight p.m., DeMarco's phone rang. He answered it, and McIntyre said, "Okay, we'll do what you want. When and where do you want to meet tomorrow?"

DeMarco said, "The Starbucks on Duval Street. I'll be in there at exactly ten a.m., and I expect to see both of you sitting inside the place when I arrive. I don't want to have to worry about one of you sneaking around behind me. I'll have the girl's phone with me, but you won't get it until I've verified there's a million in my bank account."

"Understood," McIntyre said, and hung up.

He told Emma, "Well, McIntyre said they're going to give me a million bucks."

"If they do pay you, then we've still got them. But my money is on them trying to kill you tonight."

———————

When the sun set, Sergio and Javier dressed in dark clothes and put on bulletproof vests and night vision goggles. Armed with M4 rifles equipped with night vision scopes and sound suppressors, they slithered into the bushes surrounding the house. Emma, also in dark clothes, slipped into the garage with her laptop. She had her Beretta in a holster on her right hip.

DeMarco, having nothing better to do, watched television until eleven, then turned off the lights in the house and crawled to the garage and joined Emma there. She periodically spoke to Sergio and Javier in Spanish in a low voice. She watched the feed from the surveillance cameras on her laptop.

Now it was just a matter of waiting until McIntyre and McGruder showed up.

28

As Patty drove, she made sure she stayed below the speed limit. This wasn't the night to get a ticket. When she was about thirty miles from Key West, she called McIntyre. He told her that he and McGruder were in the parking lot at Geiger Beach Park, which was near the place where DeMarco was staying, and told her how to get there.

Around midnight, Patty drove into the parking lot and parked next to McIntyre's Caddy. Before leaving the car, she looked around. The parking lot wasn't lighted, and there were no other cars except for McIntyre's. The closest houses were across the road from the park, the nearest house maybe three hundred yards away. There were lights on in a few of the houses, but most of them were unlit, indicating the homeowners had most likely gone to bed.

Patty got into the back seat of McIntyre's car and placed her purse on her lap. She felt like screaming at the two of them. It was their fault they were in this goddamn mess. They should have seen the Moore girl following them the night they killed the Bermans. They were trained FBI agents, and she was just a kid, not a damn Navy SEAL. And when they realized the girl's phone was missing, they should have found it. DeMarco had found it, and if they weren't so fucking lazy and stupid, they would have found it, too. But she decided to skip the rant. They were where they were, and they had to deal with the threat that DeMarco posed.

McIntyre, swiveling his head to address her in the back seat, said, "We got a plan. DeMarco's staying in this house about a mile from here. We know he's home because his car is parked outside. It's the last house on the road, and there's trees and bushes and shit on the back side. So we'll sneak through the brush behind the house, go in through the back door, and get the drop on him. I'll use a tire iron to jimmy the door if I have to. Then we'll make him hand over his phone and the girl's, then, well . . . then we'll pop him."

"Let's just talk things over for a bit," Patty said. "First, this could be a setup. DeMarco could be lying about trying to blackmail you, and when you go in there to get him, there could be a SWAT team waiting to take you down."

"Yeah, we thought about that," McIntyre said, "but we don't think it's a setup. We checked DeMarco out as best we could, and he told us the truth about being Mahoney's guy. We figure anyone who would work for a crook like Mahoney is exactly the kind of asshole who would try to blackmail us. The other thing is, even if it is a setup, we're screwed if he can enhance the video of us killing the Bermans. So no matter what we'll get arrested unless we take care of him and get that phone."

"You could run," Patty said. "Split to someplace that doesn't have an extradition treaty with the U.S."

"We thought about that, too, but we're Americans and we want to live in America, not in some goddamn place where no one speaks English. If we survive tonight, we're gonna get a boat and live in Florida. That's always been our plan and we're sticking to it."

McGruder said, "Plus, in order to stay in someplace that doesn't have an extradition treaty, we'd have to pay off some greasy government fucker who would bleed us dry."

Patty said, "You know, if you kill DeMarco, there's always the chance that you'll get caught even if it's not a setup. You'll leave behind fingerprints or DNA or some damn clue, and they'll nail you."

"We're not gonna get caught," McGruder said. "We're not as stupid as you seem to think we are, and we're not going to leave evidence behind, just like we didn't when we killed Moore."

"Where are your cell phones? I mean your personal cells, not your burners."

"Back at the motel where we're staying. They're not going to be able to trace us here with our phones. And after tonight, it might be smart for us to all get new burners and ditch the old ones."

"What weapons are you going to use?" Patty asked.

"We'll have to use our service weapons," McIntyre said. "We didn't have time to pick up clean guns."

Patty said, "And since you can't toss your FBI guns, if they do a ballistics test they'll nail you."

"No, they won't. Tomorrow we're going to get new barrels for our Glocks. We know a dealer in Miami. So if they do a test to see if our guns were used to kill DeMarco, we'll be good. I'm telling you, Patty, we've thought this thing through."

Patty said, "The other option we have is we just pay the damn guy like he's asking. We'd each lose about three hundred K, but we'd still have more than four million apiece. And once we pay the bastard, he becomes complicit in the crime and won't be able to talk."

"Fuck that," McGruder said. "We pay this asshole, he'll come back at us again. That's what blackmailers do. We've got to get rid of him."

"And I think we've talked about this enough," McIntyre said. "We gotta deal with him tonight. We can't spend a week developing the perfect plan."

Taking charge, McIntyre said, "Patty, you drive and drop us off close to where DeMarco's staying, and we'll sneak up on the back of the house and take care of him. While we're doing that, you play lookout and call us if you see anything. I've got a pair of night vision binocs in the glove compartment."

"Let's don't forget to set our phones on vibrate," McGruder said. He laughed and added, "I can just see us creepin' around in the dark and getting one of those spam calls."

Patty looked out at the ocean. All she could see were a few white breakers hitting the beach and a pale half-moon mostly hidden by clouds.

She sighed, then pulled the untraceable .38 from her purse and shot McIntyre in the back of the head.

McGruder yelled, "Fuck!"—but before he could do anything, she shot him in the head, too.

29

Patty clamped down hard on her emotions.

This wasn't the time to think about how she felt about killing two men who had been friends and lovers. She hadn't had a choice. They hadn't *given* her a choice. Killing them was something that had to be done to save herself—so she did it. She'd deal with her grief and her regrets and her conscience later.

Maybe their plan to kill DeMarco and get his and Moore's cell phones would have worked, but there were just too many things that could have gone wrong. If it was a setup, they would have gotten caught, and eventually they would have dealt her to get a better deal for themselves. Or if it wasn't a setup and they killed DeMarco, they still might have gotten caught because they'd overlooked something. Like McIntyre's idea to swap out the barrels on their Glocks to pass a ballistics test. He apparently didn't realize that a Glock has the serial number located in three places: on the bottom of the frame, on the barrel near the ejection port, and on the slide under the ejection port. So if someone did a ballistics test to see if their weapons had been used to kill DeMarco, the technician might have noticed that the serial number on the barrel didn't match the other two numbers and would realize that they'd changed out the barrels. It was that kind of dumb mistake—and who knows what other ones they would have made—that would have led to them getting caught, which again would lead to them cutting a deal with the cops to get a better deal for themselves.

Whatever the case, she was home free. The only real proof DeMarco had was Andie's cell phone and the video implicating McGruder and McIntyre in the Bermans' deaths. But there was nothing tying *her* to the murders, nor was there anything tying her directly to the money they'd stolen from the Bermans. The fact that she'd be able to keep all fifteen million they'd stolen hadn't really been a factor in her decision—she'd have been satisfied with five—but getting all fifteen was not a bad thing.

She looked around the parking area again. There was no one she could see, not surprising at one in the morning. The two gunshots had sounded incredibly loud inside the car—her ears were still ringing—but the windows had been closed, and it was doubtful that anyone had heard the shots. What she needed to do now was get their wallets and their cell phones to make it look like a robbery. She was glad that they'd left their personal phones in their motel rooms and there was nothing in those phones that connected them to her, as they'd been using burners to communicate ever since the Berman operation started. But she had to get the burners because they'd used them to talk to her and then, like McGruder had said, get rid of all the burner phones, including hers.

She assessed the situation. McIntyre was slumped over the steering wheel. She could see a phone sitting in the cup holder next to him; that was probably McIntyre's burner. McGruder was leaning against the passenger-side door, his bloody head pressed against the passenger-side window. The front windshield was *dripping* with blood, bone, and brain matter.

She put the pistol she'd used to kill them back in her purse, and using the hem of her T-shirt, she opened the back door on the driver's side and stepped out of the car. The whole time she'd been inside the car, she'd made sure not to touch anything on the interior. The only thing she'd touched on the exterior of the car was the back seat door handle on the driver's side. She wiped down the handle with her T-shirt.

She took a pair of latex gloves from her purse, put her purse on the ground, and donned the gloves. The gloves would prevent her from leaving fingerprints in the car. She was still wearing the baseball cap she'd worn in the airport, and hopefully it had kept DNA-traceable strands of hair from falling inside the car.

She opened the driver's-side front door, ready to shove McIntyre back into the car if he fell out, but he didn't. He stayed slumped over the steering wheel, his head on the wheel. Then she realized she couldn't reach his burner phone in the cup holder because his body was blocking her access to it, so she slipped into the back seat and got it.

Now she needed to get to his wallet, which was in his left back pocket, but there was no way she could lift him up—as heavy as he was—to pull out the wallet. She pushed him so he fell to the passenger side of the car and ended up slumped over the console between the two front seats. With him in this position she was able to extract his wallet.

She placed McIntyre's phone and his wallet into her purse, closed the driver's-side door, and went around to the passenger side. McGruder was leaning against the door. His head, which looked as if the whole top had been blown off, was pressing against the passenger-side window, which was thick with blood. She had to get to McGruder's wallet, which, like McIntyre's, was in his left back pocket, but, like McIntyre, he was too heavy to lift to pull out the wallet. So she opened the door and just let McGruder fall out of the car. He landed facedown at her feet and it was easy to extract the wallet from his back pocket. She figured his phone would be in one of his front pockets, so with some effort she rolled him over—Jesus Christ, he was heavy—and patted his pockets and found the phone in the front right-hand pocket of his pants.

She dumped McGruder's wallet and phone in her purse, then, as much as she wanted to run back to her car and speed away, she stood still and assessed the situation. Was there anything else she should do? She'd taken precautions not to leave fingerprints or DNA in the car. She got their cell phones and their wallets. What else? Footprints? She doubted her footprints would be visible on the asphalt surface of the parking area, plus she was going to get rid of all the clothes she was wearing, including her shoes. What else? What else?

She thought for a minute about rifling the car and taking anything of value—McIntyre had said there was a pair of binoculars in the glove compartment—but decided not to do that. That would just be more shit she'd have to get rid of. She didn't know if the cops would believe that the two men had been killed just for their wallets, but if they didn't, so what? The important thing was that she couldn't be tied in any way to their deaths.

She picked up her purse and, still wearing the latex gloves, got into her car and took off.

She drove in the direction that would take her back to Highway 1, the highway back to Miami. About ten miles from the park on Geiger Key, she passed a strip mall containing five retail stores. She turned into the parking lot and drove around to the back of the mall, where she saw five dumpsters, one for each store. She popped the trunk of her rental car. Inside the trunk was her carry-on bag, which contained a change of clothes. She stripped down to her underwear and put on a clean pair of jeans, a blouse, and different shoes. She tossed the clothes she'd been wearing into one of the dumpsters.

That done, she took the tire iron from her rental car and smashed McIntyre's and McGruder's burner phones into pieces, and the pieces went into another dumpster. She'd wait until she got back to D.C. to get rid of her burner because she might need the phone before she got home.

Next she removed the cash from McIntyre's and McGruder's wallets, but not the credit cards, and dumped the wallets into two different dumpsters. She doubted it would happen, but maybe someone would find the wallets in the dumpsters and use the credit cards, and then maybe that poor, unlucky bastard would be arrested for their murders.

She still had to get rid of the gun, the .38 she'd used to kill them, but decided not to throw the gun into a dumpster. She got back in her car and drove until she saw what she was looking for: a big storm drain. She removed the unfired bullets and two empty shell casings from the gun—which she'd touched when she'd loaded the gun—and wiped them clean of prints. Then she wiped every surface on the gun to remove prints from it and tossed the gun and the bullets into the storm drain. With any luck, the gun would be washed out to sea during the next hurricane, and without a doubt, this being Florida, there'd be another hurricane.

She checked her watch. It was a little after two a.m., and it would take about three hours for her to reach the airport in Miami. She knew there were half a dozen morning flights back to D.C., the earliest one leaving at six a.m. She'd head for the airport, maybe stop for breakfast at some twenty-four-hour place if there was time—for some reason she was starving—then turn in the rental car and catch the earliest flight she could get back to Washington.

As she was driving, and now that everything had been taken care of, she allowed herself to think about McIntyre and McGruder and began to tear up. They'd been good friends; they'd had some great times together. She particularly remembered McGruder's fiftieth birthday party. She'd danced with them that night, both of them moving like trained bears. At one point, they'd started talking about their exes: her ex-husband and McIntyre's and McGruder's four ex-wives. They couldn't believe how they'd all been so unlucky in love, and when McGruder told a story about his second wife soaking his clothes in gasoline and burning them on the front lawn with the neighbors watching, they started laughing so hard they couldn't stop.

She wiped away the tear that had rolled down her right cheek.

Damn it. She was going to miss the two big galoots.

30

Dawn broke, the blue sky tinged with pink, and the beach and the ocean in front of DeMarco's rental house became visible. A flock of seagulls, circling like vultures, screamed down at something on the beach. The dorsal fin of a great white shark sliced through the water as the legendary predator hunted for prey.

DeMarco was sitting on the floor of the garage, his back up against the driver's-side door of Sergio and Javier's red convertible. Emma was sitting also, her back against a wall, looking at the laptop showing the feed from the cameras that Neil and DeMarco had installed. She'd been looking at it all night and, unlike DeMarco, hadn't dozed off periodically. Sergio and Javier, the poor bastards, were still lying in the brush, unless they'd been eaten alive by mosquitoes.

DeMarco said, "Well, so much for this great fuckin' plan."

Emma said, "Yeah. I thought for sure they'd come." She spoke into the throat mic she'd used to communicate with Sergio and Javier. She said, "Stand down. Come to the house and we'll have some coffee."

She left the garage, and DeMarco followed her into the house. A few minutes later, Sergio and Javier joined them. The little guys didn't look as if a night spent lying in snake-infested brush had affected them at all. DeMarco suspected that in their pasts they'd spent worse nights in worse places and where the primary danger hadn't come from reptiles.

DeMarco made a pot of coffee. While they were drinking it, Emma said, "I was positive that they'd try to kill Joe here at the house, but it looks like I was wrong. I still don't think they'll pay him the million, but maybe they will, so Joe will meet them at the Starbucks in Key West at ten, but we're all going to go with him to make sure they don't ambush him. What we'll do is—"

Emma's phone rang. She looked at the caller ID. "It's Henry," she said to DeMarco. "I wonder why he's calling so early."

She answered the phone, saying, "Good morning, Henry."

She listened to whatever Henry was saying for a couple of minutes, interrupting him only once to say, "Where?"

She hung up, didn't speak for a moment, then said, "McIntyre and McGruder were shot last night at a park near here. McIntyre's dead. McGruder's still alive, but probably not for long." To DeMarco, she said, "You and I will head down to where they were shot and find out what happened. Their bodies were only discovered a couple of hours ago and I'm sure the cops will still be there."

To Sergio and Javier, she said, "You guys can go home. Thank you for helping me out, and I'm sorry I wasted your time."

"Not a problem," Sergio said. "It was good to see you again."

Emma took out her wallet and started to count out a bunch of hundred-dollar bills, but Javier said, "We can't take money from you, Emma. We can't ever repay you for what you did for us."

Emma, still counting out the bills, said, "Yes, you can. Buy your wives something special."

They eventually took the money, and before they left, Sergio said, "You need us again, just call."

"I will," Emma said, then added something in Spanish that DeMarco didn't understand.

A few minutes later, the red Mustang pulled out of the garage, DeMarco wondering what it was that Emma had done for the two men that they'd be willing to risk their lives for her.

He knew he'd never find out.

DeMarco packed his clothes, took out the garbage, and put the dishes he'd used in the dishwasher. There was a notebook telling him all the other stuff he was supposed to do before departing the place, but he didn't bother to look at it. He put the house keys back where he'd found them, and he and Emma took off, Emma leading the way in her car.

As he drove, he wondered if McIntyre and McGruder had been shot because he'd set them up. Probably. But who cared? They'd killed Andie Moore and deserved to get shot.

———◆◆◆———

The entry to Geiger Beach Park was blocked by a couple of sawhorses and a sheriff's deputy, standing there to keep people from entering the parking lot. DeMarco and Emma parked on the street a block away.

As they walked back to the parking lot they took in the scene. There were three Monroe County sheriff's patrol cars in the lot, blue and red lights spinning; two unmarked sedans; and one white van, which DeMarco assumed belonged to the crime scene techs. Five uniformed sheriff's deputies, one guy in a suit who was probably a detective, and two men and a woman wearing FBI windbreakers were all standing around talking, while two people wearing white coveralls examined a maroon Cadillac that DeMarco recognized as McIntyre's car. The passenger-side door of the Cadillac was open, and there was someone slumped over in the driver's seat who wasn't moving.

Emma walked up to the deputy by the sawhorses, showed him her credentials, and said, "Who's in charge here?"

The deputy pointed at a man wearing a blue windbreaker with FBI on the back in yellow letters and said, "That guy." The FBI agent was in his forties, and he was *huge*, about the size of LeBron James both in terms of height and weight.

"What's his name?" Emma asked.

"Beats me," the deputy said. "All I know is that he's an asshole."

Emma and DeMarco walked over to the agent. DeMarco noticed that he had a heavy five o'clock shadow at seven in the morning. He scowled when Emma introduced herself and showed him her credentials, which identified her as a special investigator for the DOJ Inspector General.

Looking down at Emma, he said, "What the hell's the IG have to do with this?"

Emma said, "What's your name?"

"Perkins," the agent said.

Emma said, "Agent Perkins, we were sent to Miami to investigate a case McIntyre and McGruder were involved in, a case where they made several errors and, in fact, where they may have acted illegally. As part of our investigation, we followed them to Key West and were planning to meet with them this morning."

DeMarco thought that was an accurate while amazingly incomplete and misleading explanation of what they'd been doing. He couldn't help but be proud of Emma.

Emma continued: "We may have information that's pertinent to this investigation, but all we've been told so far is that McIntyre was killed and that McGruder was badly wounded. Can you please fill us in on what happened?"

Perkins thought that over for a moment, as if he might be considering telling Emma to butt out of his investigation. But he didn't, probably because he wasn't certain how much bureaucratic clout Emma might have. Emma just *looked* like a person with clout.

He said, "About four a.m., a guy who lives a couple of miles from here was headed into Key West. He runs a bakery, and he starts work about four thirty every day. Anyway, he forgot his cell phone at home, and he pulled into the parking lot to turn around and saw a parked car in his headlights. The passenger-side door was open just like you see it now, and there was a man lying on the ground near it. The baker stopped to see if the guy was okay, and that's when he saw that the guy on the ground had had his head practically blown off and that there was another guy inside the car who'd been shot in the head, too. So he jumped in his car and went barreling back to his place, because he didn't have a phone, and called the sheriff.

"A deputy got here fifteen minutes later. He's the idiot standing over by the sawhorses. He didn't bother to see if either victim had a pulse because of the way their heads looked. He called his boss, said he had a double homicide on his hands, then stood back like he's supposed to to wait for the detectives and the CSIs. Half an hour later, one of the CSIs, for whatever reason—maybe he was checking for lividity or body temperature or some fuckin' thing—found out that McGruder had a pulse. Barely.

"While they were waiting for an ambulance to haul McGruder off to the hospital, the CSIs checked the victims for IDs. Neither guy had a wallet on him, but in the glove compartment they found a parking pass for the FBI field office in Miramar that had McIntyre's name on it. A bunch of calls were made, and they eventually got to McIntyre's supervisor in Miami. She had whoever called describe the two men, and that's how they identified the other guy as McGruder, McIntyre's partner. I was sent over to take charge because I was working on a case in Key West and was the closest senior agent available."

Emma figured that the news of two FBI agents being shot would have spread through the bureau like a California wildfire, and when Henry heard the news, he immediately called Emma. She glanced over at McIntyre's body sitting in the driver's seat. One of the CSIs was in the back seat doing something, and the other CSI was kneeling on the passenger side of the car, near the open door.

Perkins said, "All we can tell so far is that somebody sitting in the back seat shot them both in the head. The CSI guys are guessing it happened after midnight, like around one a.m. And since neither guy had a wallet, a robbery might have been the motive for the shootings. Anyway, that's all we got so far: someone sitting in the back seat shot them and took their wallets. As you can see, we're still dusting for prints and looking for more evidence."

"What hospital did they take McGruder to?"

"The Lower Keys Medical Center on Stock Island. It's about ten miles from here."

Emma said, "Do you have a card, Agent Perkins, so I can contact you if I need to?"

"Yeah," Perkins said, and took one from a case and handed it to her.

"Thanks," she said to Perkins. To DeMarco, she said, "Let's go," and turned to walk back to her car.

"Hey, wait a damn minute," Perkins said. "You said you might have some information related to what happened to them."

Without stopping, Emma said, "I'll call you later, Agent Perkins. I promise. But I have to leave now."

"Hey!" Perkins yelled again. Emma ignored him.

DeMarco thought that it was a good thing that a guy the size of Perkins didn't decide to tackle her.

Emma started jogging back to her car, and DeMarco was forced to jog to keep up with her.

"What's the rush?" he panted.

"If McGruder dies, we need to keep the hospital or the cops or anyone else from releasing that information. We want whoever shot them to not only know he's still alive but to think he might recover. I'm going to call Henry and ask him to do what he can to keep a lid on McGruder's condition. I'll see you at the hospital."

———◆———

At the hospital, they took the elevator to the ICU, Emma figuring that if McGruder was still alive that's where he'd be. She flashed her credentials at one of the nurses and asked for McGruder's room number and the name of the doctor in charge of his care.

Outside McGruder's room they saw an empty wooden chair near the door. Emma, looking like a hawk searching for a rabbit, spotted a man in a sheriff's uniform chatting up a pretty nurse.

Emma said, "Hey, you!"

The deputy spun around. "Yeah?" he said.

Emma said, "Aren't you supposed to be guarding McGruder?"

"I am guarding him," the deputy said.

"No, you're not. Get your ass back in that chair and don't let anyone into that room who isn't a nurse or a doctor. If you do, I'll get your ass fired."

"Who the hell are you?" the deputy said.

"FBI," Emma said, and the deputy was too intimidated to ask her to prove it.

Emma and DeMarco glanced into McGruder's room. All they could see were monitors measuring vital signs and a man whose head was encased in bandages. There was a bunch of tubes and wires running to various parts of his body and a machine on his face that DeMarco thought might be a ventilator. It was impossible to see the man's face. DeMarco couldn't help but think of the way McGruder had looked grinning, posing for a photo with the fish he'd caught.

Emma asked the nurse who'd been flirting with the deputy, "Where do I find Dr. Singh?"

Dr. Singh was in an office on the third floor, his feet up on the desk, speaking into a cell phone. He looked up in annoyance when Emma and DeMarco walked in but didn't stop talking into the phone. DeMarco heard him say, "I'd like a reservation for four at eight, one of your view tables. Yes, I'll wait."

Emma said, "Hang up. We need to talk to you."

Singh, apparently on hold while someone checked on the availability of a table with a view, said, "Who are you?"

"FBI," Emma said. "Now hang up. This is urgent."

Singh was dressed in dark pants, a crisp white shirt, and a multicolored silk tie that had probably cost a couple hundred bucks. On his feet were tasseled cordovan loafers. He had oily dark hair and a dark complexion. He was tall, slender, and Bollywood handsome—and reeked of arrogance. It had been DeMarco's experience that most doctors, particularly surgeons—and Singh was a neurosurgeon— were arrogant. They'd all been the smartest kid in any school they'd attended and had been fawned over all their lives and told how brilliant they were.

Singh studied Emma but didn't hang up the phone. When it appeared that Emma was about to snatch it out of his hand, he said to whomever he was talking to, "Yes, that'll be fine. I'll see you tonight." He hit the DISCONNECT button on his phone and said, "Now what do you want?" He spoke English fluently but with a noticeable accent.

Emma took a breath, most likely to stop herself from screaming at him. She said, "We're involved in an investigation having to do with your patient Mr. McGruder. We need to know his condition and his prospects for recovering."

Singh sniffed and said, "I'm not going to discuss his condition with you or anyone else who isn't a medical professional associated with his treatment. His medical condition is privileged, as I'm sure you must know."

Emma said, "Very soon, whoever runs this place will be getting a call from people at the Justice Department telling him or her how this hospital is to behave when it comes to McGruder. And I have no doubt the hospital will cooperate."

Singh shrugged. "I don't care what the administration does. I will not violate doctor-patient confidentiality."

Emma put her knuckles on Singh's desk and leaned over so that she was about six inches from his face. She said, "Let me tell you something about your patient that's also confidential. He's an FBI agent who's a killer and a thief. He was about to be arrested, but then someone tried to kill him and killed his partner. Now we're trying to catch the person who shot him and we need your cooperation. So let me ask again: What is his condition and his prognosis?"

Singh said, "You can ask all you want. I'm not going to discuss his condition with you. And now I must excuse myself. I've rounds to make."

DeMarco had had enough and decided to take a shot at Singh that could very likely backfire. He said, "Doctor, what kind of visa are you on?"

Singh hesitated, and DeMarco knew he'd hit the bull's-eye. DeMarco said, "It's an H-1B visa, isn't it?"

"Yes," Singh said.

An H-1B visa was for so-called specialty workers, for guys like doctors and the geeks that the tech companies wanted on their payroll because there weren't enough Americans with the brains to fill all the vacant positions. These were people in high demand, not poor bastards seeking asylum so they could live in America and pick fruit.

DeMarco said, "What do you think the chances are of that visa being renewed if you jerk around the FBI and the Department of Justice?"

Singh, being the brilliant guy he was, took only a second to make a decision. "Okay," he said, "I'll make an exception in Mr. McGruder's case in the interest of seeing justice done. But that's the only reason why."

That and because he preferred to practice medicine in the Florida Keys as opposed to Kolkata or wherever he was from.

He cleared his throat and said, "I'm frankly amazed that Mr. McGruder is still alive. The bullet that struck him had an upward trajectory and hit him high on the left side of his head and exited through the top of his skull. I operated on him to debride the wound and relieve the pressure on his brain, and he's currently in a coma. He's not brain dead. At least not yet. However, it's very unlikely that he'll live for more than another forty-eight hours. If he does survive, which in my opinion would be miraculous, he'll not be able to speak because the bullet damaged the part of his brain that controls speech and other motor functions. Nor will he, should he regain consciousness, be able to remember what happened to him. So that's his prognosis. Is there anything else?"

"Yes," Emma said. "Doctor, we need you to take an active role in catching the person who shot McGruder."

"What do you mean by an active role?"

"I'll get to that in a minute, but first, tell me what happens when McGruder dies."

"I don't understand what you mean," Singh said.

"I mean when he dies, I assume one of those machines that's connected to him will alarm or something. Is that right?"

"Yes. Alarms will go off at the nurses' station, and one of the nurses will check to make sure the machine hasn't malfunctioned or that a sensor hasn't come loose. If it appears that the machine is functioning properly, and after the nurse has manually checked his vital signs, the nurse will call for the physician on duty if I'm not in the hospital, after which I or another doctor will declare him dead. A death certificate will be generated, the family will be notified, and he'll be transferred to the morgue, where an autopsy will be performed."

"Yeah, that's what I thought. Doctor, I think that when the person who shot McGruder finds out that he's still alive, this person will be concerned that McGruder will recover and tell investigators who shot

him. That person may even try to kill McGruder again. So we need you
to do a couple of things.

"First, you need to tell the ICU nurses and the on-duty docs that
you're to be notified when he dies and that only you can declare him
dead. And then you don't declare him dead until we tell you to. What
I'm saying is, we want you to keep his death secret as long as possible
and leave him lying in his bed until we tell you otherwise. Can you
make that happen?"

"Yes, but I can't ensure that people won't talk."

"I understand that, but you can make sure that he isn't officially
declared dead until you sign off on him. Right?"

"Yes."

"The other thing we need you to do is tell folks, like any cops or
reporters who might ask, that McGruder is doing great after you performed surgery on him. You say you can't discuss the specifics of his
condition, but you expect him to recover, although it may be several
days before he'll be able to answer any questions."

Singh said, "Saying that will make me look incompetent after he
dies."

DeMarco said, "Only until people learn you were helping us catch
a killer. Then you'll be a hero."

Singh, after a lengthy pause, said, "Okay, I will do as you ask."

"Good," Emma said. "Now we have a whole bunch of people we
need to talk to, and you need to go talk to the nurses." Emma dropped
a card on his desk that contained her cell phone number. "You call me
the minute McGruder dies. Got it?"

"Yes," Singh said.

As DeMarco and Emma were leaving the office, Emma said, "That
was rather mean of you, using his visa to squeeze him. Good boy."

DeMarco said, "Who do you think shot him?"

"A lawyer," Emma said. "One of the first things Henry told us was
that he suspected that McIntyre and McGruder were getting advice

from a lawyer on how to screw up the Berman case. I think this lawyer was their partner and is getting a share of the money, and after we found the video of them killing the Bermans, the lawyer decided that they had to go. And I suspect that after that lawyer learns that McGruder is still alive, he or she will go batshit crazy."

Emma let out a sigh. "What we need to do now is talk to Henry and tell him what we told Singh to do and see if he can get the FBI and the hospital to cooperate. And then we need to go brief the FBI on everything we know and turn over Andie's cell phone to them. We'll just have to hope that we don't get arrested for tampering with evidence and interfering in a federal investigation."

"Oh, fuck me," DeMarco said.

31

Emma called Perkins, the FBI agent in charge of the McIntyre homicide investigation.

She said, "Agent Perkins, we need to meet immediately."

"Why?" he asked.

"To catch the person who shot McIntyre and McGruder. I told you when I met you that I had information pertinent to the case, and now you need to hear it. More importantly, I believe the person who shot McGruder may try to kill him a second time, and you need to put assets in the hospital where he's staying to catch that person."

"What in the hell are you talking about?" Perkins said.

"Not on the phone. You need to get over to the hospital where McGruder is. That's where I am. And bring a couple of your people with you. I'll meet you in the cafeteria. Hurry, Agent Perkins. There's no time to waste." She hung up before Perkins could ask another question.

DeMarco, who'd been sitting at the table with her in the hospital cafeteria, listening as she spoke to Perkins, said, "I think this is a really bad idea, and if I get arrested, I'm going to blame you."

When Emma ignored him, DeMarco said, "Well, I'm going to get something to eat while we're waiting for Perkins. That is, if I can find something edible."

"What are you talking about?" Emma said. "You're in a hospital cafeteria. Why wouldn't you be able to find something edible?"

"Did you notice that everything on the menu here is advertised as 'heart healthy' and contains zero trans fats, no sugar, and has about fourteen calories?"

—◆◆◆—

Thirty minutes later, Perkins arrived, looking annoyed. He had two other FBI agents with him, a man and a woman, the same agents who'd been with him at Geiger Beach Park. They'd replaced the FBI windbreakers they'd worn at the crime scene with sport coats to partially hide the pistols they all had in holsters on their belts.

Perkins walked over to the table where Emma and DeMarco were sitting and dropped into a chair. The big man looked tired and grumpy, which was understandable as he'd been up since dawn. The two agents with him pulled over a nearby table so they could be part of the conversation. Perkins didn't bother to introduce the agents.

"Now what the hell's going on?" Perkins said.

Emma told him. She told him everything they had done since arriving in Miami, which DeMarco thought was a *huge* mistake. She told how they'd been sent by Henry Cantor to investigate Andie's death, and the reason they were sent was because Henry believed FBI agents may have been responsible for her death and therefore didn't trust the FBI. She told how Andie Moore had been convinced that McIntyre and McGruder had deliberately tanked the case against the Bermans so they could steal what the Bermans had stolen. And all that was okay—but then she told Perkins that they searched the Bermans' house and became convinced that the house had been staged to make it appear as if the Bermans had taken a trip.

The only lie Emma told, for which DeMarco was very grateful, was she didn't say that she'd picked the lock to get into the Bermans' house. Instead she said that they found the door ajar, and because she was concerned about the Bermans, they decided to enter the house and, after that, they searched it. This was good because although she admitted to trespassing, she didn't confess to breaking and entering.

She explained how they found Andie's cell phone in the swamp with Neil's help and how they'd been able to open the password-protected device. When Perkins asked why she hadn't turned the phone over to the FBI, she said that at that point she wasn't sure she could trust the FBI. This comment did not sit well with Perkins. She showed Perkins the photo of McIntyre and McGruder walking with the Bermans the same night Andie was killed, the night the agents claimed they were both home alone. She told how DeMarco had met with McIntyre and McGruder in Key West and pretended to blackmail them, hoping that they'd attempt to kill him and give her an opportunity to apprehend them. Lastly, she mentioned that she'd told Dr. Singh to falsely claim to anyone who asked that McGruder was likely to recover, hoping that might lure McIntyre's killer to the hospital.

As she was telling all these things, Perkins reminded DeMarco of a cartoon character with steam coming out of its ears. At one point he screamed, "I can't believe you fuckin' people! I'm gonna—"

"Boss, you need to lower your voice," the female agent who'd accompanied him said.

Emma concluded with: "The person who probably shot McIntyre and McGruder is the lawyer who helped them throw the Berman case, although we don't know that for sure. What you need to do is make sure

McGruder is protected while he's here in this hospital in case whoever shot him takes another crack at him, and he needs to be protected by someone other than a sheriff's deputy."

Perkins sat for a long moment glaring at Emma, then took a breath and said to the male agent, "Go up to intensive care and make sure the deputy who's supposed to be guarding McGruder is doing his job. In fact, stay up there with him." The agent got up and quickly departed.

To Emma, he said, "I've got to go make a bunch of phone calls to tell people what you two have done. You just sit here until I get back." To the female agent, he said, "If they try to leave before I get back, shoot them. I mean it."

Perkins was gone for almost an hour.

While waiting for him to return, DeMarco chatted with the female FBI agent. She had short blond hair and freckles dusting her cheekbones, and she was pretty in a tomboyish sort of way. When DeMarco learned that she was single and also a golfer, he became even more attracted to her and started asking her about courses around Miami where she lived and played. Emma, who spent the hour looking at her phone, rolled her eyes when DeMarco said, "You know, if there's time, maybe we could play a round before I head back to D.C."

Perkins returned to the cafeteria, took a seat, and said, "We'll decide later what to do about you, but I'm recommending that you be charged with obstruction of justice. You withheld evidence, you tampered with evidence, you illegally searched the Bermans' house, and you set up McIntyre and McGruder, which most likely got McIntyre killed. But what I want right now is Moore's cell phone, and then you're going to write up a statement documenting everything you did."

"I'm not writing up shit," DeMarco said, while Emma simultaneously said, "I'll be happy to give you a written statement, Agent Perkins, but I'd like to know what the bureau is planning to do next."

Perkins said, "I'm not going to tell you a damn thing about what we're doing next. You two—"

"Agent Perkins, I'm working for the inspector general," Emma said. "And in that capacity, I didn't do anything illegal, although I can see that you might think otherwise. And regardless of what I've done, it's still probably not in your best interest to withhold information from the IG's representative."

Perkins, scowling, and most likely thinking that bucking the IG might not be good for his career, said, "We're going to put a couple of agents in the ICU dressed as nurses and see if we can spot someone taking an interest in McGruder. If someone tries to kill him, we'll catch him. We're also going to look at McIntyre's work history, his computers and phones, and search his apartment to see if we can tie him to a shady lawyer. Since he's dead, we don't need a warrant to do that. Because McGruder is still alive, we'll have to get a warrant to look at his stuff and we're already working on that. And while the FBI is doing all those things, you two are *not* going to do shit. Do you understand me? Now go write up the statement I asked for and call me when it's done, and I'll have someone pick it up. Then I'd strongly suggest you get the hell out of Florida, because if I get my way, you're going to be arrested."

———◆———

As they were leaving the hospital, DeMarco said, "Well, that went real fuckin' well."

Emma said, "Actually, it did go well. We now have the FBI protecting McGruder and ready to catch whoever shot him if he or she tries again. And I'm also glad that the FBI will start looking for the lawyer who helped tank the Berman case."

DeMarco said, "Well, I wouldn't write up any sort of statement if I were you. And I'm sure as hell not going to write one. I don't know if we criminally obstructed justice or not, but if you write down everything we did, that's not going to leave the lawyers we're going to have to hire a whole lot of wiggle room. We can always deny what we told Perkins or say he misunderstood us, but we won't be able to deny anything if you give him a written confession."

"I have no intention of providing Perkins with a statement," Emma said. "I just said that to get him off our backs."

"So then, what are we doing? What we ought to do is head back to D.C. now that the bureau's involved. They can track down whoever shot McIntyre and McGruder better than we can."

"We're not going back to D.C. yet. I want to see if we can get a lead on this lawyer who helped them."

"And how are we going to do that?"

"I was thinking we might search McGruder's apartment. You heard what Perkins said. He needs to get a warrant to search it, and it'll probably take him a while to get one, so maybe we can search it before he does."

DeMarco said, "Emma, there's no way in hell I'm breaking into the apartment of a wounded FBI agent. But I am willing to be a character witness at your trial."

Emma, sounding as if she was thinking out loud, said, "Whatever lawyer helped them, it had to be someone close to them, somebody they trusted completely. And this person was most likely the one who moved the money the Bermans stole, and they wouldn't have trusted just anyone with fifteen million dollars. Plus, they let this person get close enough to kill them, never suspecting that they'd get shot. So before we do anything else—"

Meaning: *Before I break into McGruder's apartment.*

"—I want to talk with the people McIntyre and McGruder worked with in Miami and see if they can point us toward someone."

DeMarco said, "Why do we have to do anything, Emma? Let Perkins follow up on finding the lawyer. He can question people as well as we can."

"For one thing, Perkins doesn't know as much about the case as we do, and we're more likely to find something than he is. The other thing is, we don't know how many bad apples there are in the FBI when it comes to the Berman case, and for all we know, someone who assisted McIntyre and McGruder might be assigned to find the lawyer."

"Oh, bullshit," DeMarco said. "You just want to solve this thing before Perkins does."

Emma didn't respond—and DeMarco knew he was right.

32

As Emma had predicted, Patty McHugh went batshit crazy.

She got back from Miami at about two in the afternoon the same day she shot McIntyre and McGruder. She suspected that their bodies would be found sometime that morning and that their deaths would make the national news. She listened to the radio as the cab was taking her from Dulles to her apartment, but nothing was said about them. A pipe bomb had gone off in Times Square—nobody was killed, and nobody knew who had set it off or why—but that's all the newscasters were talking about.

When she got home, she took a shower to wash off the grime of airline travel and any bits of blood and brain matter from McIntyre and McGruder that might have ended up on her. She put on a fluffy white bathrobe, made herself a margarita, and turned on the news.

The talking head on CNN—a blonde who had the cheekbones of a fashion model—was talking about the bombing in New York. The FBI and Homeland Security either didn't know anything or hadn't shared anything with the media, so the blonde was eating up airtime talking about past terrorist attacks and making baseless speculations about who was responsible for the current one. Then she said, "In other news of the day, two FBI agents were shot while sitting in their car in

Geiger Key, Florida. We'll have more on that after we come back from a short break."

Patty had to listen to four commercials, all of them pushing various drugs with what sounded like really dangerous side effects. Finally, the blond newscaster came back on and said, "Two FBI agents were found in their car at approximately four this morning at a beachfront park on Geiger Key, which is a few miles from Key West. The agents' names haven't been released, but we know that one agent is dead and the other is in critical condition. At this time, we have no information on what the agents were doing on Geiger Key or why they were shot. But this appears to be another case of law enforcement personnel being targeted."

Patty came off the couch as if she'd been propelled upward by a jack-in-the-box spring and spilled half her drink down the front of her robe. She screamed, "Son of a bitch!" and threw her glass at the television. Luckily for her, the glass bounced off the screen without cracking it.

How the hell could one of them have lived?

She'd practically blown their goddamn heads off their shoulders. The windshield and the passenger-side window had been *covered* with blood. The only good news was that whoever had lived was in critical condition—which you'd expect with a massive head wound—and there was a possibility that he would die. But which meant that there was also a possibility that he might live.

What the hell should she do? What could she do?

The first thing she needed was information. It didn't matter which of the two dumb bastards had lived. Whoever it was, if he could talk, there was no doubt he'd tell the cops that she was the one who shot him. And Florida had the death penalty and liked to use it. But could he talk? Obviously, he hadn't talked yet, because if he had, she would have been arrested. She also figured that the likelihood of a guy with a gunshot wound to his head talking any time soon was small. But what were the chances of him recovering so he could talk eventually? She needed more information.

She figured that the news of two FBI agents being shot would have gone through the Hoover Building like a flash flood, and by now agents in the building would know a lot more than the media did. Certainly, they'd know the agents' names and which one had survived. They might even know more about the medical condition of the survivor.

She called an agent she was currently working with on a money-laundering case, talked about the case with her briefly, then switched the topic to those poor FBI agents who'd been shot in Florida—and learned that McGruder was the survivor. The agent she spoke to, however, didn't know anything about McGruder's condition other than what had been reported on the news, just that he was in critical condition.

Thinking about it, she wasn't surprised that it was McGruder who'd survived. When she shot McIntyre, he'd been sitting still and his head had been only about six inches from her outstretched arm. McGruder, however, had been moving after she shot McIntyre; he'd twitched sideways and had been a bit farther away from her. He'd been the lucky one.

But she needed to find out what condition he was in. Maybe he was brain dead and they were just waiting to pull the plug on him. Or maybe he was in a coma and would be in one for weeks or months or, with any luck, forever. Whatever the case, she needed to find out if he would be able to recover enough to say who shot him. On the upside was the fact that most people who suffered a severe head trauma often had no memory of the event that had caused the trauma. She could only hope that that was the case with that hardheaded son of a bitch McGruder.

She'd just had this thought when a voice emanating from the television penetrated her reverie.

"We have some breaking news on the FBI agents who were shot in Florida. The neurosurgeon who operated on the agent, a Dr. Angit

Singh, made a statement to reporters. Dr. Singh said he couldn't provide specifics about the agent's condition other than to say that the operation he performed was successful and, although the agent is in a coma, it's possible that he might make a full recovery. Our thoughts and prayers are with the agent."

"Fuck your thoughts and prayers!" Patty screamed.

33

Traveling in separate cars, Emma and DeMarco began the three-hour ride from the Keys to the federal building in Miramar. Captivated by the scenery and the balmy spring weather, DeMarco spent part of the drive wishing he had a time-share in Florida, a place to go to when the weather in Washington turned cold and cruel.

He turned on the radio just in time to hear the newscaster relay a story about Mahoney and the Republican leader in the House calling each other a liar, a cheat, and a scoundrel, something they did about every other day. DeMarco knew, however, that when not engaged in political theatrics, the two men would sit in Mahoney's office, drinking Mahoney's booze, and were actually friends— probably because they were so much alike. He turned off the radio.

Emma was thinking about what she planned to do once they reached Miami—she hadn't totally excluded breaking into McGruder's apartment—when her phone rang. It was Deputy Fisher, the man leading the investigation into Andie's murder for the Collier County sheriff. It was the fourth time he'd called her—she hadn't returned any of his previous calls—and the last voice mail he left had ended with: "Lady, if you don't call me back this time, I'm going to put out an APB to have you detained so I can talk to you."

Emma answered the phone. "What can I do for you, Deputy?"

Fisher said, "Ma'am, I need you to explain something to me. We tried to find that girl's cell phone, and we traced it from a spot in the Glades close to where she was killed, and from there it went to the Naples morgue, but after that it went dead and we couldn't trace it any further. The funny thing is, it was at the morgue at the exact time you visited the morgue. I think you found her phone and—"

"I did find it, Deputy. And I apologize for not turning it over to you, but, well, it's complicated."

"Complicated, huh? That's what you feds always say whenever you pull some stunt to shut out the locals."

Emma saw no reason to explain she really wasn't a fed. She said, "Deputy, I've turned the phone over to the FBI, an agent named Perkins, and I'm sure he'll be happy to share with you everything he knows."

"Yeah, right," Fisher said, and hung up.

Emma thought it might be wise to avoid Collier County in the near future.

⸻

They took the elevator to the floor of the federal building where McIntyre and McGruder had worked and went to see their supervisor, but Brooks wasn't in her office. DeMarco figured the poor woman was probably visiting her oncologist. Since Brooks wasn't there, they walked into the bullpen area where a few agents were sitting, and Emma went over to one of them, a young guy looking at a computer screen showing used cars for sale. DeMarco doubted that he was chasing down a ring of car thieves.

Emma flashed her credentials and said, "We're from the inspector general's office looking into something McIntyre and McGruder were working on before they were shot."

"Yeah, I heard about you," the agent said.

"Where are their desks at?"

"Why do you want to know?"

"Because we're going to search their desks. We've already talked to their supervisor, and she's agreed that's within the scope of our investigation, which is still ongoing. If you don't believe me, ask her."

"For Christ's sake," the agent said. "McIntyre's dead and McGruder's in critical condition, and you're still going after them? What the hell's wrong with you people?"

"We're not going after them at all," Emma said. "And we're sorry about what happened to them. We're looking into the actions of a lawyer who was involved in the case. Now which desks are theirs?"

The agent pointed and said, "That cubicle over there."

As they were walking, DeMarco said, "I thought we were going to talk to people."

"We will," Emma said, "but let's see what's in their desks."

In the cubicle were two desks facing each other. The owners of the desks were identified by small stick-on metal labels on the sides. Emma sat down at McIntyre's desk, so DeMarco plopped down in the chair behind McGruder's.

"What are we looking for?" DeMarco asked.

"Hell, I don't know. Anything related to the Berman case or the money or lawyers they knew."

"You think there's going to be a file labeled 'crooked lawyers'?"

"Just shut up and look."

Emma turned on McIntyre's computer, then muttered, "Shit. You need a password."

The desks were government issue, constructed of gray-painted sheet metal. DeMarco opened the middle drawer. All that was inside it was the usual crap you find in desks: pencils, pens, paper clips, and so forth. In one of the side drawers, he found a stack of magazines all related to fishing and a bunch of advertisements for boats that were for sale. The only thing that struck him was that the boats McGruder had been looking at were not cheap, some of them having million-dollar price tags.

In a deep file drawer was a bunch of files, all apparently related to cases McGruder had been working on, all cases dealing with various sorts of fraud. None of the files related to the Berman case, and DeMarco figured they must have been active cases. He flipped through the files quickly and nothing leaped out at him, other than the fact that there were a lot of people committing fraud. In another drawer, he found a bunch of personal stuff: an electric razor, a bottle of mouthwash, a wrinkled necktie, a shoeshine kit, a tape recorder with dead batteries, and a pint of scotch that was half full (explaining the mouthwash). He sat back and noticed that on top of the desk were a couple of photos. In one of them, McGruder was grinning and holding a salmon that looked as if it might weigh fifty pounds, which made DeMarco remember one time when Mahoney had caught a salmon and later lied about how big it was, adding twenty pounds to the actual size.

The other photo showed McIntyre and McGruder sitting at a table in what appeared to be a restaurant or a bar. In between them sat a woman with long blond hair who appeared to be about their age. All three people were holding brandy snifters and were glassy-eyed from drink. On the table in front of them was a birthday cake, and stuck into the top of the cake, like two candles, were the numbers 5 and 0. It appeared as if the trio was celebrating someone's fiftieth birthday party.

He looked up to see what Emma was doing. She was holding a small spiral-bound notebook in her hand and appeared to be studying it.

"What's that?" he asked her.

"An address book. Apparently, McIntyre wasn't one of those people who put all his contacts information into his phone."

DeMarco showed Emma the birthday party photo that he'd found on McGruder's desk. "I wonder who the woman is."

Emma glanced at the photo. "Maybe it's one of his ex-wives. He was married twice."

"Yeah, maybe," DeMarco said, but was wondering why anyone would want to celebrate a birthday with an ex-wife. He certainly wouldn't have invited his ex to any of his birthday parties. DeMarco's one and only wife was a woman he'd met when he was about fifteen. She was his first love. She was the first woman he ever slept with. She divorced him when she had an affair with, of all people, DeMarco's cousin, a guy who was better looking than most movie stars. DeMarco was not on speaking terms with his ex or his cousin.

Emma started taking photos of the pages in the address book with her phone. She said, "I didn't find anything in his desk that was useful, but I'm going to get the information in this book to Neil and have him find out who all the people are. He can do that faster than we can."

When she finished, Emma said, "Let's go," and walked over to the agent they'd first spoken to. He was still looking at used-car ads.

She said, "Who were McIntyre and McGruder's closest friends?"

The agent said, "Hell, I don't know. They mostly just hung out with each other. The guys in this unit are a lot younger than them and married and didn't socialize with them at all. So I couldn't tell you. Oh, wait a minute. There's a guy down on the second floor. A bank robbery guy. He worked with one of them before they were stationed in Miami. I've seen them with him a few times."

"What's his name?"

"I don't know. But he's as bald as a cue ball and looks old enough to retire."

They started toward the stairs, when Emma said to DeMarco, "Take a photo of that photograph you showed me, the one with the woman in it. She's obviously someone close to them. Maybe we can ID her and talk to her if we need to."

On the second floor they found the unit that caught bank robbers. It must have been a slow day when it came to robbing banks because most of the desks in the area had people sitting at them. They found one guy in a cubicle with a smooth, perfectly round bald head. Some guys look good bald, and this guy was one of them. He was on the phone, and DeMarco heard him say, "Look, I'm telling you, Leon isn't in any trouble. I just need to talk to him about a guy he knows. And tell him if he doesn't call me, I'm going to have the Miami cops pick him up, because he owes like five hundred bucks for parking tickets, and if he's arrested that will violate his parole."

He hung up and said to Emma and DeMarco, who were standing in the doorway to his cubicle, "Can I help you?"

"Maybe," Emma said. "What's your name?"

"Sinclair. Jim Sinclair."

Emma said, "Agent Sinclair, I'm from the inspector general's office." She showed Sinclair the ID that Henry had given her. "Did you know McIntyre and McGruder, the agents who were shot in Geiger Key?"

Sinclair shook his head. "Yeah. I still can't believe that McIntyre's dead. I just hope McGruder makes it. What really gets me is that they were only a few months from retiring. Talk about shitty luck. Do you have any idea why they were shot?"

"No. We're not involved in that investigation. That's being handled by an agent named Perkins working out of Key West. I'm reviewing a case that McIntyre and McGruder were involved in last year. I'm very sorry about what happened to them, but I still need to complete my review."

"So what do you want from me? I never worked on anything with them. I knew McIntyre from when we were both stationed in Phoenix, and we'd go out for drinks or lunch sometimes. I went fishing with them once, but I got so seasick I never went again."

Emma said, "We're trying to identify a lawyer who was close to them, someone who they would have trusted."

"Did they do something wrong?"

"No, and I can't get into the specifics, but this lawyer may have. So can you think of anyone?"

"Well, hell, they knew a lot of lawyers. Anyone who works in the bureau does. It seems like there's ten lawyers involved in every case we work."

"I realize that," Emma said, "but this lawyer would most likely have had a personal connection to them. Like I said, they would have trusted this person, and a lot more than they'd have trusted the lawyers they encountered randomly on the cases they were working."

Sinclair shook his head. "I can't think of anyone like that, and they didn't have a high opinion of lawyers in general."

"Can you give me the names of anyone else they were friendly with here at work?"

"No. I mean, I would if I could, but as far as I know they didn't hang around with anyone here other than me, and I didn't see them socially all that often. Mostly they just palled around with each other."

DeMarco said, "Do you know the woman in this picture?" He showed Sinclair the photo he'd taken of the birthday party photo that had been on McGruder's desk.

Sinclair said, "Yeah, her name's Patty something. In fact, I'm the one who took that picture. McIntyre set up a surprise fiftieth birthday for McGruder at a bar. Most of the people there were retired FBI who'd settled in Miami or guys they fished with. But she flew down from Washington for the party."

"What does she do in Washington?" DeMarco asked.

"I don't know. All I remember is McGruder saying he and McIntyre met her at Quantico."

"So she's an FBI agent," Emma said.

"No, I don't think so, but I can't tell you why I think that. That party was more than five years ago. I got the impression she was just good friends with them, like maybe an ex-girlfriend, but I couldn't tell if she was McIntyre's or McGruder's ex."

"Do you know her last name?" Emma said.

"No. All I know is they called her Patty. She was a kick. I danced with her a couple of times, but then my wife started giving me the look."

"Now what?" DeMarco said after they left Sinclair's office.

"I don't know. I'll decide after I hear back from Neil on the names in the address book."

DeMarco was relieved. At least, for the moment, she wasn't planning to break into anyone's home.

34

Patty paced her living room, the hornets in her head buzzing.

Somehow, someway, she had to make sure McGruder didn't recover. There was no doubt that if he regained consciousness and was able to speak, he'd give her up in a heartbeat. Hell, he might not even have to speak. They could probably come up with some way that he could blink his fucking eyes to spell out her name.

She stopped pacing. She knew what she had to do. And she had to do it quickly.

She packed a bag with a few things she might need, then again using the Bowerman credit card, she made a reservation on a seven p.m. flight to Miami. Fortunately, tomorrow was Saturday, and she didn't have to come up with an excuse for not going to work.

She arrived in Miami around ten, rented a car, made the drive to Stock Island, and, at two in the morning, was sitting in the parking lot of the Lower Keys Medical Center. She knew McGruder was in the medical center because she'd googled Dr. Angit Singh and found out that was where he practiced.

Now what?

She needed to find McGruder's room and see if he was being guarded, which was a very good possibility since he'd been shot. In her suitcase, she'd packed a disassembled automatic—the SIG Sauer that normally was in the nightstand next to her bed—and a silencer that fit the weapon. There had been no time to get a clean gun. If McGruder wasn't being guarded, and if it looked as if she could get out of the hospital quickly and without being seen, maybe she could just shoot him a couple more times in the head and run. Another possibility was if she could get into his room, posing as a nurse or a visitor, maybe she'd be able to inject an air bubble into his IV line and stop his heart. She'd have to get a syringe and needle from someplace—like maybe a drugstore that sold shit for diabetics—but that was doable. Or maybe she could just put a pillow over his fat face and smother him; in his weakened condition that should be easy. The problem with that bright idea was she suspected that he was hooked up to monitors and an alarm would go off at the nurses' station, and she could just see some nurse running into the room as she was snuffing out McGruder's life.

The truth was that all those ideas were extremely risky, and the likelihood of being able to pull any one of them off without getting caught was minuscule—but she had to try. If McGruder came to, she was going to end up on a death row gurney with someone sticking a needle into *her* arm.

But first things first. She needed to see where they were keeping him and if he was being guarded.

She noticed while she'd been sitting in the parking lot that the hospital's front doors were locked—which was understandable at two in the morning—and when a person dressed in scrubs, like a nurse or a lab tech, wanted to get in, he or she pushed a button by the door, and the graveyard shift security guard opened the door. That wasn't good. Not only would the guard get a good look at her, but she'd have to come up with some explanation for why she was visiting the hospital at two in the morning.

Maybe it would be better to wait until the stores were open and go into Key West and see if she could find a place that sold scrubs like the ones the orderlies and nurses wore. She'd also go to a drugstore and buy some big glasses with plain lenses to further obscure her face. And if she could find a place that sold wigs, she'd get a wig, too. Then she'd come back to the hospital during the day when there were a lot of people in the place, go up to the ICU, and wander down the halls looking like a nurse and check out McGruder's room. If it looked feasible to shoot him or inject him with an air bubble, she'd do it—which again made her think that the odds of pulling that off were small to nil.

Then something else occurred to her. The hospital was probably just like the DOJ's building, and there was someplace where the smokers hung out like a bunch of lepers. She'd go find the smoking area, and when someone came out to have a smoke, maybe she could slip into the building after him and take a look around the ICU. At this time of day there wouldn't be many people wandering around, and the nurses would most likely be sitting at their station BS-ing, and maybe she'd be able to get a shot at McGruder. Literally, a shot at McGruder.

She stuck the silenced pistol in the back of her jeans, put on a windbreaker to cover the gun, and grabbed a pack of cigarettes from her purse. It was one of the few times she was glad she smoked. She got out of the car and walked around the medical center, and on the back side of the building, near a door, she saw a guy puffing on a cigarette. There were three folding lawn chairs near the door and two standing ashtrays. An outdoor light shined down on the chairs. Yeah, this was the place where the lepers congregated.

She walked toward the smoker—and as she was walking another idea occurred to her.

The smoker was a skinny, thin-faced Latino guy wearing blue scrubs, his black hair in a short ponytail. She thought he looked sort of sly and weaselly, but maybe that was just wistful thinking on her part. She took a seat on one of the folding chairs, pulled out a cigarette, and lit it.

She said to him, "Hi, how you doin'?"

"Okay," he said.

"What's your name?"

He hesitated. "Horatio."

"You a nurse?"

"Orderly," he said.

Orderly was good. Orderlies were the guys who pushed patients around in wheelchairs and mopped up the puke when someone puked. Orderlies didn't get paid for shit.

"Horatio, how would you like to earn a hundred bucks?"

"Doing what?" he asked.

"I'm a reporter for the *Miami Herald*, and I'm down here covering those two FBI agents who were shot on Geiger Key. You know about that?"

"Yeah, sure."

"Well, we can't get any information out of the bureau about the agent who survived, the one that's here in this hospital. We don't even know his name. So I'll give you a hundred bucks if you'll do a couple of things for me. First, get me his name and find out what his condition is. He's supposedly in a coma, but I'd like some more facts, like is he likely to recover, how long might he be in the coma, if he recovers will he be able to talk, that sort of thing. You know, some details I can put in my article. I'd also like to know if he's being guarded, meaning I'd like to know if the FBI is worried about anyone trying to shoot him again. And what I'd really like is a photo of him. So you take your phone, snap a couple of pictures of him, look at his chart, BS with the nurses, and come back here and tell me what you find out. How does that sound to you?"

This was Patty's new plan: she'd let the orderly do a recon for her. When he came back to collect his money, she'd ask him if it was possible for her to sneak into McGruder's room herself and see him. If Horatio said yes, she'd shoot him with the silenced pistol so he wouldn't be able to ID her later and prop him up in one of the smokers' chairs. Then she'd sneak into McGruder's room and kill him, too. If Horatio said it wasn't possible for her to get into his room for some reason, like if an agent was sitting right outside his door, then, well, she didn't know what she'd do. She might be completely screwed.

The whole time she'd been talking, she'd noticed that Horatio had a small smile on his weasel face. For whatever reason he found what she was saying amusing, but she couldn't understand why.

She said, "Well, what do you think? You interested or not?"

He said, "You give me a hundred right now, I'll tell you all about his condition."

"You actually know his condition? You're an orderly, not a doctor, so how would you know?"

"For a hundred bucks, I'll tell you how I know."

"Okay, fine," Patty said, and pulled out her wallet and handed him the money.

"I don't know the guy's name. But what I do know is that he's dead. He died about an hour ago."

"You're shitting me," Patty said, a wave of relief washing over her.

"Nope. He's dead. I was in the ICU when it happened. I was in the room right across from his. Some old fart's catheter bag broke and I was cleaning up his piss, when an alarm went off and I see nurses run into the guy's room, like four of them. Later one of the docs shows up. Anyway, I finish up and ask one of the nurses if the guy had died, and she tells me he's the FBI agent who got shot. Not only that, she tells me two of the nurses who I saw go into the room were really FBI agents disguised as nurses guarding him."

Patty thought, *Jesus, I'd have been nailed for sure if I'd tried anything.*

Then remembering she was supposed to be a reporter, she said, "Does anyone outside the hospital know he's dead yet?"

"Beats me," Horatio said. "But probably not. Looks like you got yourself a scoop."

She walked back to her car thinking, *It's finished. I've won.*

She'd managed to kill McIntyre and McGruder without getting caught, and the fifteen million in the bank that she would have had to split with them was now hers alone. She'd still wait a year—let everything cool down when it came to McIntyre and McGruder and Andie Moore—and then she'd start to live the life of the rich and famous. Well, not the famous, but the rich.

She'd launder the money carefully—and being an expert at money laundering, that wouldn't be a problem. She'd buy a small starter home in Sedona, wait a few months, then sell it and buy a grander one on a golf course. She'd take lessons from a handsome pro and improve her game. She'd buy a Mercedes convertible because she'd always wanted one, and she could picture herself driving down the highway, the top down, her blond hair flying in the wind. Oh, life was going to be so good.

35

Emma's phone rang, waking her from a sound sleep. It took a few seconds for her to realize that she was in a hotel room in Miami.

She answered the phone, saying, "Yes."

"This is Dr. Singh. As you requested, I'm calling to let you know that Mr. McGruder died."

"But you haven't declared him dead yet, have you?"

"No. As you may know, there were two FBI agents in the ICU pretending to be nurses and guarding McGruder. They were present when he died. The agents have instructed the nursing staff to leave McGruder lying in bed and connected to the monitoring equipment until they're told otherwise."

"Good. And thank you for your help, Dr. Singh."

Emma thought for a moment, then went back to sleep. There was nothing for her to do. Either the person who shot McGruder would take another crack at him or he wouldn't.

At six, Emma woke up. Her alarm didn't ring; that was just when she always woke up. She brushed her teeth, then checked her phone to see if there was any news about the FBI catching a killer at the Lower Keys Medical Center and saw that no such thing had been reported. She dressed in shorts, a T-shirt, and running shoes and went for a five-mile run. When she returned to her room, she took a shower, then went down to the hotel restaurant and had a cup of coffee and half a grapefruit. She looked at her watch and saw it was seven thirty and decided that DeMarco had slept long enough. She called his room and told him to meet her in the hotel restaurant.

Fifteen minutes later, DeMarco arrived, unshaven, looking grouchy. "What's going on?" he asked.

"McGruder died last night. Dr. Singh informed me about two this morning."

DeMarco said, "Yeah, well, that was to be expected. So what?"

"I'm going to call Perkins and ask him what he plans to do next."

"And you decided to wake me up so I could be here while you talked to Perkins?"

"No. I wanted you here so we can decide what to do after I've talked to Perkins. And it was time for you to get up anyway. Nobody should sleep so late."

"Late! It wasn't even eight o'clock."

⬥

Perkins was not happy to hear from Emma.

She said, "I know that McGruder died last night and—"

"How do you know?"

"I just do," Emma said. "I also know that they're leaving his body in the ICU and that you have two agents waiting to see if anyone tries to kill him. I'm assuming that no one tried last night. Is that correct?"

"Hey. I'm not going to discuss this case with you any further."

"Why not?" Emma said. "I've been very cooperative with you."

"Because I don't trust you," Perkins said.

"Agent Perkins, do I have to remind you again that I'm working for the inspector general? All I want to know is what you're planning to do next so I can tell my boss, and if you won't tell me, I'll call my boss and he'll call your director. I don't think you want that to happen."

"Hey, I don't give a shit who you—"

Perkins stopped as his brain caught up with his mouth. He'd been around long enough to know that antagonizing the DOJ Inspector General was rarely a smart thing to do.

He took a breath and said, "I'm going to leave the body where it is for another twenty-four hours. I can't leave it lying there any longer than that. The hospital's already pissed that we got a corpse decaying in one of their ICU beds. If nothing happens by tomorrow at this time, then we're moving the body to the morgue."

"What do you plan to do if no one makes a run at McGruder?"

"I don't know. And that's the truth. I'll figure something out. And, hey, where's the statements you and DeMarco were supposed to give me?"

Emma said, "I'm still working on mine because I'm trying to be thorough. As for Joe's, well, you see, Joe's dyslexic and he's doing his best, but he has a hard time using a computer."

"Look, I want those statements and I want them today."

"Agent Perkins, if there's anything I can do to help, don't hesitate to call." Emma hung up.

"Dyslexic?" DeMarco said.

Emma shrugged.

"So now what?"

Emma didn't answer; she was making another call.

"Who are you calling now?"

"Neil," she said. "I want to see what he's learned about the people in McIntyre's address book."

"What did you do? Tell him to stay up all night working on it?"

Emma didn't answer.

On the fifth ring, Neil answered the phone, saying, "Hello." His voice sounded hoarse.

Emma said, "Well?" She put the phone in speaker mode so DeMarco could hear.

Neil said, "I'm not finished yet. I've still got a couple of names to go. Anyway, most of the men's names in the book are FBI agents about McIntyre's age. I'm guessing they're friends, guys he used to work with. Most of them are retired. The others are still working and scattered all over the country. A bunch of the numbers are for fishing guides or for guys who run charter boats or fishing camps or something related to fishing. The women's names in the book are, I'm guessing, old girlfriends. Two are waitresses. Another one sells real estate. There're also a couple of relatives. A brother in Colorado, a cousin who lives in Idaho, and an uncle who's in a nursing home."

"So you didn't find any lawyers," Emma said.

"I'm not finished," Neil said. "I found two. One's the lawyer who handled McIntyre's second divorce. He lives in Minnesota and all he's ever done is divorce work. The second lawyer is the one that will interest you. She's a woman named Patricia McHugh. She works at—"

"Patricia?" Emma said. "Was she identified in the address book as Patricia or Patty?"

"Well, Patty, but her given name is Patricia. Anyway, like I started to say, she works at DOJ. She's the one I'm still researching. But what I've got so far is that she's a former FBI agent who's a lawyer, and she transferred from the bureau to DOJ about twenty-five years ago."

"Did you find a photo of her?"

"No, but I wasn't looking for a photo."

Emma thought for a second, then said, "You said the address book contained the names of agents McIntyre used to work with. Are any of them located in or near Miami?"

"Yeah, a couple of them."

"Give me their names, phone numbers, and addresses."

Neil did as instructed, and Emma wrote the information down.

"Now, I want you to see if you can find a photo of the McHugh woman and send it to me. Do that first, then keep researching her."

"Okay. But I need to get a couple hours of sleep, Emma. I'm runnin' on fumes here."

"Sleep after you find the photo," Emma said, and hung up.

To DeMarco, she said, "I'm going to call these retired agents and see if they can tell us anything. I figure that McIntyre might have socialized with the ones who live near Miami."

DeMarco said, "Great. Sounds like a plan."

He got up from the table and started to leave. Emma said, "Where are you going?"

"While you're calling these guys, I'm going to shave and take a shower, then I'm going to get something to eat, and then, since I've got nothing better to do, I'm going to follow up on an assignment Mahoney gave me."

"What assignment?"

"Oh, just something related to a congressman who didn't vote the way Mahoney told him to."

"Well, I'm glad to see that there's at least one Democrat in the House with a spine who that bastard can't intimidate."

DeMarco saw no reason to tell her that he suspected Congressman Stanley Freeman really didn't have a spine or, if he did, only recently acquired it. He said, "If you learn something from these agents or from Neil, give me a call."

Although it hadn't been too early to wake DeMarco, Emma decided not to call the retired agents until nine a.m. To kill time, she ordered another cup of coffee, then called her partner, Christine, whom she also woke up. Fortunately, Christine, unlike DeMarco, was a cheerful morning person and they chatted for half an hour, Christine going on and on about the National Symphony's new conductor, who she said was a megalomaniac and a tyrant, which was the same complaint she'd had about his predecessor. Although Emma pretended to be sympathetic, she'd always thought that managing the large but fragile egos of talented musicians would be more difficult than herding cats.

At nine, she called the first agent whose name Neil had given her. He didn't answer his phone, so Emma left a message. She said, "I'm sure you've probably heard about the two FBI agents shot in Geiger Key. One of the agents was your friend, McIntyre. I'm working the case. Call me. I need to talk to you."

The second agent, a man named Keller, answered his phone. Emma identified herself as an FBI agent working on the shootings of the two agents in Geiger Key and said she'd gotten his name from McIntyre's address book. After the retired agent got over the shock of learning that his friend was dead, Emma said, "The reason I'm calling is that I'm pursuing a lead related to a lawyer that McIntyre may have known. I don't have a name. All I know is that McIntyre would have been close to this lawyer, someone that he would have confided in. I was hoping that you might know someone like that."

Keller said he didn't. When Emma asked if he knew a woman named Patty McHugh, Keller said, "Not really. I met her once at a party a few years ago. About the only thing I know is she's someone McIntyre met when he first started at the bureau. But I don't know anything else about her other than that she was close to Mac, like maybe an ex-girlfriend."

The first agent called her back. He didn't know anything about anything and sounded hungover. She'd just finished talking to him when her phone chirped with a text from Neil. Accompanying the text was a photo of Patricia McHugh taken when McHugh appeared as an expert witness in a money-laundering case—and Emma thought, *Hmm*. It was the same woman in the birthday party photo that had been on McGruder's desk.

———◆———

DeMarco decided to sit outside by the hotel pool to continue his pursuit of Stanley Freeman. He didn't want to go to the restaurant because Emma might still be there and because he was hoping that maybe he'd encounter the divorced teacher, Marcie, from Vermont again. No such luck. There was no one in the pool area but one lady who appeared to be about eighty swimming laps. DeMarco was impressed by her stamina; he would have drowned had he tried to swim as far as she did.

He opened his laptop, reread the two-line article in the *Sprague Journal* again, then found a phone number for the newspaper.

A man answered, and DeMarco said, "Can I speak to the editor or whoever's in charge?"

"That'd be me," the man said. "Editor, journalist, and janitor. What can I do for you?"

"I saw an article in your paper that was posted about a year ago having to do with a man named Stanley Freeman discharging a firearm, and—"

"That crazy son of a bitch. What's he done now?"

"Nothing that I'm aware of," DeMarco said. "I was just curious about the story you published."

"Why's that?" the editor said.

DeMarco decided a lie might be appropriate. He said, "I work for a company that does background research on people applying for jobs. Freeman's an applicant, and I was assigned to check him out, and the only thing that popped up that surprised me was the fine he got for discharging a gun. I'm just trying to make sure this guy isn't some sort of nut who might pose a danger to others."

The editor was happy to tell him what he knew about Freeman, and it became apparent that he had no idea that Freeman was a congressman from Rhode Island. All he knew was that Freeman was a maniac who owned a cabin on a creek near the town, which he visited maybe a dozen times a year. DeMarco didn't bother to say that Freeman's sister actually owned the place, but it was the cabin on the creek that led to the firearms fine—and that also explained Freeman's vote on the wetlands bill. DeMarco would have to make a couple more calls to confirm what he'd learned—he'd probably have to talk to the cops in Sprague—but as soon as he hung up, he started laughing.

His phone rang. It was Emma.

"Where are you?"

"Sitting by the pool."

"Go pack, we're leaving. I want to catch the next plane to D.C. Neil found a photo of the McHugh woman. She's the woman in the photo on McGruder's desk. And she's a lawyer. I've told Neil to get a couple of hours of sleep but after that to do more research on McHugh. By the time we get back, he'll have more information for us."

"But we have no evidence that McHugh is the lawyer that assisted McIntyre and McGruder."

"No, but she's the only lawyer we've been able to find that was close to them. So hurry up."

36

DeMarco had never been inside the National Security Agency's head-quarters at Fort Meade in Maryland, but he'd always imagined that the offices of the NSA technicians who did sneaky things, like hacking into computers located in North Korea, looked just like Neil's office.

At Neil's workstation were three jumbo-size monitors. One of them showed nothing but constantly changing lines of what DeMarco guessed was raw computer code, and the screen reminded him of the ones he'd seen in that movie, *The Matrix*—making him wonder if Neil was real or a hologram. Beneath the workstation were five computer towers and half a dozen black boxes with blinking green lights. He had no idea what the black boxes did. The cables connecting all the various devices made the floor look like a snake pit.

Neil was dressed as DeMarco had last seen him in Florida. In fact, he may have been wearing the same clothes: a wrinkled Hawaiian shirt, cargo shorts—the pockets bulging with God knows what—and sandals on his fat splayed feet. His face looked haggard from fatigue, and his pupils were the size of buttons from the amount of caffeine or amphet-amine he'd taken to stay awake.

Emma's sympathetic reaction to his condition was: "What did you learn?"

Neil said, "Like I told you before, McHugh worked for the FBI for five years before she transferred to Justice. She started at the bureau the same day McIntyre and McGruder did, but she was never stationed where they were after she completed her training."

"What does she do at Justice?"

"The last ten years she's mostly been involved in money-laundering and tax-evasion cases. She's not a trial lawyer, but she helps build the cases to prosecute people or go after banks. A lot of the work she's done has been connected to drug cases. You know, going after cartel money stashed in U.S. banks and convicting the people laundering the money. She's apparently pretty good at what she does. While she's been at Justice, she's been promoted steadily, and she's now a GS-14 and supervises a couple of people. She's got in thirty-plus years of government service and could probably retire any time she wants."

"Her finances?" Emma said.

"Because of her rank and the kind of work she does, she's required to file a financial disclosure statement. Her annual salary is a little over a hundred grand, her retirement savings are tied up in her government 401(k), and she's got another hundred grand in cash, stocks, and bonds. I'm surprised she doesn't have more in savings, and I'm guessing she's probably made a few bad investments along the way. She's paying off a three hundred and fifty K mortgage on her condo in Arlington but other than that doesn't have any debt. My guess would be that her net worth is about three-quarters of a million, with a good chunk of that being the equity in her condo. So she's doing okay financially, but she's not rich. If she were to retire now, her pension would probably be around seventy grand before taxes."

"Her personal life?"

"She was married for about fifteen years to another lawyer at Justice. She divorced him ten years ago. She lives alone. Based on her phone records, I don't think she currently has a boyfriend. I mean, there isn't some guy she calls frequently."

"What do her phone records show when it comes to McIntyre and McGruder?" Emma asked.

Neil said, "Now here's where it gets interesting. McHugh talked fairly often to McIntyre and McGruder until about a year ago, meaning they'd call her or she'd call one of them every couple of months. But she hasn't called them in a year. Maybe they had some sort of falling out, but the date she stopped communicating with them roughly coincides with the time McIntyre and McGruder were assigned to the Berman case. Which also coincides with another event.

"A year ago, she took a flight to Miami, and the three of them apparently split the bill at a restaurant there. What I'm sayin' is, all three of them had a credit card charge for the same amount on the same night at the same restaurant, as if they split the bill three ways. But also based on her credit card records, she hasn't traveled to Miami since then, and she didn't fly down there on the day McIntyre and McGruder were shot."

Emma said, "If they communicated in the last year, they could have been using burners. And I suppose it's possible she could have driven to Miami, but I doubt it. It's a fifteen-hour drive, then another three hours to Key West. Maybe she has a fake ID."

Neil said, "Yeah, maybe, but to prove she flew down there, you'd have to get airport surveillance footage to see if a camera picked her up. That's something I can't do."

"The FBI could get the footage," DeMarco said.

Emma said, "Yes, but the FBI would have to have a reason for doing so, and right now we don't have anything that would make them believe that McHugh's done anything illegal. All we can prove is that the three of them were friends, which isn't enough for the FBI to get warrants or launch an investigation."

"We also have a problem when it comes to motive," DeMarco said. "If she was involved with McIntyre and McGruder, she had a motive for killing them when we tied them to Andie's murder. But what was her motive for getting involved with them in the first place? Like Neil said, financially she's doing okay, so why would she steal the money the Bermans stole and risk going to prison?"

"Because people are greedy and always want more," Emma said. Case closed.

They all sat in silence, the only sound being Emma's polished fingernails tapping on Neil's desk. Neil closed his eyes, and it looked as if he was about to fall asleep. DeMarco stared out a window, looking at the Pentagon, which he could see from Neil's fourth-floor office, making him wonder what the Department of Defense thought about having Neil as a neighbor.

"Well, there is one thing we can do," DeMarco said. "We can't prove she killed McIntyre and McGruder, but we can probably prove that she didn't."

"What are you talking about?"

"McIntyre and McGruder were shot at about one in the morning. On a Friday morning, meaning on a workday morning. If she shot them, she'd have to have flown down on Thursday and then driven three hours to Geiger Key, then she'd have to drive three hours back to Miami and catch a plane back to D.C. What I'm saying is, if she killed them, she probably wasn't at work on Friday and left work early on Thursday. If we can prove she was at work on those days, then that will at least eliminate her as a suspect."

"I don't know why I didn't think of that," Emma muttered.

DeMarco said, "Call Henry and tell him to find out if she took time off from work on those days. The IG's office has the authority to see if an employee took annual leave or sick leave on a particular day."

Emma did as DeMarco suggested and told Henry they had a lead connecting McIntyre and McGruder to a DOJ lawyer and gave Henry McHugh's name and asked him to see if she was at work on the days in question. Ten minutes later, Henry called back and informed them that McHugh had taken three hours of sick leave on Thursday afternoon and eight hours the following day.

Emma smiled. She said, "Henry, can you do something else for me? Can you get the TSA to see if she flew to Miami on Thursday and flew back on Friday?" Although Neil had said that McHugh hadn't used a credit card to charge a flight to Miami, Emma was thinking that maybe she'd used cash.

"That shouldn't be a problem," Henry said.

Thirty minutes later, Henry called back. By then Neil was sound asleep. "There's no record of her taking a flight to Miami. I mean, not on a commercial airline. I suppose she could have chartered a plane or flown under a different name, although that seems unlikely."

"Well, poop," Emma said. "Henry, I'll get back to you."

DeMarco said, "So. Do we let the FBI take it from here?"

Emma's lips compressed into a thin, stubborn line. "No, not yet. I want to talk to this woman first. If she killed McIntyre and McGruder, they almost certainly told her that we were down in Miami investigating them and she'll know who I am. So I want to see what she's like. I want to get a sense of her. I want to see how she reacts when I question her."

"Maybe she'll react by shooting you," DeMarco said.

37

Patty looked up from her desk to see a tall, slender woman with short grayish-blond hair standing in her office doorway. She had a high forehead, a perfectly straight nose, and extraordinary pale blue eyes. There was an aura of authority about her. Her clothes, although simple, were expensive. Patty paid attention to fashion even if she couldn't afford the fashions she liked. The slacks the woman was wearing had probably cost five hundred bucks; they looked tailored, not something you'd buy off the rack at Macy's. And she was wearing Mephisto walking shoes that retailed for over three hundred dollars. Patty knew this because she'd always wanted a pair like that but hadn't wanted to spend so much on casual shoes. Once she moved to Arizona, she'd buy a dozen pairs of Mephistos.

"Can I help you?" she said.

The woman said her name was Emma and that she was from the IG's office and doing some sort of review related to sick leave—but Patty had stopped listening to what she was saying as soon as she heard "Emma."

Oh, shit, oh, shit, oh, shit. This was the woman who'd been investigating McIntyre and McGruder down in Florida. How in the hell had she connected her to them?

She tried to freeze her face into showing no emotion whatsoever but wasn't sure she'd pulled it off. She said, "I'm sorry. Could you repeat that? You said you're doing an audit of sick leave versus annual leave usage, is that right?"

"Yes," Emma said. "Our records show that you took three hours of sick leave last Thursday and eight more hours on the following day. First, I want to verify that our records are correct."

"Yeah, but so what? I got the flu or something, was throwing up and had diarrhea and a horrible headache, so I took a couple of days off."

"Did you see a doctor?"

"No. If I'd gotten sicker, I would have, but I didn't. Why in the hell would the IG care if I took sick leave?"

Emma said, "First of all, relax. You're not in any trouble."

"I am relaxed," Patty said, even though she wasn't.

"The IG is concerned that employees are sometimes taking sick leave when they're not really sick and should be using their annual leave. Now I'm sure a person with your time in federal service knows that sick leave is like an insurance policy. You don't want to waste your accrued sick leave hours because someday you might get really sick and need every hour you have. Also, sick leave hours add to your retirement. That is, every hour of unspent sick leave increases your total time in federal service, which affects your pension."

Everything the woman had said was true when it came to the reasons federal employees shouldn't waste their sick leave hours, and at the same time, Patty knew it was all total bullshit. This woman wasn't here to ask if she'd used her sick leave inappropriately; she was here to confirm that she hadn't been at work when McIntyre and McGruder were killed.

Patty said, "Yes, I know all that. And like I said, I didn't use my sick leave hours inappropriately."

"Well, okay then," Emma said. "Thank you for your time."

When Emma worked at the DIA, she'd never been used as an interrogator. The reason for this was that a good interrogator has the ability to develop a level of rapport with a subject and can come across as being genuinely sympathetic, compassionate, and understanding of the subject's behavior even when the behavior is terrorism and mass murder. Emma just couldn't do that; she just couldn't pretend to be sympathetic. She had, however, taken classes given to interrogators by psychologists and other eggheads who taught the interrogators how to tell when someone was lying. There were physical indicators, such as body language, and eye, mouth, and hand movements. There were patterns of speech and the way a liar would take a breath or pause or purse his lips. The techniques taught had been useful to Emma both professionally and personally. They weren't foolproof, however. For example, even though she knew John Mahoney lied almost every time he opened his mouth, he rarely displayed the telltale signs of a liar. The only reason she knew he'd lied on CNN about getting kickbacks from the federal building contractors in Boston was because she knew that was exactly the kind of thing he'd do. With DeMarco, on the other hand, she could always tell when he was lying.

And when it came to Patty McHugh, she knew that McHugh had lied to her when she said she was sick on the days that she'd taken sick leave.

She knew that Patty McHugh had killed McIntyre and McGruder.

But now what? Even though she was certain McHugh had lied to her, she had no evidence to prove she'd killed anyone, and as defense lawyers always say, *It's not what you know but what you can prove.*

Just knowing she was right about McHugh was a step forward.

But what was the next step?

Patty left her office, telling her secretary that she was going outside to have a smoke.

Her secretary said, "You've been smoking quite a bit lately. Are you stressed out about something?"

She had to stop herself from screaming, *Oh, go fuck yourself!* Instead she said, "Yeah, you're right. I need to stop altogether. It's just the Pemberton thing. I'm spinning my wheels on it and need to clear my head."

The Pemberton thing was a case involving a guy named Albert Pemberton who owned a chain of dry cleaners in Maryland and was laundering money through them for a drug lord in Baltimore. She wasn't spinning her wheels on the case; she just didn't give a shit about it.

She took the stairs down to the first floor and went out the east side of the building to Ninth Street. Across the street was the grand structure housing the National Archives. In all the time she'd lived in D.C., she'd never been inside the building.

She took a seat on a bench and lit a cigarette. She hadn't noticed the guy when she sat down, but a few feet away from her was a bearded bum wearing a badly stained olive-green army fatigue jacket, despite the fact that it was almost eighty degrees outside. She could smell his body odor from ten feet away. He had a cardboard sign around his neck that said PLEASE HELP. NEED BEER MONEY. He was apparently one of the funny bums.

He said, "Hey, can I get a smoke from you?"

She said, "No. And get the hell away from me."

"Sheesh," the guy said. "You don't have to be so mean about it."

"If you don't leave, I'm going to call the security guards inside the building and tell them you're threatening me."

"Hey, fine, and go fuck yourself," the guy said. He got up and started walking away, then turned and said, "I'm a veteran, you know."

"Tell it to someone who gives a shit," Patty said.

The bum flipped her the bird but went on his way.

What should she do?

That woman, Emma, obviously suspected that she'd killed them because she'd asked about the days she went down to the Keys *to* kill them. But how in the hell had she connected her to them? One scary possibility was that she had actual evidence tying her to the murders, but that was unlikely. If she'd had any evidence, she wouldn't have shown up at her office. The FBI would have shown up instead and arrested her. More likely, she'd done some sort of deep dive into people whom McIntyre and McGruder had known and come up with her name, and she'd probably zeroed in on her because she was a lawyer who could have helped them tank the Berman case.

But so what? Knowing them wasn't proof that she'd killed them, so what had the damn woman been trying to achieve? Maybe she'd just wanted to see her reaction. Or maybe she was hoping that she'd panic and do something that would lead her to actual evidence.

There was evidence, of course, like the gun she'd used to kill them, but they'd never find the gun. And if by some fluke they did find it, they wouldn't be able to trace it to her. She supposed that if they put enough manpower on it, they could prove that she'd flown to Miami. Even though she'd used a fake name, they could look at airport cameras, talk to rental car people. But again, so what? If they could prove she'd flown to Miami, that would definitely make her a "person of interest," but they'd still have to prove that she was a killer.

She dropped the cigarette she'd smoked down to the filter and immediately lit another.

So what should she do?

The answer was obvious. The answer was: *Do nothing.*

She'd done everything she could have done to keep from getting caught, and she'd just have to hope that she'd done enough. She'd stick to her plan. She'd retire, wait a year, and then start to launder the money. If they caught her—well, then they caught her.

But she didn't think they would.

She got up from the bench and headed back toward her office, feeling kind of bad for yelling at the bum—if he actually was a veteran.

38

DeMarco and Emma met Henry at his home in Falls Church.

Henry's home was on a quiet residential street. It was two stories and had a large front yard with several flower beds. Across the street from his house was an elementary school, probably the school his late son had attended as a child. DeMarco imagined maintaining the house and grounds would be a burden for someone Henry's age, and he wondered if the reason he was still living in it, and not in a small apartment or a facility for seniors, was that he couldn't bear to leave the place where the people he'd loved had lived. The house was his last connection to them.

Emma rang the bell, and Henry let them in. He was wearing the pants from the suit he'd worn to work and a white shirt without a tie. On his feet were soft slippers. He moved slowly, and somewhat stiffly, as he led them into the living room. DeMarco was struck by how gaunt Henry looked. It looked as if he'd lost ten pounds in the short time since he'd seen him last.

"Would you like something to drink?" he asked.

Before DeMarco could speak, Emma said, "No, we're fine."

Emma and DeMarco sat down on a worn, but comfortable, floral-patterned couch; Henry sat across from them in an overstuffed chair that matched the couch. DeMarco estimated that all the furniture in the room was at least two decades old. He imagined that everything had been purchased by Henry's late wife, and he hadn't changed a thing in the room since she'd died. On a side table were several framed photographs of his family. One photo was of a beautiful, bright-eyed young girl who looked a lot like Andie Moore; the girl had to be Henry's granddaughter.

DeMarco also noticed that there was nothing in the room related to Henry's military career. His Congressional Medal of Honor wasn't on display, nor were there any photos of the young men he'd served with in Vietnam. It appeared as if his military service was something he didn't want to be reminded of.

Emma said, "Henry, I'm about ninety percent sure that this DOJ lawyer, McHugh, conspired with McIntyre and McGruder on the Berman case, but I can't prove it. I also think she killed them, and I know she wasn't at work when they were killed, but I can't prove she flew to Miami. And the FBI found no physical evidence tying her or anyone else to the murders."

"So what makes you think she's guilty?" Henry asked.

"Because she lied to me when I asked her why she'd taken sick leave."

"How do you know she lied?"

Emma said, "I just do."

"I see," Henry said. Emma's answer sounded weak even to DeMarco.

Emma said, "What we need is for the FBI to look at airport cameras to see if she flew to Miami using another name, but I don't think the bureau would be willing to make the effort in the absence of any evidence. That she was lifelong friends with McIntyre and McGruder isn't an adequate reason, and the fact that she apparently hasn't had any contact with them in a year makes it even less likely that the FBI would want to get involved. So I'm stuck, and I can't think of what to do next."

Henry may not have realized it, but DeMarco knew that Emma saying that she didn't know what to do next was a rare and astounding admission.

Henry started to say something, but then he inhaled sharply as if he'd just experienced a sharp pain.

Emma said, "Henry, are you all right? You don't look well."

"Oh, I'm fine," he said. "Just a bit tired."

He didn't look tired; he looked dead on his feet.

He said, "I suppose I could speak to the FBI director about this woman. I know he'd listen to me, but frankly I'm reluctant to do that. I don't want to tarnish her reputation or cause her problems if she's innocent, and the fact she lied to you doesn't prove she's a killer. Maybe she lied for some other reason, like maybe she did something embarrassing on the days she took leave and didn't want to admit it."

Surprisingly, Emma didn't tell Henry he was wrong, and DeMarco knew why: because Henry wasn't wrong. And his concern for not damaging McHugh's reputation—which an FBI investigation could certainly do, even if the FBI ultimately found out that she'd done nothing wrong—was an indicator of his decency. As a senior employee working for the inspector general, Henry had certainly damaged some reputations and ended more than a few careers, but he probably never did so unless he was a hundred percent—not ninety percent—certain that he was right.

Henry rose slowly to his feet, and DeMarco and Emma rose with him.

Henry said, "I want to thank you for everything you both did. You went far beyond what I expected, and I'm not asking you to do anything else. At least I know who killed Andie and why, and they've paid for what they did. As for catching the person who killed McIntyre and McGruder, we'll just have to hope that the bureau can catch whoever did it, whether it's this woman or someone else. But, again, thank you for everything you did."

Emma, clearly not satisfied and feeling as if she'd failed, looked as if she was about to say something else, but then nodded and turned to leave. She turned back and said, "Henry, is there anything I can do for you? I mean, on a personal level. Do you have anything around here you need help with, any errands I can run for you, anything like that?"

"Oh, no," he said. "But thank you for offering."

As they were walking back to their cars, DeMarco said, "He didn't look good at all. What do you think's going on with him?"

"I think he's dying," Emma said.

39

DeMarco arrived at the Italian restaurant in Georgetown at ten as instructed and saw a CLOSED sign on the door. Peering through the window in the door, he could see there were no other customers in the place except for Mahoney, who was sitting at a table with two other men. All three of them were holding drinks in their hands and—contrary to city ordinances—smoking cigars. DeMarco recognized the two men with Mahoney; they were members of the Boston City Council.

DeMarco suspected that if a casting director was looking for two characters to portray corrupt politicians in a movie, he would have picked these two. They were overweight and had small, cunning eyes. Their faces were red from too much booze and too little exercise, and they just *looked* like a couple of guys on the take. In other words, they somewhat resembled Mahoney—who was definitely on the take.

DeMarco wondered why they were meeting with Mahoney in D.C. and suspected it had to do with some nefarious scheme to either make Mahoney money or keep him in power. On the other hand, they could have been meeting with him for some perfectly legitimate reason; after all, they were Mahoney's constituents.

Nah. If they were meeting with Mahoney privately, in an empty restaurant at ten o'clock at night, it was for some sneaky, underhanded reason.

DeMarco rapped hard on the window, and Mahoney looked over at him, then turned and said something to someone DeMarco couldn't see. A moment later a pretty woman with long dark hair, wearing a red dress and lipstick that matched, walked toward the door. She appeared to be about forty and had an outstanding figure. She unlocked the door and said, "John said that he'd be with you in a moment. Go sit at the bar. Help yourself to whatever you want to drink."

Because she was attractive and because she'd called Mahoney "John," DeMarco wondered if she could be Mahoney's current mistress. DeMarco had never been able to understand why so many women found Mahoney attractive, and this woman was young enough to be his daughter. Maybe he was reading too much into the fact that she'd called the old lecher by his given name.

He walked over to the bar as instructed, went behind it, and studied the booze selection. He pulled a bottle of Grey Goose vodka off the shelf, poured two fingers into a glass, and added a single ice cube. Then he took a seat at the bar to wait impatiently for Mahoney to finish plotting whatever he was plotting with the two Boston pols.

He'd called Mahoney earlier and asked if he wanted an update on the Andie Moore investigation. Also, he needed to tell him what he'd learned when it came to Congressman Stanley Freeman. Mahoney said he definitely wanted to hear what DeMarco had to say, but the only time he could meet with him was at ten p.m. in the restaurant where DeMarco was now sitting.

Finally, the two men who'd been with Mahoney left the table and walked to the front door of the restaurant. As they passed DeMarco, they looked at him suspiciously; they didn't like the fact that he was a witness to their meeting with Mahoney. DeMarco got off the barstool and strolled toward Mahoney's table. As he was doing so, the woman in the red dress walked over to Mahoney. He placed a meaty paw familiarly on her hip and said something to her, and she tilted her pretty head back and laughed. DeMarco shook his head; he just didn't get it.

As DeMarco neared the table, he heard Mahoney say, "Tell your dad thanks for letting me use the restaurant tonight. I'll call you later."

The woman headed toward the kitchen, most likely to clean up after Mahoney's dinner. DeMarco took a seat. Mahoney's eyes were glassy; God knows how much bourbon he'd consumed.

DeMarco said, "You want me to give you a lift home when we're done here?"

"Nah. George is out back."

George was Mahoney's driver. It didn't bother Mahoney a bit that poor George had been required to sit in a car for two or three hours while Mahoney was inside drinking, smoking cigars, and stuffing himself.

"So. What have you and Emma been up to?" Mahoney asked.

"First, let me tell you about Congressman Freeman. That won't take long."

Mahoney shrugged and took another sip of his drink.

"Freeman's sister has a cabin on a creek in Connecticut, but it's basically Freeman's cabin because he's the only one who uses it. It's his retreat, where he goes to get away from his wife, where he goes when he wants to be alone and relax. The thing is, Freeman has a thing for beavers. He absolutely hates the bucktoothed bastards."

"Beavers? What the fuck are you talking about?"

"Every year beavers build a dam on the creek that runs by Freeman's cabin, and when it rains, the dam causes the creek to rise and it floods the cabin. The beavers have flooded it half a dozen times, and Freeman's had to replace hardwood floors and rugs and half the furniture in the place. So every year, he goes on a beaver-killing spree. He shoots the critters; he catches them in traps; once somebody blew up the beaver dam with a stick of dynamite and the sheriff was sure it was Freeman, although he couldn't prove it. One time he got caught shooting at the beavers and was fined, which was how I found out about the cabin."

"But what the hell does this have to do with him not voting for the bill?"

"The bill had a provision in it that basically protects native wildlife in wetland areas, which includes the creek that runs near Freeman's cabin."

"It did?" Mahoney said. Like most of the bills passed in the House of Representatives, the bill was hundreds of pages long, and Speaker Mahoney hadn't bothered to read it.

"Yeah. And that's what Freeman objected to, although he wouldn't admit it. He hates the fucking beavers so much he didn't want anything to protect them."

"Well, shit," Mahoney said. "That's just stupid. He could have voted for the bill and killed the beavers anyway."

"Yeah, I suppose," DeMarco said. "But he's likely to get arrested the next time he shoots one. Anyway, he's probably not going to cause you a problem in the future unless he's voting on something beaver related."

Mahoney shook his head. "So what's the story on the girl who was killed?"

DeMarco told him everything he and Emma had done and learned. He talked about breaking into the Bermans' home and using a dead girl's thumb to open her cell phone and Emma bringing in two hard-looking little Latino guys armed to the teeth to protect DeMarco in case McIntyre and McGruder tried to kill him. Henry may have been shocked by the things he and Emma had done, but Mahoney wasn't. He knew DeMarco and Emma and the extent that they—and particularly Emma—would go to if they felt it was necessary.

When DeMarco finished, Mahoney said, "So you're telling me that this fuckin' woman is likely to get away with killing two men and stealing fifteen million dollars."

"Yeah, maybe," DeMarco said. "But I've got an idea. Got it while I was waiting at the bar. The problem is I'm not sure if Henry will be willing to go along."

The next morning DeMarco drove to Emma's place. He found her sitting on her patio, drinking coffee, enjoying the view of her perfectly groomed backyard. She didn't look peaceful—she looked annoyed—and DeMarco figured she was still stewing about the McHugh problem. He could hear a cello playing from the house; it was Christine practicing. DeMarco recognized the piece: it was one of the songs from *The Phantom of the Opera*, the one titled "The Music of the Night"—and he found it vaguely, eerily disturbing on a sunny spring morning.

"I've got an idea when it comes to McHugh," he said.

He told her what his idea was.

Emma said, "Henry could get killed."

"Then I guess it's our job to make sure that doesn't happen."

Emma didn't say anything for a moment, her fingernails tapping on the patio table. Christine was now playing another song from *Phantom*. DeMarco recognized it, too; it was called "The Point of No Return."

"All right," Emma said. "Let's talk to Henry."

40

There was a rap on the door frame, and Patty looked up to see a slight, gray-haired man in a dark suit standing outside her office. It was Henry Cantor.

She'd never met Cantor before, but she knew who he was. She also knew why he was there. He wasn't coming to ask if she was using her sick leave properly. He was there because he believed—like that bitch, Emma, believed—that she had killed McIntyre and McGruder. What other reason could there be?

He said, "Good morning, Ms. McHugh. My name's Henry Cantor. I work for the inspector general."

"I know who you are, Mr. Cantor. What can I do for you?" She kept her face expressionless, her tone neutral.

"May I sit down?" Henry said.

"Of course," Patty said.

Henry took a seat in one of the chairs in front of her desk. She thought he looked frail and unhealthy, but she'd heard stories about how persistent he could be when it came to doing his job. He was a dangerous man.

Henry said, "I'll get right to the point. I've been led to believe that you conspired with two FBI agents named McIntyre and McGruder to ruin a case involving Medicare fraud. One of my employees told me this and then she was killed."

Patty started to say—actually to *scream—That's outrageous!* but Henry held up a hand stopping her. "Let me finish, please."

Henry said, "I've also been led to believe that you killed the two FBI agents to silence them and keep them from implicating you in any crimes."

Now Patty screamed. "This is outrageous! I don't care who you are. How *dare* you accuse me of doing those things? I'm going to lodge a complaint with—"

Patty stopped. Who would she lodge a complaint with? She obviously couldn't complain to the inspector general.

"—with HR. Or I'll hire a lawyer and sue you and the Justice Department for making baseless accusations that could damage my career. I've given thirty years of my life to public service, and I will not allow you to tarnish my reputation."

Henry said, "I don't have any intention of accusing you formally of committing any crimes, Ms. McHugh, and the Justice Department Inspector General's Office is not going to be involved at all. I mean, I would accuse you if the evidence was there, but the problem is that you're a very smart woman and there's no proof that you've done anything wrong. So I'm not here in an official capacity. In fact, I just submitted my resignation and will be leaving the department the day after tomorrow."

"Then what—"

"This is personal for me, Ms. McHugh—the young woman who was killed meant a lot to me—and what I plan to do is make sure that you don't profit from your crimes. Right now, there's fifteen million dollars sitting in some shady foreign bank, and I imagine that what you're planning to do at some point is start spending that money on yourself. The problem you'll have is that you'll have to find a way to launder the money so you won't have issues with the IRS. Now I've been told that when it comes to money laundering, you're an expert, so I'm sure you've already given considerable thought as to how you'll clean the money. Maybe you'll start a business and launder it through the business. Maybe you'll launder it through casinos."

That's exactly what she'd been planning to do.

"But I'm not going to let you do it, Ms. McHugh. As I'm sure you know, it's often difficult to convict people of money laundering because they use middlemen and the banks don't cooperate. But you're not a drug cartel. You don't have layers of people between you and the money. You're going to have to launder it yourself.

"Well, Ms. McHugh, I intend to devote the rest of my life to watching you. I'll be retired and have nothing better to do, and I've got quite a bit of money myself and no one to leave it to, so I can afford to spend it on hiring people to help me. And what I'm going to do before I leave the department is put your finances under a microscope. I have the authority to do that. I'll get your tax returns, run credit checks on you, find out how much money you have in banks and investment firms. The reason I'm going to do that is so I'll know exactly how much money you have before you start to launder the money you stole. Then after I retire, I'll turn that information over to some people who will help me watch you. And I'm a man with lifelong connections, not only in the DOJ but also at Treasury, and even after I've retired there are people who will listen to me. So I'm going to be watching, Ms. McHugh. I'm going to be watching every move you make. And my friends at the IRS will audit you, they'll audit you every year, and the people doing the audits won't be rank-and-file bean counters. They'll be the heavy hitters from Treasury's criminal division."

Patty said, "You're making a big mistake, and I'm not going to stand for—"

Henry stood up. "No, the big mistake was killing Andie Moore. If that hadn't happened, I wouldn't be here. I'm not going to let you lead a life of luxury when that girl never had a chance to live her life at all."

Patty wanted to scream at the top of her lungs to give vent to her fury. But she didn't. She sat motionless, her jaw clamped so tight her teeth hurt, and tamped down on the anger and the panic and all the other useless emotions she was feeling. When she was calm enough to think clearly, she told her secretary that she was going outside for a smoke.

Her secretary said, "You have a meeting that starts in fifteen minutes."

She ignored her secretary, left the building, and took a seat on the bench where she'd sat before, the one with a view of the National Archives building. She looked around to make sure there weren't any nearby bums to hassle her, then lit a cigarette.

Now what? What should she do?

Her plan had always been to retire and then disappear from Washington and lead a mostly anonymous life. She would have laundered the money slowly, patiently, carefully, and only very gradually began to display the trappings of affluence: a lovely home, a luxury car, membership in a country club, tailored designer clothes. But with that little bastard, Cantor, watching her, how would she be able to pull it off? Like buying a house. The sort of house she was thinking about eventually buying in Sedona—four thousand square feet, a view, a swimming pool, manicured landscaping—would cost over two million even before she started buying artwork and furniture. But she could just see some vicious little gnome from the IRS saying, *Can you please explain something to me, McHugh. Your annual pension, before taxes, is seventy thousand dollars, meaning your monthly income, before taxes, is approximately six thousand dollars. How are you able to afford a home where the mortgage is approximately nine thousand dollars a month?*

And when she tried to launder the money that would explain how she could afford the home she wanted, Cantor would catch her if he did what he said.

The first step in money laundering is to get the tainted money into a bank. If you're a drug cartel and your profits are in the form of boxcars filled with cash, getting the money into a bank is tricky. The regulators tend to notice a guy with a suitcase filled with ten million in crumpled twenty-dollar bills making a deposit.

But Patty didn't have that problem because the Bermans had accomplished the first step for her. When Medicare had sent money to their nursing home account for some medical procedure that was never performed, the Bermans had vectored the money to an offshore bank, a bit at a time, over a five-year period. All Patty had had to do was move the Bermans' money to a different bank, a bank that knew the money was dirty but didn't care, and one that wouldn't cooperate with the U.S. government. The bank, of course, charged her a hefty fee for holding her money.

The next phase of the cleansing process was to turn the dirty money into what appeared to be a legitimate income stream, one that could be explained to the IRS—provided the IRS didn't look too closely. What Patty had been planning to do was buy a small business in Sedona, like a boutique or one of the little shops that sold crap to tourists. She would get the loan to buy the business from the bank who held her money. That is, the bank would give her *her* money and take a small slice for doing so. Once she had the business, she'd be able to inflate its revenue by tallying up sales that never happened, thus increasing her income to one that would match her lifestyle. To minimize her taxes, there would be business remodeling and maintenance expenses that never occurred, and the money supposedly spent on those items would be spent on herself.

Then there were the casinos in nearby Las Vegas. She'd been planning to make a couple dozen trips a year between her bank and Vegas. She would get cash from her crooked banker and then turn the cash into casino chips. For example, say she started with twenty thousand in cash. She'd turn the twenty thousand into chips, gamble recklessly for an hour, lose a couple thousand, and then cash in the remaining chips. Not only would she walk away with eighteen thousand squeaky-clean dollars, she'd have a record from the casino to show how she'd earned it. The casino, of course, would be happy to cooperate. It had just made two grand.

But none of this would work if Henry Cantor had people watching her. If she bought a business, he'd know how much revenue the business really generated and he'd know that expenditures she claimed had never occurred. If she was followed to a casino, whoever followed her could document that she didn't start with a couple thousand bucks and turn two thousand into eighteen. Instead there would be a video of her starting with twenty and walking away with eighteen.

Her fifteen million dollars—the fifteen million she'd sweated, schemed, and killed for—would effectively rot inside the bank, and she wouldn't be able to enjoy the fruits of her labor.

The only good news was that making her life miserable appeared to be a personal mission for Cantor. And if he was retired, then it wouldn't be the government coming after her; it would just be him.

She supposed she could just sit back and wait until he died. He was in his seventies, and she was only fifty-six, and he didn't look all that healthy. So she'd definitely outlive him, but what if the son of a bitch lived for ten more years? Fucking doctors these days could keep people living well past the point when they should have expired, and that would mean she'd have to leave her money untouched for ten years and live the life of a penny-pinching, retired civil servant for a decade.

That wasn't acceptable.

She flicked the cigarette away.

The answer was obvious: she couldn't allow Henry Cantor to live ten more years.

And she needed to move quickly. She couldn't allow him to put together a file on her finances, then pass off what he knew to whomever he planned to have help him. She wondered if that woman Emma might be involved; her gut told her that she might be, and Patty sensed that she was even more formidable than Cantor.

So Cantor had to go—and he had to go soon.

41

Patty returned to her office and told her secretary to cancel all her appointments and that she was leaving for the day. She didn't bother to say why she was leaving, and her secretary, sensing her foul mood, was afraid to ask.

Most of the people who worked at the DOJ's main building used public transportation to get to work, including Patty. To get a parking spot in the building's garage, you had to be three or four pay grades above hers. So while she hated traveling in a cramped subway car with the grubby masses, she used the Metro to commute to work. If she'd driven her car to work, she would have had to pay an outrageous amount for parking and would have had to park several blocks from her office. The life of a midlevel bureaucrat in Washington basically sucked.

She took the thirty-minute Metro ride to her apartment in Arlington and changed out of the suit she'd worn to work and into jeans, a T-shirt, running shoes, and a lightweight jacket. She also put on a plain blue baseball cap and sunglasses. She checked her watch. Four p.m. Cantor would most likely be getting off around five.

She took the Metro back to the DOJ building. She knew where Cantor's office was located and which door he'd most likely use to leave the building. She took up a position on the street near that exit.

She hadn't taken her car because she knew she'd never be able to find a place to park.

Her mission today was simple: she wanted to see how the little bastard commuted to work and she wanted to see his house. She figured that, like her, he'd use the Metro. She'd looked up his address and saw he lived in Falls Church and not that far from a Metro stop. If he drove to work, then she'd find out where he parked and come back tomorrow in her car to follow him. But she was almost certain he'd take the Metro.

At five thirty, he came out of the building. She fell in behind him, and sure enough he walked to the Federal Triangle Metro Station. She waited until he boarded one of the subway cars, but she didn't get into the same car that he did. She was sure, based on his address, that he'd get off at the West Falls Church Metro Station.

Thirty minutes later, Cantor got off the subway, and she followed him up the escalator and watched as he walked, with a throng of other people, to a nearby parking lot used by commuters. Unfortunately, it was an outdoor lot and not an underground parking garage. She saw him get into a pearl-gray Prius.

Okay. She knew how he got home from work, where he parked, and the car he drove.

She jogged over to a line of taxis near the Metro station, hopped into a cab, and gave the Sikh driver Cantor's address. She said, "You make it there in less than ten minutes, I'll give you a twenty-buck tip." She wanted to beat Cantor home. The cabbie stomped on the gas and drove like a maniac, going through a couple of lights that turned from yellow to red as he passed beneath them.

She had the cabbie drop her off on the corner closest to Cantor's house. His house was in the middle of the block, and directly across the street was a soccer field that was part of an elementary school. On the other side of the soccer field, on a raised elevation, was a playground with swing sets, slides, teeter-totters, and an elaborate structure with ladders and rings for the little monkeys to climb on. It was now past six, and the playground and the soccer field were empty. Patty jogged across the soccer field and over to the playground and took a seat on one of the swings; from there she could see directly into Cantor's house across the street.

She noticed that the playground was surrounded on three sides by rhododendrons and azaleas. She swung around on the swing and looked behind her and saw a parking lot. There were four cars parked in it, probably janitors or teachers staying late. There were street-lights spaced at fifty-foot intervals around the parking lot. The lights weren't on yet; they were probably activated by timers or light-sensing switches and would come on when it got dark. On the other side of the parking lot was the school, a one-story structure that was almost a block long.

She swung around again so she could see Henry's house. She esti-mated that the distance from the playground to his place across the soccer field was about two hundred yards. She wasn't worried about Cantor seeing her: all he'd see was a woman sitting on a swing wearing a baseball cap, and she'd keep her head down so the bill of the cap would obscure her face. Plus, he was in his car and driving, and she doubted he'd even look over at the playground.

Cantor arrived home a few minutes later and pulled his car into the one-car garage attached to the house. She thought, *If I can get into that garage, I could pop him when he parks his car.* She'd heard about gizmos that could duplicate a garage door remote, but she had no idea how she'd get her hands on one of those.

Five minutes after he parked, Henry came into view again. She could see him through a picture window that looked into what was most likely his living room. He'd taken off his suit coat and tie and was wear-ing the suit pants and white shirt he'd worn to work that day. He was holding something in his right hand, maybe a soft drink or a beer. He sat down in a recliner and picked up something—a remote?—and she guessed he turned on a television set, although she couldn't see the screen. He was probably watching the evening news.

She sat for a few more minutes, swinging gently back and forth, watching Cantor as he watched TV, then swung around again and looked at the parking lot and the school building. She realized then that the parking lot was on the *back side* of the school. The main entrance was on the other side of the building, where a street ran past the school's front. The parking lot was most likely used by the teachers, and the parents dropped their brats off on the other side of the building. The good thing, from her perspective, was the school building blocked people passing by on the street in front of the school from seeing anyone behind the school— or, more important, from seeing anyone in the playground area. The view of the playground was also blocked from the streets running along the sides of the school by hedges, trees, and chain-link fences, and then the playground itself was surrounded by bushes. All this meant that the playground was clearly visible only from the street running in front of Cantor's house, and even then, a person crouched or lying down behind the rhododendrons and azaleas would be almost impossible to see.

She swung around again and looked at Cantor's house. Or rather, she looked *into* his house. He was still watching TV. She thought about the streetlights around the parking lot and decided they could be both a blessing and a curse, depending on what she decided to do.

She went back to the corner where the cab had dropped her off and then walked around Cantor's block. She saw that his house butted up against the backyard of the neighbor behind him, and a six-foot cedar fence separated the two backyards. She concluded that approaching Cantor's house from the back side would be tricky. She'd have to sneak through the neighbor's backyard and go over the fence separating the two yards. It would be doable at night, but not ideal. She completed her walk around the block and then called for another cab. As the cabbie was taking her back to her apartment—she'd have the guy drop her off a couple of blocks away—she thought about possible scenarios.

It might be feasible to get him walking from the DOJ building to the Metro station after he left work tomorrow. She wished she had an umbrella, one that would inject a polonium pellet into his ass, but since she wasn't a Russian spy, she didn't have one. She could just come up behind him while he was walking and shoot him in the back with a silenced pistol—the pistol she'd intended to use to kill McGruder—but that would be risky. There would be a lot of people around, and silenced pistols weren't completely silent. And in D.C., thanks to all the fucking terrorists, there were cameras everywhere and she was liable to be videoed committing murder.

The parking lot near the Metro station in Falls Church where he parked his car was another possibility. She could walk behind him as he walked to his car or wait for him by his car and shoot him. But again, there were liable to be a lot of people around unless, for some reason, he stayed really late at work, and it was unlikely that on his last couple of days at Justice that he'd be staying late.

She concluded the best place to kill him would be at his house. She really liked the idea of waiting for him inside his garage but again couldn't figure out how to open the roll-up garage door. She'd have to see what Google and YouTube had to say about that. Another option was to simply knock on his door after it got dark, and when he answered the door, shoot him and run. Or, even better, if she could talk her way into his house, she could kill him inside. The problem with both of those options was that she couldn't control the possibility of someone driving by on the street in front of his house, or one of his neighbors walking by with a dog or looking out a window as she was executing him or as she was leaving his house. She supposed she could get around that problem with a simple disguise, like wearing a hoodie, but it would be best if she wasn't seen at all.

The other thing she could do was snipe him from the school playground. She could park in the parking lot behind the school, close to the playground, then drop down behind the rhododendron and azalea bushes and take the shot from there, and then hop back into her car and take off. As it was only about two hundred yards from the playground to his house, it would be an easy rifle shot. She'd wait until dark, say nine o'clock, when there wouldn't be anyone using the playground, and when he walked into his living room or sat down in front of his television set as he'd done today, she'd put a bullet right through his picture window and into his head. With the streetlights in the school parking lot and the lights on in Henry's living room, she didn't think she'd need a night vision scope. The only drawback she could see with shooting him from the playground was that someone might notice her car as she drove into the parking lot. The car wouldn't be visible once she was parked, but if someone saw a car drive into the lot behind the school after dark and when the school was closed, they might get suspicious and call the cops.

Hmm. She needed to do some more thinking about which option would be best. Sniping him from two hundred yards away was more difficult than shooting him right in his doorway, but there was less chance of anyone seeing her if she killed him from a distance.

It would also be good if she could come up with an alibi for where she was when he was killed—and then it occurred to her that that was easily doable. Her alibi would also solve the problem if someone should happen to see the car she was driving.

As the taxi took Patty back to her apartment in Arlington, she closed her eyes and pondered her options for killing Henry. She never noticed the car following the cab, a black Mercedes being driven by a woman. Nor had it occurred to her as she followed Henry from the DOJ building to his home in Falls Church that someone might follow her. She never saw the short Latino man riding on the subway with her, nor did she see another Latino man watching her as she sat on the swing in the playground.

42

Two days before Patty McHugh followed Henry home, DeMarco and Emma had gone to see Henry to discuss DeMarco's plan.

DeMarco had begun with: "We might be wrong about McHugh, but if we're right, there's one thing we know for sure. She's willing to kill to protect herself. When I braced McIntyre and McGruder down in Key West and showed them the video from Andie's phone, I think they called McHugh and told her that we were onto them. And in spite of the fact that those two guys were her friends, she killed them because she was worried that if they got caught, they'd eventually give her up. So she whacked them.

"Now, as Emma told you the other day, I don't think there's any way we can prove she killed them or conspired with them to steal the money the Bermans stole, but what we might be able to do is provoke her into trying to kill again."

"How would you do that?" Henry asked.

"We'd tell her—and by *we* I mean *you*, because you're the only one who would be a credible threat—that you're going to watch her like a hawk, and when she tries to spend the money she stole, you'll get her. You'll get her for tax evasion or money laundering or wire fraud or whatever you get people for who spend money they couldn't have possibly earned."

"Yes, that would be possible," Henry said, "provided we're watching every financial move she makes."

DeMarco said, "But I don't think we'll have to watch every move she makes because I think she'll try to kill you first. She's not going to let you stop her from spending the money she stole, and she's not going to give you a chance to catch her laundering the money."

Henry nodded.

Emma said, "You understand that this could be risky."

Henry said, "Yes, but I like the idea." Henry was silent for a bit. "I'll do it, but not as an employee of the Justice Department. I won't use my official position to do something like this. I'll retire tomorrow—my boss has been expecting my resignation, so he's prepared for my departure—and then I'll go see Ms. McHugh. I suppose the worst thing that can happen is that you're wrong about her and she doesn't take the bait."

"No," DeMarco said. "The worst thing that can happen is that she takes the bait and kills you."

Emma decided there was one major flaw in DeMarco's plan—that flaw being DeMarco.

Emma was trained and had experience in following people. She was trained on how to kill, had several firearms and knew how to use them. DeMarco, on the other hand, had no military or law enforcement experience and he didn't own a gun. He'd fired a gun only a couple of times in his life and probably couldn't hit the broad side of a barn if he was inside the barn. Emma concluded that rather than trying to train DeMarco to be useful, it would be better to bring in people who were already trained and she knew to be competent.

She called her pals Javier and Sergio, and they flew up from Miami.

Emma placed herself in Patty McHugh's shoes and thought of all the ways she could kill Henry—and came up with even more options than Patty did two days later. She thought about killing him commuting to or from work; sneaking into his garage and shooting him when he drove his car into the garage; knocking on his door and shooting him when he opened it; sneaking through his backyard, breaking into his house, and shooting him inside the house; sniping him through his living room picture window from the elementary school across the street. She even considered McHugh driving by on the street and using a weapon like an AR-15 and unloading a thirty-round clip through his front window. She thought about more exotic killing methods, like setting fire to Henry's house or planting explosives in his car, but concluded McHugh most likely wouldn't have the expertise or access to the materials required for such means of murder.

The first thing that Emma did was buy a bulletproof vest for Henry. She bought him the best lightweight vest that money could buy. The vest was hot and uncomfortable, and Henry didn't like wearing it, but Emma insisted and he eventually relented.

She had Neil install a simple security system in Henry's house, as Henry didn't have one. The system would send a signal to Emma's phone if anyone tried to breach Henry's house or garage when he wasn't there. The security system wouldn't sound an alarm if someone broke into Henry's house because Emma didn't want to scare an intruder off. She wanted to catch him—or, in this case, her—after she broke in.

Lastly, she called a man named Miguel Rivera. Miguel was a master craftsman, and he'd done a lot of work on Emma's house, fixing things that needed fixing and replacing things she wanted replaced. Miguel loved working for Emma because she overpaid him.

Emma had noticed that Henry's front entrance consisted of a wooden door and screen door. The screen door had glass on the top half that could be replaced with a screen when the weather was warm. She had Miguel replace the glass in the screen door with bulletproof glass and install another large piece of bulletproof glass behind the glass in the picture window in Henry's living room. Miguel worked ten hours without stopping. To obtain the glass required on such short notice, Emma took advantage of women she knew who worked in procurement at the Pentagon.

When Henry tried to pay for the vest, the security system, and his new windows, Emma said, "Don't worry about it. I'm filthy rich, and Neil works for free."

It was on the day after all these precautions had been taken that Henry went to see Patty McHugh and told her that he was the hound from hell who would never let her spend the money she stole. When Patty left work and went home to change into her stalking clothes, Sergio followed her. When Patty followed Henry to the Metro stop, Sergio was about five yards behind her for most of the way, and if she'd pulled out a gun to shoot Henry, he would have shot her if he couldn't find some other way to stop her.

When McHugh sat on the swing in the school playground to examine Henry's house, Javier had been watching her through binoculars. And when McHugh caught a cab to return to her apartment, Emma had followed the cab in her car.

43

Once McHugh was back inside her apartment building after casing Henry's house, Emma conference-called her team, which included DeMarco. She said, "Joe, I want you and Sergio watching McHugh's place tonight. I think today she was doing reconnaissance, checking out Henry's house and seeing how he commuted to work. I don't think she'll try anything tonight because she needs to figure out exactly what she's going to do, but I could be wrong. So we need to watch her. Javier and I will stay close to Henry in case she does try something, and if she leaves her apartment tonight, call me, and then you and Sergio follow her."

Back at Henry's place, Emma and Javier walked over to the playground at the elementary school.

Javier said, "She sat on a swing for a long time looking at Henry's place and looking at the school and the parking lot behind her."

Emma looked at the rhododendrons surrounding the playground. "These bushes would make for a good hunting blind."

"Sí," Javier said.

Emma's stood for a moment, then said, "I would think that shooting him with a rifle would be her last option. It's not a long shot, less than a couple of hundred yards, but that takes some skill. If I was her, I'd want to shoot him at close range, the way she shot McIntyre and McGruder. I think she'll park in front of his house so she can get away quickly. She'll wear some sort of disguise and probably mask the plates on her car. Then I think she'll knock on the door, and when Henry doesn't let her into the house, she'll shoot him through the window in the screen door."

Javier nodded.

Emma went silent again as she considered McHugh's killing options. "But we have to be prepared for every possibility. I'll stay in the house with him in case she comes through Henry's neighbor's backyard and tries to break into his house. And I'll be there if she knocks on his front door. But if she tries to snipe him, the best place to shoot from is these bushes near the playground. So if she heads this way tonight, you'll hide someplace close to the playground, like over near the base of the school. At night, with the streetlights on in the parking lot, there will be a lot of shadows, and what you'll do is hide someplace close to the playground and then get her after she shoots."

Javier shrugged, the shrug meaning: *Not a problem.*

When Javier had worked with Emma in Colombia, he once had to cross a lighted runway that was patrolled by guards armed with machine guns to plant a tracking device on a small plane. Javier had moved from shadow to shadow; he *became* a shadow. He blended into the asphalt runway, moving an inch at a time, sometimes not moving for several minutes, until he reached the plane. Then he slithered back out again, invisible to more than a dozen men. He'd have no problem at all hiding near the playground and sneaking up on McHugh and taking her after she took the shot.

And Emma wanted McHugh to take the shot. If she tried to shoot Henry through either the screen door window or the picture window, the bulletproof glass that Miguel had installed would protect him, and McHugh would be arrested for attempted murder.

After they finished taking a look at the school and the playground, Emma and Javier walked over to Henry's place and he let them in.

They went into Henry's kitchen, and Emma told him how McHugh had followed him home from work, cased his house from the school across the street, and walked around the block to see how to approach the house from the back side.

Emma said, "So she's planning something, and right now, Joe and Sergio are watching her place, and if she leaves, they'll call me and follow her.

"I think what she'll do is knock on your front door and ask you to let her in, and when you don't, she'll try to shoot you through the screen door. You'll be protected by the glass, of course, and then we'll apprehend her. She could use a rifle and fire from the school across the street. There's a place near the playground that makes for a perfect shooting blind. In case she chooses that option, Javier will be hiding near the shooting blind, and he'll take her after she takes the shot. But I'm betting on her shooting through the screen door, as that's the simplest thing to do."

Emma said, "I'm going to stay here inside the house with you tonight, and Javier will be outside, so if she leaves her apartment tonight, we'll be ready for her."

"Well, okay," Henry said. "It sounds as if you've thought of everything. Now would either of you like something to eat or drink?"

So far Henry hadn't shown the least concern about the possibility of being killed. Obviously, he wasn't a coward; he'd proven that fifty years ago. And fifty years ago, he had been shot at and almost killed by people a lot more lethal than a D.C. lawyer, and he hadn't had Emma and two ex-mercenaries protecting him then. So maybe he really wasn't worried about Patty McHugh killing him, but Emma had the feeling that there was something going on with him—that he was keeping something from her—but she couldn't imagine what that could be.

44

Back inside her apartment, Patty checked her watch. It was seven thirty, and the sun would set around eight thirty.

She had a lot of things to do in the next hour.

The first thing she did was go to the storage area in the basement of her building to retrieve her dad's hunting rifle.

The rifle was a classic bolt-action Winchester Model 70, one of the most popular hunting rifles ever made. Winchester started making them in 1936 and was still making them. Her dad's rifle was sixty years old, and the last time Patty had fired it was probably twenty years ago, the last time she'd gone hunting with her dad. And when Patty cleaned out the house after her dad died, she decided to keep the rifle. Partly she did so for sentimental reasons: she'd enjoyed hunting with her dad and had fond memories of those times. The other reason she'd kept it was that she hated to give up a good weapon and thought that maybe she'd go hunting again someday. She never did.

The rifle was in a hard-shell case designed to protect the weapon and the attached scope. Also inside the case was a cleaning kit. She took the rifle to her kitchen and examined it. As she'd known would be the case, it was spotless because her dad had always cleaned it after using it. She disassembled the weapon, applied gun oil to some of the parts, reassembled it, and dry fired it half a dozen times. Everything appeared to be fine with the rifle.

It was time to go see her neighbor.

Patty's neighbor across the hall from her apartment was a woman named Maggie Lawton. Maggie was eighty-four years old. She rarely left her apartment, as she had difficulty walking, and she had her groceries and her medications delivered. She had a daughter who lived in Arkansas and a son who lived in Nebraska, and they visited her three or four times a year, but most of the time she was alone. All her friends were dead. She spent virtually every waking hour watching television.

Mentally, Maggie wasn't doing too bad. Her short-term memory kind of came and went, like a bad radio signal, but she wasn't totally senile. She did tend to repeat things numerous times during the same conversation and didn't realize it. Patty knew that her kids wanted to put her in an assisted living facility, but the old bat refused to go into one. And now Patty was glad she'd refused, because Maggie could provide three things that Patty needed.

Patty didn't have a lot of contact with Maggie, but she was friendly toward her, and if she needed help with something—like replacing the batteries in her hearing aids or opening a jar that she was too weak to open—Patty would give her a hand.

Patty checked the TV guide to see what shows were playing tomorrow night, found the perfect one, then walked across the hall and knocked on Maggie's door. She waited patiently, knowing it would take the old lady forever to make the twenty-foot walk from her television-watching chair to the door. Finally, Maggie called out, "Who is it?"

"It's me, Patty," Patty said.

Maggie opened the door and beamed at Patty, delighted to have some-one to talk to. The old woman was less than five feet tall thanks to a spine permanently curled into the shape of a question mark from osteoporosis.

Patty said, "Do you have a stapler I could borrow? Mine just broke."

"Oh, sure," Maggie said. "I've got one on my desk. Let me get it for you."

"No, no, I'll get it," Patty said. "I know where your desk is. You just sit down."

She didn't go to the old lady's office in the second bedroom. Instead, she went into Maggie's bedroom. Three or four years ago, Maggie had bought a wig to cover her thinning gray hair, but she hardly ever wore it. It took Patty only a minute to find it in a box on the top shelf of the bedroom walk-in closet. She shoved the wig under her blouse and then went to Maggie's desk and picked up the stapler.

Maggie said, "Would you like some tea?"

"I wish I could, but there's something I need to finish for work tonight."

"Oh," Maggie said, disappointed.

Patty said, "But I happened to notice that they're showing an old Fred Astaire–Ginger Rogers movie called *Swing Time* tomorrow night at eight. It's on the TCM channel. You've told me before how much you enjoy watching Fred and Ginger."

"Oh, I do," Maggie said. "Did I ever tell you that my Jack and I used to do ballroom dancing when we were young?"

Only about a million times.

"Yes, and that's why I was thinking we should watch the movie together. I'll make us some popcorn."

"That sounds absolutely *marvelous*," Maggie said, clapping her hands.

Patty said, "Great. I'll see you tomorrow."

As she was leaving Maggie's apartment, she scooped up the old lady's car keys that sat in a bowl on a table near the door.

Patty hadn't been too concerned about anyone seeing her when she followed Henry and checked out his house. She hadn't done anything illegal. But she had to make sure that no one saw what she was planning to do next.

———◆———

She returned to her apartment and put her dad's rifle into its carrying case. She put on Maggie's curly gray wig. She was surprised the wig was a bit big on her; she hadn't realized the old lady had such a large head. Next, she put on a pair of reading glasses and looked at herself in the mirror. She was recognizable in the light in her apartment, but it was now almost dark outside. The wig in place, she grabbed the rifle and a folding tray, the type you set your dinner on while watching TV, and headed for the parking garage.

Maggie's car was a fifteen-year-old Mazda that she hadn't driven in five years; she was way too old to be out on the road and no longer had a driver's license. But Patty wasn't worried about the car starting or the battery being dead, because Maggie's children used the car when they came to visit her, and they made sure it stayed in working condition.

She put the rifle and the TV tray in the trunk of the car, hunched down in the seat to approximate Maggie's height, and took off.

———◆———

DeMarco and Sergio barely noticed the blue Mazda pulling out of the parking garage. They were both looking for the black Toyota RAV4 that McHugh owned. And it was dark out, and they could barely see the person driving the Mazda. DeMarco just caught a glimpse of what appeared to be a gray-haired woman.

Sergio and DeMarco had been sitting there together since six p.m. It was now close to nine p.m.

After three hours they'd run out of things to talk about. DeMarco had learned that Sergio was married and had two daughters, one a doctor, the other a lawyer. When he wasn't helping Emma, he and Javier ran a private detective agency that catered primarily to the Latino community in Miami and mostly to ex-Cubans. The Cubans, Sergio said, tended to have a lot of drama in their lives. It turned out that DeMarco and Sergio had one thing in common, that one thing being baseball, and most of the time they spent talking about the Nationals and Marlins being able to field decent teams.

At one point, DeMarco asked, "How did you meet Emma?"

"In Colombia."

"Really. Are you originally from Colombia?"

"No."

After it became apparent that Sergio wasn't going to say where he was from, DeMarco asked, "What were you and Emma doing down there?"

Sergio just looked at him.

Patty drove to a hardware store in Arlington that she knew stayed open until nine and found a sheet of double-paned window glass. The pane was about three feet by three feet, but she had the hardware guy use a glass cutter to cut out a six-inch square. He told her she'd have to pay for the entire sheet of glass, which she said was fine, and when he asked why she wanted the six-inch square, she said, "Oh, it's for some dumb thing my husband's doing." She also bought a tube of Krazy Glue, a five-foot-long, half-inch-diameter metal rod, and a hammer. She paid for everything in cash.

From the hardware store, she drove to a supermarket and bought a small watermelon that was about the size of a volleyball. Not that it mattered, but the melon was organic.

Her next stop was a shooting range near Manassas that was open until midnight to accommodate the guys who liked to go there after work and fire the weapons in their ready-for-Armageddon arsenals. The parking lot was more than half full, and when she opened the door it sounded as if there were a war going on. Part of the range was indoors and used for shooting handguns. The outdoor part of the range was five hundred yards long and used by the long gun shooters. It was lit up like a football stadium.

She paid the shooting range fee and also bought a box of cartridges for the Winchester. She paid in cash.

The outdoor range had targets at various distances, like one hundred, two hundred, and three hundred yards. She lay down in a prone position—the position she would be shooting from—looked through the scope, and fired a shot at the two-hundred-yard target. The bullet missed the bull's-eye. It was about two inches too high and one inch to the right. She didn't know if the scope was off or if her aim was bad—it had been a long time since she'd fired a rifle—so she fired a second shot and got the same result. She adjusted the scope and fired again. Bull's-eye. She smiled. She hadn't lost her touch. She fired a dozen more rounds and hit the bull's-eye ten out of twelve times. The two times she missed, they were by fractions of an inch. Now that she was confident of her aim and the rifle was sighted in, she had one thing left to do.

She headed southwest out of Manassas, along State Route 28. There was a lot of open land out that way—horse pastures and farms—but she had to drive around for forty minutes before she found what she wanted: an open field with no nearby houses. A road bisected the field; it didn't lead to any houses and was most likely used only when they were farming the field.

She parked her car but left the headlights on so she could see what she was doing. She knew that someone might drive by and see the lights but considered it unlikely, as it was close to midnight and the road she was parked on didn't go to anyone's home. Plus she didn't plan to be there more than five minutes.

She grabbed her five-foot dowel rod, her tube of Krazy Glue, her new hammer, and her six-inch pane of glass. She paced off two hundred yards, hammered the metal rod a foot into the ground, and glued the pane of glass to the top of it. She went back to her car and got the folding TV tray and the organic watermelon, walked out into the field again, set up the TV tray about ten yards behind the pane of glass, and put the melon on the tray. She walked back to her car again, removed the rifle, dropped into a prone position, and looked through the scope. She hoped her car's headlights, aimed the way they were—at an angle to the field—would provide the sort of illumination she'd get from the streetlights near the playground and on the street in front of Henry's house.

She aimed at the melon, took a breath, and gently squeezed the trigger.

The melon exploded.

All she'd been trying to do was prove that the pane of glass—like the double-paned glass most likely installed in Cantor's picture window—wouldn't significantly affect the flight of the bullet. It didn't. Had the melon been Henry Cantor's head, Cantor would be dead.

DeMarco and Sergio barely noticed the blue Mazda drive back into the parking garage. It was now after one in the morning, and DeMarco was struggling to keep his eyes open.

He called Emma and said, "I don't think this is going to happen tonight."

"Yeah, I think you're right. But stay there anyway."

"For how long?" DeMarco asked.

Emma hung up.

———◆◆◆———

Patty, back in her condo, cleaned her dad's rifle and went to bed. She slept like a baby.

45

Sergio nudged DeMarco's arm. DeMarco was sleeping in the driver's seat; there was drool running down his chin.

Sergio said, "She's leaving the building."

DeMarco pried his eyes open and looked. Sure enough, there was McHugh, dressed in a lightweight beige suit, carrying a purse, marching down the steps of her apartment building. He looked at his watch; it was seven a.m.

DeMarco said, "It looks like she's going to work."

"Sí," Sergio said. "She took the subway home from work the other day. That's probably where she's headed now. I'm going to follow her. You stay here. If I need you to pick me up, I'll call you. And call Emma and tell her what's going on."

With that Sergio left the car and took off on foot after McHugh.

DeMarco called Emma as directed and told her that McHugh appeared to be headed in to work.

Henry left for work right after DeMarco called Emma. It would be the last full day he would spend at the Justice Department, and he would spend it turning over his assignments to the woman who would most likely replace him. Even though it was probably unnecessary, with McHugh being followed by Sergio, Emma and Javier escorted him to work.

Once Henry and McHugh were both inside the Justice Department building, Emma called DeMarco and Sergio, and they all met at a small café a couple of blocks away. Emma was confident that McHugh wouldn't try to kill Henry while he was at work, inside the building.

DeMarco was exhausted after catching only a couple of hours of fitful sleep in the car outside McHugh's building, but it appeared as if Sergio, Javier, and Emma could keep going for hours. DeMarco had seen those sci-fi movies where mad scientists altered the DNA of soldiers so they'd become *super* soldiers. He wondered if he was sitting with three of the government's experiments.

"So what's the plan for today?" DeMarco asked, suppressing a yawn.

"I don't think she'll try anything while Henry's at work, but if she leaves the building, we need to follow her and see what she does. Like maybe she'll leave early to set up some sort of ambush for Henry or go to his house and break in before he gets home from work. So we need to watch her. We'll split up into two teams. Javier and I will take the first watch while you and Sergio get some sleep. You come back here and relieve us at one. When Henry leaves today, Javier and I will escort him home, while you and Sergio follow McHugh. Then we'll do like we did last night. You and Sergio will stake out her apartment, and if she leaves, you'll follow her and call me. Javier and I will stay with Henry."

"How long are we going to keep this up?" DeMarco asked.

"For as long as we need to," Emma said.

"And what if McHugh decides not to do anything?"

"She'll do something," Emma said. "I know she will. She wouldn't have cased Henry's house if she wasn't planning something."

At five, Sergio followed McHugh home on the subway. DeMarco drove to her place and was waiting near her apartment building when she arrived, and then Sergio and DeMarco sat together in DeMarco's car, waiting—hoping—that McHugh would leave.

After Emma and Javier escorted Henry home from work, they had dinner together. Javier prepared the dinner, a marvelous, spicy dish consisting of rice, chicken, and beans.

Emma said, "This is wonderful, Javier. I didn't know you could cook."

"I had to learn," Javier said. "If I'd left the cooking to my wife, my children would have lived off pizza and frozen dinners." Emma had met Javier's wife; she was a beautiful woman, but Emma would have described her as "high-maintenance."

As they were eating, Henry said, "They had a small party for me at work today. You know, a cake and punch and a few people made nice speeches. The attorney general herself showed up. I'd never even met the woman and was surprised she came."

Only a man as modest as Henry would have been surprised. Emma wasn't surprised at all. And had he not retired so abruptly, she imagined that the people he worked with would have wanted to hold a grand retirement party for him. There would have been a formal dinner, plaques would have been presented, and maybe even a letter signed by the president.

When it got dark out, Emma told Javier to tour the neighborhood and the school across the street. Like a roving watch. She was feeling apprehensive, and her gut was telling her that McHugh would try something tonight. Javier slipped out through Henry's back door and vanished into the night.

Emma noticed that Henry had barely touched his dinner and that it had been a struggle for him to eat as much as he did.

After Javier left, she said, "Henry, I can see you're ill. What's going on with you?"

Henry looked away, then directly into her eyes. "Abrupt liver failure," he said. "It's called 'abrupt' because it comes on suddenly and without much warning. I got the diagnosis about two weeks before Andie was killed. My doctor says that at this point, there's nothing that can be done."

"A transplant?" Emma said.

Henry shook his head. "For various reasons, that's not feasible."

"How long do you have?"

"Maybe a couple of months."

"I'm sorry," she said.

Henry shrugged. "I've had a long life. And until my son and daughter-in-law and granddaughter were killed, I would have said that I'd had a very good life, a very lucky life. I had a wonderful family. Steady employment. A job I could be proud of. I have no regrets."

She believed him.

Henry got up from the table and said, "I'm sorry I didn't do justice to the wonderful meal your friend prepared, but now I'm going to have some ice cream. For some reason, ice cream seems like the only thing I feel like eating these days. I have vanilla with pralines and mint chocolate. Would you like some?"

"I'll have the vanilla," Emma said.

When Henry turned to get the ice cream, she wiped the tears from her eyes.

She wondered what the hell McHugh was doing.

46

Patty was sleeping.

She took a nap as soon as she got home from work because she had a long night ahead of her and needed to be sharp. At seven she woke up and dressed in a black long-sleeved T-shirt, black jeans, and black running shoes. She also had a black watch cap she'd put on later to cover Maggie's wig.

She put on a pair of thin black leather gloves and disassembled the hunting rifle and wiped every part clean of prints. Although she was sure she would need only one bullet, she cleaned three and loaded them into the rifle. She took the elevator to the parking garage, placed the rifle in the trunk of Maggie's car, and dropped the leather gloves on top of it. She'd put the gloves on again when she left and wouldn't take them off until the job was done.

She'd decided to leave the rifle at the scene. No one would be able to trace a sixty-year-old hunting rifle back to her, and it would be better not to have the rifle in her possession in case she was stopped by a cop on her way home or considered a suspect in Cantor's murder. And afterward, she'd get rid of all the clothes she'd worn in case there was gunpowder residue on them.

Back in her apartment, she checked her watch. A quarter to eight. It was almost time to go see Maggie. She crushed two sleeping pills into powder and put the powder in a plastic sandwich bag. She'd been given a prescription for the pills a couple of years ago when she had a bout of insomnia that just wouldn't stop. She knew from personal experience that the pills would put a person's lights out in minutes.

She made a large bowl of microwave popcorn and headed across the hall to Maggie's place. She wondered if Maggie would remember that they had a date to watch the Fred and Ginger movie. She did. The old lady was beaming when she opened the door. She said, "I've been looking forward to this all day."

"Me, too," Patty said.

Patty found the TCM channel, and they started to watch the movie. At eight twenty, she said to Maggie, "I'm going to make us some chamomile tea." Chamomile was the old woman's favorite. She boiled the water and poured the ground-up sleeping pills into Maggie's cup. Fifteen minutes later the old lady was snoring. She'd sleep through the night.

After she'd dealt with Cantor, she'd come back and put Maggie to bed, and she was confident the old gal would say that Patty had been with her when Cantor was killed. Maggie was her alibi.

She took Maggie's apartment keys, returned to her place, put on her reading glasses and Maggie's wig, and headed for the garage.

That little bastard was *not* going to ruin her life.

———◆———

Sergio pointed and said, "Same car left yesterday about this time." It was nine p.m.

"Could you see the driver?" DeMarco asked.

"Barely," Sergio said. There was a light near the exit to the parking garage, but the car had passed through it quickly. "Looked like an old woman, gray hair, glasses, but I just got a glance at her. Why would she be leaving at the same time again?"

"Maybe she's got a night job, and this is when her shift starts," DeMarco said.

"Yeah, maybe," Sergio said.

Sergio called Emma. "Any way we can find out if McHugh has a second car?"

"I'll see if Neil can find out. I'll have him check the DMV's database if he can. But he might not be able to get anything until tomorrow."

What Emma meant was that Neil didn't always hack into databases to get information. Instead, he got a lot of what he needed from people he paid who worked inside government institutions and private sector businesses, like the IRS and telephone companies, and at nine o'clock at night the people who could help him wouldn't be at work.

Sergio said to DeMarco, "I wonder if she could be planning to use another exit."

There were several exits to McHugh's apartment building, but Sergio and DeMarco were watching only the garage exit because Emma was convinced that McHugh would use her car to drive to Henry's place. She wouldn't take a cab to commit a murder, not unless she was stupid, and McHugh wasn't stupid.

Sergio got out of the car and looked up at the third floor, where McHugh's apartment was located. The lights were on, but from the street, he couldn't see if anyone was moving around inside the apartment.

He got back into the car. He said to DeMarco, "I just got this feeling."

DeMarco shrugged; the only thing he was feeling was tired.

DeMarco's phone rang. It was Emma.

"I want you to see if she's still in her apartment."

"She hasn't left in her car and the lights are on in her place," DeMarco said.

"I don't care. Go see if she's there."

It appeared as if both Sergio's and Emma's intuitions, developed over years of doing God knows what, were screaming that something was amiss with McHugh. Or, back to his theory that their DNA had been modified in some military laboratory and maybe they shared some sort of telepathic connection.

"How do you want me to do that?" DeMarco asked.

"I don't want you to do it. Tell Sergio to knock on her door, and if she answers, to pretend he can barely speak English. He can say he's the maintenance guy and came to check on a plumbing problem or something."

"Okay," DeMarco said.

———◆◆◆———

The building's garage had a roll-up door operated by a keypad near the door. It also had a conventional door near the roll-up door—and Sergio, like Emma, had no problem with the lock on the door. He took the elevator to McHugh's floor and stood outside her apartment, listening to see if he could hear anyone inside. When he didn't hear anything after a couple of minutes, he knocked on the door. No one answered. He knocked again, louder. No one answered.

He called Emma. "She's not answering the door."

Emma paused, then said, "See if she's inside. Be careful."

"Sí," Sergio said.

Sergio picked the lock on McHugh's door and slowly pushed the door open. The lights were on in the living room and in the kitchen, but he sensed that the apartment was empty. He stepped inside and quietly and quickly walked through the place. He had no idea what he'd say if McHugh appeared. She didn't.

He called Emma. "She's not here."

"Shit," Emma said. "You and DeMarco come back to Henry's place. She might already be here, but we haven't seen her. Hurry."

She called Javier, who was still lurking outside Henry's place in the dark. She said, "She's not in her apartment, but Sergio never saw her leave. Go wait up near the school."

"Okay," Javier said. He jogged across the soccer field, through the playground, and past the parking lot and found a spot at the base of the school that was in a deep shadow cast by the streetlights in the parking lot. If McHugh drove into the lot, he'd see her. He squatted down on his haunches; he could sit in that position, unmoving, for hours. He remembered one time when he sat unmoving for so long in a South American jungle that a rat sat on his shoulder like a pet.

—◆—

Emma was standing in Henry's kitchen, her nerves tingling, her gut telling her that something was going to happen. She had too much experience to ignore her gut. She checked the backyard through the kitchen window and peeked through a bedroom window that looked out toward the elementary school. She didn't see a thing. She returned to the kitchen where she could see Henry sitting in the recliner in his living room.

Emma had told him to sit there. She wanted him to be visible through the front window, so if McHugh drove by, she'd see that he was home. She noticed that he was flipping through a photo album. He was looking at pictures of his family, the family he no longer had.

Emma's phone vibrated. It was Javier. "There's a person at the south end of the block, walking down the sidewalk in the direction of Henry's place. Whoever it is is wearing a hoodie, and I can't see a face, but I think it's a woman and I think it's her. She's McHugh's height and has the same build, and she's holding something in her right hand, down by the side of her leg. I think it's her," Javier said again.

"Good," Emma said, a thin smile on her lips. "Get down here and we'll take her like we talked about."

Javier, like Emma, was armed. Emma had her Beretta, Javier a Glock. Neither weapon was silenced and intentionally so. Emma and Javier were both wearing bulletproof vests, as was Henry. When McHugh knocked on Henry's front door, Emma would tell Henry to go to the door and open the wooden door but not the locked screen door. McHugh might ask Henry to open the screen door, or she just might shoot him as soon as she saw him. When McHugh shot and saw that the bullet didn't penetrate the glass, she'd be puzzled and would most likely shoot again—and when the second bullet still didn't shatter the glass, she'd run. But by then Javier would be close to her, on the street in front of Henry's house. He'd fire a round into the air and tell McHugh to drop her gun. At the same time, Emma would push past Henry, go out Henry's front door, and McHugh would be trapped between her and Javier. Emma would also be screaming at McHugh to drop her weapon. If McHugh elected not to drop her gun and took a shot at Emma or Javier . . . well, then they wouldn't have a choice and McHugh would most likely die.

One stray thought passed through Emma's head: Where had McHugh parked? Why wouldn't she have parked in front of Henry's house so she could get away quickly?

47

Shit happens.

Emma was in Egypt not long after 9/11. She wasn't in charge but was part of a ten-person team about to raid a house and nab a terrorist mastermind the Egyptians refused to arrest. The raid was complicated because of the guy's security and because if the Egyptians found out about it, there'd be an international uproar.

She never forgot the man leading the raid: a grizzled colonel who resembled the eagles on his shoulder boards. He held a briefing, going over everybody's job for about the tenth time, and when he was done, he said, "But don't forget, shit happens. It always happens." What he meant was that no matter how much redundancy was built into a mission, no matter how well an operation was planned and rehearsed, that events could occur that couldn't have possibly been anticipated and that were totally out of anyone's control.

He gave a number of examples: a rockslide, for no reason other than God being whimsical, blocking the only road for extracting a team on a mission in Iraq; a power blackout caused by rodents eating into a transmission line five miles from the site of an operation in Libya; a car that had been checked and double-checked by the best mechanics in the army failing to start because a new part, installed to *prevent* problems, had a manufacturing defect that didn't present itself until the tenth time the car was started. The colonel said that when shit happens, the game plan goes totally out the window, and then you have to do the last thing the military ever wants you to do: improvise.

That night in Falls Church, sixteen-year-old Carrie Reynolds, who lived down the block from Henry, and who was tall and blond, decided to go see her friend Amanda. She told her mom that she and Amanda had to work on a school project together, but what they were really going to do was smoke a joint that Amanda had stolen from her brother's stash. She put on her hoodie, and just as she was leaving the house her mom said, "Carrie, take that umbrella, the black collapsible one that's by the door. It belongs to Amanda's mom."

Shit happens.

Javier left the shadow at the base of the school where he'd been hiding and started jogging in the direction of Henry's house. He didn't run directly across the soccer field but ran along the side of the field because he didn't want the person he thought was McHugh to see him, and she might notice a man running across the field. She was now about fifty yards from Henry's house. He was thinking he needed to pick up his speed or she'd get to Henry's door before he reached the street in front of Henry's house.

As he was running, he heard a sound behind him—and he stopped. The sound had come from the parking lot near the playground. Then he heard the same sound again. Sound carries well in the night, and he knew the sound he'd heard was of a car door shutting. Twice. He looked back at the playground.

McHugh turned into the driveway leading to the parking lot behind the school and stopped near the playground/shooting blind. She needed to move quickly. Before she'd driven to the parking lot, she'd driven past Cantor's house and saw him sitting in his living room. God had decided to drop the little shit right into her lap. But she had to move fast. She had to take the shot before he got up from his recliner.

She popped the trunk latch, got out of the car, shut the driver's-side door, took the Winchester out of the trunk, shut the trunk lid, and hustled toward the shooting blind.

She didn't realize it, but she was smiling slightly.

———— ◆◆◆ ————

Javier saw the silhouette of a person in the playground pushing the swings out of the way. The person was holding a rifle. He couldn't see the person's face because the streetlights in the parking lot were behind her, but he realized immediately that he'd made a mistake. The woman in the hoodie walking toward Henry's house wasn't McHugh. McHugh was now in the shooting blind.

He called Emma, and because he was excited, he spoke in Spanish. "I was wrong," he said. "The person coming down the street isn't McHugh. McHugh just went into the shooting blind. She might shoot before I can get into a position to stop her from leaving."

Emma's plan had been that if McHugh tried to snipe Henry from the playground, Javier, who would have been hiding near the base of the school, would let her take the shot, then would stop her from fleeing. If he had to, he'd shoot the tires on her car. But now Javier wasn't close enough to stop her from driving away and McHugh might get away with attempted murder, because even though they knew it was McHugh who'd taken the shot, they might not be able to prove it was her.

Shit happens.

Emma called DeMarco. "Where are you and Sergio?"

"About five blocks from Henry's place."

"Hurry. McHugh's about to take a shot at Henry. You need to get to the school and stop her from driving out of the parking lot."

———◆◆◆———

McHugh dropped into a prone position between two bushes. Then she noticed a person in a hoodie walking down the sidewalk that passed in front of Henry's house. In a minute, whoever it was would be in her line of fire. She needed to shoot immediately, before the hoodie person blocked her shot.

She placed the crosshairs of the scope on the left side of Henry's head.

———◆◆◆———

Javier was running as fast as he could to get back to the school parking lot, but he doubted that he was going to make it on time. He was fifty years old, and he wasn't an Olympic sprinter.

———◆◆◆———

Emma, who was in the kitchen so McHugh wouldn't be able to see her, said to Henry, "Henry, she's in the playground across the street. She's going to take a shot at you any second now. Don't move. And don't worry. The glass will protect you."

"Okay," Henry said. She noticed that Henry was completely calm. He didn't appear to be the least bit concerned. He dropped the photo album he'd been looking at on the floor next to his recliner.

She called DeMarco. "Where are you?"

"A block away."

"Hurry up, goddamnit!"

———◆◆◆———

McHugh took a breath, exhaled, and applied pressure to the trigger. But then—

———◆◆◆———

Henry got up from the recliner.

Emma said, "Henry, what are you doing? Sit back down."

———◆◆◆———

"Son of a bitch," McHugh muttered. Why the hell did he get up? She thought about taking the shot anyway, but he was moving, and she was afraid she'd miss. She hoped he would sit back down, but he didn't. He—

———◆◆◆———

Henry walked quickly toward his front door.

He could hear Emma yelling, telling him to stop. He ignored her.

He opened the front door, unlocked the screen door, and stepped out onto his front porch.

He stood completely still.

He closed his eyes.

McHugh saw the front door open and Henry step onto the porch.

She smiled.

She moved the rifle barrel slightly to the left and placed the crosshairs on the center of Henry's forehead.

48

It was a glorious spring day.

The temperature was in the mid-seventies. There wasn't a cloud in the blue sky. A gentle breeze, like a soft kiss, carried the perfume of blooming trees.

It was a day for picnics, a day for taking your kids to a baseball game, a day for walking hand in hand with your lover along the banks of the Potomac.

It was a day suitable for outdoor weddings, a day to celebrate beginnings.

It was not a day for laying those you cherished to rest.

Henry's flag-covered casket was pulled from a gleaming black hearse and placed on a caisson drawn by six black horses. A young army officer, seated on a separate black horse, led the caisson down a winding path to the grave site, passing row after row of white headstones. There seemed to be no end to the rows of headstones. They went on forever, eternal tributes to a fraction of those who had died fighting America's wars.

'The casket was removed from the caisson by six pallbearers, all of them tall, young soldiers. They wore the army's dress blue uniform, the one with a yellow stripe running down the leg, and peaked hats. The soldiers were from the Third Infantry Regiment stationed at Fort Myer. The Third Infantry Regiment is also known as "the Old Guard," and it's the regiment that provides the sentinels for the Tomb of the Unknown Soldier.

They carried the casket to the grave, walking slowly, their movements precise, synchronized, ceremonial.

———◆———

At the grave site stood more than a hundred people.

In addition to Henry's coworkers and his friends and neighbors was a large contingent of Vietnam War veterans, a few who had served with Henry, but most who had only known of him and wanted to honor him. Representing the Department of Justice was the deputy attorney general and its current inspector general.

DeMarco was present, as was John Mahoney. Mahoney, a man who almost always sought to be the center of attention, stood quietly in the middle of the crowd, his eyes downcast, his white hair moving ever so slightly in the breeze. DeMarco knew that his boss, the consummate political actor, could feign any emotion, but this time he had no doubt Mahoney was genuinely grief-stricken.

Emma, tall and elegant, wearing a black Armani suit, stood slightly apart from the gathering. Her face was impassive, but DeMarco was certain she was heartbroken.

DeMarco wondered if both Emma and Mahoney felt that they were witnessing their future. They were both veterans, and they'd mentioned to him that they intended to be laid to rest at Arlington. DeMarco believed Emma, but he suspected that Mahoney would change his mind.

Arlington National Cemetery is the great leveler. The graves of generals and privates, of admirals and ordinary seamen, were marked by identical white headstones, and usually the only things inscribed on the headstones were the deceased's name, date of birth and death, the highest military rank achieved, and the wars he or she had fought in. DeMarco found it hard to imagine that Mahoney's ego would be satisfied with such brevity. Emma, on the other hand, ever the enigma, he knew would welcome the anonymity.

After Patty McHugh took the shot, she dropped her rifle and sprinted to her car. She was already speeding toward the exit by the time Javier arrived at the parking lot, too late to stop her from fleeing. Javier pulled his Glock, aimed at her left rear tire, fired, and missed.

Patty was going almost forty miles an hour as she exited the parking lot—and T-boned DeMarco's car.

The cops arrested McHugh after Emma called them, only telling them that a man had been shot and where they could find the shooter. They found McHugh still sitting in her car in the school parking lot, being guarded by Sergio and Javier. She was sobbing, and blood was trickling from her nose, which had been struck when her car's airbag exploded.

DeMarco was also still sitting in his car when the cops arrived. He'd been bruised and shaken by the accident, but not seriously injured. He just couldn't get out of his car because of the damage to the driver's-side door. Firemen eventually freed him using a long crowbar.

With Javier as an eyewitness—he'd seen the muzzle flash when McHugh fired the shot that killed Henry, and he saw her drop the rifle and run from the shooting blind—there was no doubt McHugh would be convicted of first-degree murder.

And that's what Henry had wanted.

Emma had been shocked by what Henry had done—but upon reflection, not surprised. Had Henry let nature take its course, he would have lasted only a couple more months and died a slow, painful death. By allowing McHugh to kill him, he'd achieved two things. He had died quickly and with dignity, and instead of Patty McHugh going to prison for a dozen years for attempted murder, she'd spend the rest of her life behind bars.

She would pay the full price for Andie Moore's death.

Seven soldiers fired a twenty-one-gun salute in three volleys, the rifle shots startling the mourners even though they'd known they were coming. DeMarco flinched with each volley; most of those present did.

The flag covering the casket was removed and folded into the thirteen folds of the traditional triangle. Normally the flag would be presented to the deceased's next of kin, but as there was no next of kin, Emma accepted the flag. She had made all the arrangements for Henry's funeral. She had also arranged for the flag, Henry's Medal of Honor, and a short description of what he'd done to earn the medal to be placed in a small case at the National Museum of the United States Army at Fort Belvoir.

Emma knew the small case commemorating Henry would go mostly unnoticed, just as Henry had gone mostly unnoticed during his lifetime. But it was the best she could do to honor a man who'd been truly honorable.

When Special Agent Perkins learned of Henry Cantor's death, he wanted to arrest Emma, DeMarco, Javier, and Sergio—and Perkins's position was not totally unreasonable.

As far as he was concerned, Emma should have told him that she suspected McHugh had killed McIntyre and McGruder and then should have let him and the FBI take it from there.

Perkins screamed at Emma: "You used the guy for live bait, and now he's dead."

Then there was the fact that sixteen-year-old Carrie Reynolds, an innocent bystander, could have been injured or killed had something gone wrong. Felony reckless endangerment was one of the charges being considered in addition to interfering in a federal investigation, lying to the FBI, and obstruction of justice.

Emma countered that she had done nothing illegal. She never lied; she just didn't tell Perkins everything she knew. She argued that had she told the FBI about McHugh, McHugh would most likely have never been arrested because the bureau—being the cautious, plodding, ass-covering organization that it was—wouldn't have had the nerve to do what she did. Moreover, she'd taken every precaution to safeguard Henry, pointing out the bulletproof glass she'd installed in his house and bringing in two ex-commandos to protect him. Her only error, which was not a crime, was that she hadn't anticipated that Henry would make the decision to sacrifice himself, for which she said she was truly remorseful.

Actually, she wasn't the least bit remorseful. It had been Henry's right to end his life the way he had.

In the end, thanks to Emma's very expensive, very competent lawyer, and a lot of heavy pressure applied by Emma's powerful and influential D.C. friends, and John Mahoney, who cut a side deal with the attorney general, no one was arrested other than Patty McHugh.

As for DeMarco, he was happy that he hadn't been arrested but pissed off because his insurance company had totaled his car and wouldn't give him enough money to fully pay for a new one.

As the casket was lowered into the grave, a bugler played the mournful sound of taps, the haunting notes echoing through the cemetery.

You have to be made of stone for taps not to move you.

Tears streamed down John Mahoney's florid face.

DeMarco's eyes filled with tears.

Only Emma remained clear-eyed.

She wasn't made of stone.

She would wait until the others had left the cemetery, then walk through the white headstones alone.

Only the souls of the fallen would be allowed to see her grieve.

Author's Note
and Acknowledgments

———◆———

It has never been my intention to push any particular political agenda with the DeMarco books—I'm writing to entertain, not to proselytize—but when I began the DeMarco series with the first book, *The Inside Ring*, I made John Mahoney the Speaker of the House and I made him a Democrat. As time has gone on over the period of writing the sixteen books in this series, I've tried to reflect political reality when it came to Mahoney, meaning that when the Republicans took back the House around 2010, I demoted Mahoney, and when the Democrats regained the majority in 2020, I promoted him back to Speaker again. In this book Mahoney is still the Speaker, but as I noted in the dedication, this book was completed in the spring of 2022—when the Democrats controlled the House—but it's being released in 2023, meaning after the midterm elections in November 2022. And what all this means is that although Mahoney is still the Speaker in this book, come the next DeMarco novel, I might have to demote him again, which will certainly be traumatizing for him.

———◆———

Lastly, I want to acknowledge the work of the copyeditors who have worked on all my books. I've been extremely fortunate that my publisher, Grove Atlantic, has always assigned outstanding copyeditors to find the many typos and grammar errors and all the other mistakes I make. I can't imagine how embarrassed I'd be if my novels were ever published without their sharp eyes reading the books first.